THE FAMILY JENSEN

THE VIOLENT
LAND

D0173490

THE FAMILY JENSEN
THE VIOLENT LAND

WILLIAM W. JOHNSTONE

with J. A. Johnstone

PINNACLE BOOKS
Kensington Publishing Corp.

www.kensingtonbooks.com

PINNACLE BOOKS are published by

Kensington Publishing Corp.
119 West 40th Street
New York, NY 10018

PUBLISHER'S NOTE
Following the death of William W. Johnstone, the Johnstone family is working with a carefully selected writer to organize and complete Mr. Johnstone's outlines and many unfinished manuscripts to create additional novels in all of his series like The Last Gunfighter, Mountain Man, and Eagles, among others. This novel was inspired by Mr. Johnstone's superb storytelling.

All Kensington titles, imprints, and distributed lines are available at special quantity discounts for bulk purchases for sales promotions, premiums, fund-raising, educational, or institutional use. Special book excerpts or customized printings can also be created to fit specific needs. For details, write or phone the office of the Kensington special sales manager: Kensington Publishing Corp., 119 West 40th Street, New York, NY 10018, attn: Special Sales Department; phone 1-800-221-2647.

ISBN-13: 978-0-7860-2811-5
ISBN-10: 0-7860-2811-4

First printing: May 2012

10 9 8 7 6

Printed in the United States of America

BOOK ONE

Chapter One

The seven men rode into Big Rock, Colorado, a few minutes before noon. Nobody in the bustling little cow town paid much attention to them. Everyone went on about his own business, even when the men reined their horses to a halt and dismounted in front of the bank.

Clete Murdock was their leader, a craggy-faced man with graying red hair who over the past ten years had robbed banks in five states and a couple of territories. He had killed enough men that he'd lost track of the number, especially if you threw Indians and Mexicans into the count.

His younger brothers Tom and Grant rode with him. Tom was a slightly younger version of Clete, but Grant was the baby of the family, a freckle-faced youngster in his twenties who wanted more than anything else in the world to be a desperado like his brothers.

Until a year or so earlier he had lived on the family farm in Kansas with their parents. But illness had struck down both of the elder Murdocks in the span of a few days, so Grant had set out to find his black-sheep brothers and throw in with them.

Ed Garvey was about as broad as he was tall, with a bristling black spade beard. He wasn't much good with a handgun. That was why he carried a sawed-off shotgun under his coat. As long as his partners in crime gave him plenty of room, he was a valuable ally. They were careful not to get in his line of fire when he pulled out that street sweeper.

The tall, skinny towhead with the eye that sometimes drifted off crazily was Chick Bowman. The loco eye gave him the look of somebody who might not be right in the head, but in reality Chick was fairly smart for an outlaw who'd had very little schooling in his life.

The one who wasn't all there was Denny McCoy, who followed Chick around like a devoted pup. Denny was big and barrel-chested, and he had accidentally killed two whores by fondling their necks with such enthusiasm that they couldn't breathe anymore. Chick had gotten Denny out of both of those scrapes without getting either of them lynched.

The member of the gang who had been with Clete the longest was a Crow who called himself Otter. He had worked as a scout for the army, but after coming too damned close to being with Custer when old Yellow Hair went traipsing up the Little

Big Horn to his death, Otter had decided that the military life wasn't for him. He knew Clete, who had been a sergeant before deserting, and had looked him up. Clete's prejudice against redskins didn't extend to Otter, the only man he knew who took more pure pleasure in killing than he did.

As the group tied up their horses at the hitch rack in front of the bank, Otter moved closer to Clete and said quietly, "Lawman."

Clete followed the direction the Crow's eyes were indicating and saw a burly, middle-aged man moving along the boardwalk several buildings away.

"Yeah, I see him," Clete said. "His name's Monte Carson. Used to have sort of a name as a fast gun, but he's been totin' a badge here for several years and people have pretty much forgotten about him. I wouldn't underestimate him, but I don't reckon he poses much of a problem for us, either."

"Anything goes wrong, I'll kill him first," Otter said.

Clete nodded in agreement. Otter would stay with the horses and watch the street. If shots erupted in the bank, the Crow would lift his rifle and drill Sheriff Monte Carson immediately, so he couldn't interfere with the gang's getaway.

Otherwise, Otter would wait until the other outlaws left the bank, and if anyone tried to follow them and raise a ruckus, *then* he would kill Carson.

Either way, there was a very good chance the sheriff would die in the next few minutes.

Clete glanced at everyone else and got nods of

readiness from all of them except Denny, who just did what Chick told him to, anyway. The six of them stepped up onto the boardwalk and moved toward the bank's double doors.

Otter's head turned slowly as his gaze roamed from one end of the street to the other. This town had been peaceful for too long, he thought wryly. If that hadn't been the case, someone surely would have noticed the seven human wolves who had ridden in together, not even trying to mask their intentions as they closed in on the bank.

Otter frowned slightly as he thought about the name of the town. Big Rock . . . There was something familiar about that. He knew he had heard of the place for some reason. But he couldn't put his finger on exactly what it was.

It didn't matter, anyway. After today Big Rock would be famous because the Murdock gang had cleaned out the bank and killed a few of the citizens.

A broad-shouldered, sandy-haired man in range clothes rode past on a big gray stallion. Otter noticed the horse—a fine one, indeed—but paid little attention to the rider, even when the man reined in and spoke to the sheriff. Otter couldn't hear the conversation between Carson and the broad-shouldered man.

He didn't think any more about it, convinced of its utter unimportance.

* * *

"Matt and Preacher are coming here?" Sheriff Monte Carson asked with a grin.

"That's right," Smoke Jensen said as he rested his hands on his saddlehorn and leaned forward to ease his muscles after the ride into Big Rock from his ranch, Sugarloaf. "In fact, they should be riding in today, according to the letter I got from Matt."

"I'll be glad to see 'em again," Monte said. "Good Lord, Preacher must be a hundred years old by now!"

Smoke chuckled.

"He's not quite that long in the tooth yet, and he never has looked or acted as old as he is. I reckon he'll slow down one of these days, but the last time I saw him he seemed as spry as ever."

Sometimes it seemed to Smoke that he had known the old mountain man called Preacher his entire life. It was hard to remember that he had been sixteen years old when he and his pa first ran into Preacher, not long after the Civil War. Preacher had been lean, leathery, and white-haired even then, and he hadn't seemed to age a day in the years since.

It was Preacher who had first called him Smoke, after seeing young Kirby Jensen handle a gun. So fast that the sight of his draw was as elusive as smoke, Preacher claimed. The young man's hand was empty, and then there was a gun in it spitting fire and lead, and there seemed to be no step in-between. Preacher had predicted then that Smoke would become one of the fastest men with a gun the frontier had ever known, and he was right.

But Smoke was one of the few men who had over-come his reputation as a gunfighter and built a re-spectable life for himself. Marrying the beautiful schoolteacher Sally Reynolds, whom he had met while he was living the life of a wanted outlaw under the name Buck West, probably had a lot to do with that. So had establishing the fine spread known as Sugarloaf and settling down to become a cattleman.

Despite that, trouble still had a way of finding Smoke. He had to use his gun more often than he liked. But he hadn't been raised to run away from a challenge, and anybody who thought that Smoke Jensen wasn't dan-gerous anymore would be in for an abrupt awakening if they threatened him or those he loved.

An abrupt and usually fatal awakening.

Preacher wasn't the only visitor headed for Big Rock. He and Matt Jensen had agreed to meet in Denver and come on to the settlement together. In the same way that Preacher was Smoke's adopted father, Matt was his adopted brother, although there was nothing official about it in either case. Smoke had taken Matt under his wing when the youngster was still a boy, the only survivor from a family mur-dered by outlaws, and with Preacher's help had raised him into a fine young man who took the Jensen name when he set out on his own.

Although still relatively young in years, Matt had gained a wealth of experience, both while he was still with Smoke and afterward. He had already drifted over much of the frontier and had worked as a deputy, a shotgun guard, and a scout. He had tangled with outlaws, renegade Indians, and bad men of every stripe.

Twice in the fairly recent past, Smoke, Matt, and Preacher had been forced by circumstances to team up to defeat the schemes of a group of crooked politicians and businessmen that had formed out of the ashes of the old Indian Ring. This new Indian Ring was just as vicious as the original, maybe even more so, and even though they seemed to be licking their wounds after those defeats, Smoke had a hunch they would try something else again, sooner or later.

He hoped they wouldn't interfere with this visit from Preacher and Matt. It would be nice to get together with his family without a bunch of gunplay and danger.

Those thoughts were going through Smoke's mind as he realized that Monte Carson had asked him a question. He gave a little shake of his head and said, "What was that, Monte?"

"I just asked what time Matt and Preacher are supposed to get here," the sheriff said.

"I don't know for sure. They're riding in, and I figure they'll be moseying along. Preacher doesn't get in a hurry unless there's a good reason to. I thought I'd go over to the café, get something to eat, then find something to occupy my time while I'm waiting for them."

Monte grinned.

"Come on by the office," he said. "We'll have us a game of dominoes."

Smoke was just about to accept that invitation when gunshots suddenly erupted somewhere down the street.

Chapter Two

There were several customers in the bank when Clete and his men walked in, but they didn't appear to be the sort to give problems. The men looked like storekeepers, and a woman stood at one of the teller's windows, too, probably some clerk's wife depositing butter and egg money.

The two tellers were the usual: pale, weak hombres not suited for doing a real man's work, or anything else. At a desk off to one side sat the bank president, fat and pompous in a suit that wasn't quite big enough for him.

Clete hated all of them, just by looking at them. They were sheep, and he was a wolf. They deserved to have their money taken away from them, to his way of thinking.

And their lives, too, if they got in his way.

The banker glanced up from his desk as the men entered the bank, then looked again with his eyes widening in shock and fear as he obviously realized what they were and what was about to happen. He started to get to his feet, but Clete already had his gun out and pointed it at the man.

"Stay right where you are, mister," Clete ordered. "We're just here for the money, not to kill anybody."

What he left unsaid was that he and the others wouldn't hesitate to kill anybody who interfered with them getting that money.

The other five men spread out and closed in around the customers. Ed Garvey swung his sawed-off toward the tellers, both of whom raised their hands in meek, fearful surrender.

Clete raised his voice and said, "Everybody just take it easy. No trouble here, no trouble. We just want the money. Tellers, clean out your drawers. Put everything in the sack."

With practiced efficiency, Tom Murdock had taken a canvas bag from under his coat. He shouldered aside the townie at one of the windows and thrust the bag across the counter toward the stunned teller.

"In the sack," Tom snarled at the teller, who swallowed hard and started plucking bills from his cash drawer and stuffing them into the bag.

Denny approached the female customer, who was fairly young and pretty. She was pale and trembling at the moment. She tried to shrink away from Denny as he stepped up to her, but she had her back against the counter and there was no place for her to go.

"Pretty," Denny said. His gun was in his right hand, but his left was free. He raised it and started to take hold of her neck. There was nothing he liked better than caressing a pretty woman's neck.

Chick said, "Not now, Denny, we ain't got time for that."

"Pretty!" Denny insisted, as if that explained everything.

"I know that, but—"

The woman screamed as Denny's hand was about to close around her throat.

Chick exclaimed, "Dadgum it, Denny!"

And on the other side of the counter, the teller shouted, "Leave her alone, damn you!"

His hand dropped below the counter, and when it came up, there was a Colt Lightning in it. The teller jerked the trigger three times fast, and the double-action revolver sent all three .41 caliber rounds crashing into Denny's face. The bullets turned the big man's features into a hideous red smear as his head rocked back.

"Denny!" Chick cried. Enraged, he started firing. His bullets sprayed the woman and the teller, knocking them both off their feet as blood welled from their wounds.

"Son of a bitch!" Clete bellowed. "Tom, grab all the money you can!" He turned back to the bank president, who had started impulsively to his feet, and shot the man in the belly.

Grant looked around wildly, unsure what to do. He had taken part in several robberies with his brothers, but none of them had gone this bad, this quickly. None of the gang had even been wounded in those jobs, let alone killed. Denny wasn't dead yet—he had fallen to the floor, where he was thrashing around— but he couldn't last long, shot in the head like that.

The other teller had thrown himself on the floor and lay there behind the counter with his arms held protectively over his head, as if that would stop a bullet. Tom Murdock didn't take the time to shoot him. Instead, as Tom leaned over the counter, he reached into the cash drawer and grabbed as many greenbacks as he could, stuffing them into the canvas sack. They would get *something* out of this foul-up, by God!

But who could have predicted that that meek little teller would try to turn into Wild Bill Hickok? The fella must have been sweet on the woman, and all he had thought about was protecting her from Denny.

The air inside the bank was thick with gunsmoke now. The sharp tang of it stung Clete's nose as he swung toward the doors.

"Let's go, let's go!" he called. He was confident that Otter would be covering their retreat.

"But Denny—" Chick began.

"He's done for!" Clete yelled. "Come on!"

The five men charged out through the double doors, guns up and ready for trouble.

They weren't ready for what they got.

Reacting instantly, Smoke twisted in the saddle to search for the source of the shots. They were coming from the direction of the bank, and as Smoke spotted the seven horses tied at the hitch rack in front of that establishment, his mind leaped to the conclusion that the bank was being robbed.

The sight of a stranger, a tall, lean Indian in a black hat, standing next to those horses was more evidence supporting that theory.

The fact that the Indian jerked a rifle to his shoulder and pointed it at Monte Carson confirmed the hunch.

That lookout was aiming at the wrong man. He should have paid more attention to the hombre on the big gray stallion. Smoke's Colt appeared in his hand as if by magic, and two shots blasted from it so close together they sounded like one.

Even though Smoke was firing from the hip and the distance was fairly long for a handgun, his almost supernatural abilities sent both slugs hammering into the Indian's chest. The rifle in the Indian's hands went off as his finger jerked involuntarily on the trigger, but the barrel was already pointing harmlessly at the sky as he toppled backwards against one of the horses.

The animal shied and bumped into the other horses, and they got skittish, too. All seven mounts started jerking at their reins, trying to get loose and bolt.

Monte drew his gun and broke into a run toward the bank, but instead of dismounting Smoke heeled his horse into motion. The stallion pounded down the street. Smoke arrived in front of the bank just as several men burst out through the doors.

The strangers were all carrying guns. The one in the lead saw Smoke and opened fire on him. Smoke ducked and snapped a shot at the man. The slug caught the bank robber in the shoulder and drove him halfway around. He stayed on his feet, though, and continued shooting.

One of the other men, a short, bearded, thick-bodied varmint, bulled forward and swung up a sawed-off Greener. Smoke saw the scattergun and went diving out of the saddle just as the awful weapon boomed like a huge clap of thunder. One of the horses screamed in pain as buckshot peppered its hide.

Smoke landed in the street, rolled over, and came up on one knee. He had to throw himself to the side in order to avoid being trampled.

At the same time, bullets were still flying around him. Clouds of dust swirled, kicked up by the hooves of the fear-maddened horses. It was utter chaos in the street and on the boardwalk, as gun battles often were.

From the corner of his eye, Smoke caught a glimpse of Monte Carson kneeling behind a rain barrel and firing at the outlaws. One of the bank robbers, a tall, lanky man with fair hair under a thumbed-back hat, clutched at his middle and folded up as one of Monte's bullets punched into his belly.

Smoke had two rounds left in his Colt, since he always carried the gun with the hammer resting on an empty chamber unless he knew he was about to encounter trouble. He fired again and saw one of the outlaws go spinning off his feet as the bullet tore through his thigh.

Smoke shifted his aim and fired his last shot. It went into the chest of the man whose shoulder he had broken with a bullet a few seconds earlier. The man dropped his revolver, staggered a few steps to the side, and pitched off the boardwalk to land on his face in the street.

That left two of the outlaws on their feet, including the man with the sawed-off. He had broken the weapon open and was trying frantically to thumb more shells into it.

The remaining outlaw had a canvas bag clutched in his left hand and a Colt in his right. He threw a couple of shots at Smoke and lunged toward the horses, obviously hoping to grab one of them and make a getaway.

Smoke had to dive forward onto his belly to avoid the shots as the slugs whipped through the air above his head. He looked up and saw that the man had gotten hold of a horse and was trying to swing up into the saddle.

Smoke surged up onto his feet and jammed his empty Colt back in its holster as he went after the man trying to escape. With a diving tackle, he crashed into the outlaw and drove him away from the horse and off his feet. Both men sprawled in the dusty street as iron-shod hooves danced perilously close to their heads. Greenbacks flew from the canvas bag as it hit the ground.

The bank robber lashed out in desperation at Smoke, who avoided the first blow, but then caught a knobby fist on the jaw. He threw a punch of his own, hooking his right into the man's belly. The man gasped and tried to lift his knee into Smoke's groin, but Smoke twisted aside and took the blow on his thigh. He swung his left and landed it solidly on the man's nose. Blood spurted hotly across Smoke's knuckles.

The man arched his back and threw Smoke off. As Smoke rolled away, the outlaw grabbed up the gun he had dropped and aimed it at Smoke.

A shot blasted from the boardwalk, and the man crumpled, dropping the gun again. Smoke glanced over and saw Monte Carson lowering his revolver after the shot that had probably saved Smoke's life.

But that still left the shotgunner, who had snapped his weapon closed again and now swung it toward Smoke and Monte. Smoke's Colt was empty, and so was the sheriff's, as became evident when Monte jerked the trigger and the hammer fell with a harmless click. Smoke and Monte were close enough together that the outlaw might be able to cut them both down if he fired both barrels.

"You damn meddlin' sons o' bitches!" the outlaw roared as he brought his sawed-off to bear.

Before he could jerk the triggers, his head seemed to explode in a gory spray of blood, bone fragments, and brain matter. The scattergun fell unfired from his nerveless fingers, and his body dropped to the ground right behind it.

Unsure of what had happened, Smoke looked along the street and saw two men sitting on horse-back a couple of blocks away. One of them, a lean, white-bearded figure in buckskins and a broad-brimmed felt hat, lowered a Sharps carbine from the barrel of which curled a tendril of powder smoke.

The old-timer hitched his horse forward, rode up to Smoke, and grinned as he said, "You just can't stay outta trouble for any time at all, can you, boy?"

Chapter Three

"Preacher!" Smoke exclaimed. "You sure know how to show up at the right time."

"Always have," Preacher said, still grinning. "Might should've showed up a few minutes earlier, though, since you only left one of the varmints for me to kill. Heard the shots as we was ridin' in. Sounded like a right smart fracas. How come you was killin' 'em?"

"They tried to rob the bank," Smoke explained.

Preacher nodded.

"Thought it might've been somethin' like that when I saw all them greenbacks scattered around."

Preacher's companion galloped up, threw himself out of the saddle, bounded onto the boardwalk, and swung a fist that crashed into the jaw of the lone surviving outlaw, who had pulled himself up onto his knees and was trying to lift his gun with a trembling hand. The young owlhoot went over backwards, knocked cold by the powerful blow.

"While you two were flapping your gums, that varmint was about to shoot Preacher in the back," Matt Jensen said, looking exasperated.

"No, he wasn't," Preacher replied. "I figured you'd take care of him, Matt."

With a shake of his head, Matt asked, "What if I hadn't been paying attention?"

"I knew you would be," Preacher said simply. "Smoke and me taught you well enough."

"Well, I suppose that's true," Matt said with a shrug.

He was the tallest of the three men, a fair-haired, handsome youngster in a black Stetson and a faded blue bib-front shirt. Most women naturally took a liking to Matt Jensen, and he returned the feeling.

With troublemakers, it was different. Matt carried a holstered Colt .44 double-action revolver on his right hip, and a Bowie knife was sheathed on his left. He didn't hesitate to use the weapons when he needed to, and he was almost as fast and deadly with a gun as his adopted older brother Smoke.

As Smoke thumbed fresh cartridges into his Colt to replace the ones he had fired, he said, "We're much obliged to both of you for your help, aren't we, Monte?"

"We sure are," Big Rock's sheriff agreed. He was reloading, too. As he snapped the cylinder of his gun closed, he went on, "I'd better check on the rest of those varmints and make sure they're all dead. Gonna be wounded in the bank who need tending to as well, I'll bet."

"Why don't you go see about that?" Smoke suggested. "Preacher and Matt and I will take care of the chores out here."

Monte nodded and said, "Thanks." He hurried into the bank, which was ominously quiet.

Smoke and Matt went quickly from body to body, checking for signs of life. The young outlaw Matt had knocked out was the only one of the bank robbers still alive. He was wounded in the left leg and had lost quite a bit of blood, but Smoke thought he would probably live.

He rolled the unconscious outlaw onto his belly, pulled the man's arms behind his back, and used the outlaw's own belt to lash his wrists together for the time being. That way if he came to, he wouldn't be able to cause a problem.

Dr. Hiram Simpson, the local sawbones, came running from his office and joined several other townspeople in crowding into the bank to see what they could do to help. Monte Carson emerged from the building a few minutes later, his features pale and drawn.

"It's pretty bad in there," he told Smoke, Matt, and Preacher. "Jasper Davenport, who just took over running the bank, is dead. Didn't even make it in the job for a month before those blasted outlaws gunned him down. Mitchell Byrd's dead, too, and Elaine Harris is wounded. Got a dead outlaw in there with most of his face shot off. I reckon that's probably what started the battle. Appears that Mitch got his hands on a gun and shot the desperado."

Smoke trusted Monte's assessment of the situation. He asked, "Does it look like Miz Harris will make it?"

"The doc didn't say," Monte replied with a shake of his head.

Smoke pointed a thumb at the unconscious outlaw.

"Well, when he's through in there, this fella's going to need some attention. Matt and I can go ahead and haul him over to the jail for you if you want, though."

Monte nodded and said, "That'd sure be giving me a hand. I'm obliged to you boys."

"Get his feet, Matt," Smoke said.

Smoke and Matt were both very strong, so they didn't have any trouble lifting the bank robber and toting him down the street to the sturdy building that housed Monte Carson's office and Big Rock's jail. All the cells were empty at the moment, so they carried the man into the one nearest the cell block door and placed him on the bunk. As soon as they had stepped out, Monte swung the barred door shut, closing it solidly.

Preacher had followed them into the sheriff's office.

"Beats me why you don't just let the rapscallion bleed to death," he commented when Smoke, Matt, and Monte left the cell block. "Saves the bother and expense of a trial and a hangin'."

"That's not the way the law works, Preacher,"

Monte said. "It's mighty good to see you again, by the way. You, too, Matt."

"It's good to be here," Matt said. "It's been too long since the three of us have gotten together."

Monte asked, "You fellas want some coffee?"

"I figure we'll go over to the café and have some lunch before we head out to Sugarloaf," Smoke said. "So no thanks to the coffee, but we're obliged for the offer. Were you able to find out what happened inside the bank, Monte?"

The sheriff nodded.

"There were a couple of customers who didn't get hit when the bullets started flying, and the other teller, Fred Reeves, was all right, too. They all hit the dirt, or the floor, rather, when the shooting started. Seems the outlaw who was still inside the bank tried to molest Mrs. Harris. Mitch Byrd had a Colt Lightning on the shelf under his counter. He grabbed it and shot the owlhoot, but that set off the others. I reckon it's only pure luck that it wasn't an even bigger massacre in there."

Smoke shook his head regretfully.

"It's too bad we weren't able to save more of the citizens," he said. "But at least the gang didn't get away."

"Did you recognize any of the bank robbers, Monte?" Matt asked.

"A couple of them looked familiar to me," the lawman said. "I must've seen their pictures on reward dodgers. I've got a big pile of those posters in the desk. I'll go through them later and see if I can match up any names with the faces. Could be you and Preacher have some rewards coming, Smoke."

The old mountain man snorted disdainfully.

"I don't care about no dadblamed ree-ward," he said. "I've had fortunes come an' go through my fingers so many times over the years, money don't mean nothin' to me as long as I've got enough for a meal and a snort o' whiskey now and then."

"And Sugarloaf's doing just fine," Smoke put in, "turning a profit every year and I expect that to keep up as long as we don't have a bad drought. Maybe Matt should claim the rewards."

"Me?" Matt exclaimed. "I didn't do anything except wallop one of them."

"Those wanted posters all say dead or alive," Monte pointed out. "You ought to at least get paid for the one you laid out, Matt. I'll look into it."

"All right," Matt said, "but I didn't do it for the money. I was just trying to save Preacher's scrawny old hide."

"I told you, I knowed he was back there—"

Smoke cut in on the old-timer's protest.

"Come on, let's get something to eat, and then we'll head for the ranch."

They were about to leave the sheriff's office when the door opened and Dr. Simpson came in.

Smoke paused long enough to ask, "How's Miz Harris doing, Doc?"

"I think there's a good chance she'll pull through," Simpson replied. "She was wounded in the arm and the hip. The arm wound should heal cleanly. The injury to her hip may result in her having a permanent limp. It's too soon to say. She's been taken down to my house, and my nurse is looking after her." The sawbones turned to Monte Carson. "I was told you have a wounded prisoner here, Sheriff."

"Sure do," Monte agreed. "I'll take you back to his cell." He raised a hand in farewell to Smoke, Matt, and Preacher. "See you boys later."

When they were on the boardwalk outside, Matt chuckled and said, "Sheriff Carson must be having trouble with his eyes if he called you a boy, Preacher."

"I reckon so," the old mountain man agreed, "since he didn't notice you was a snot-nosed, wet-behind-the-ears kid, neither."

Smoke grinned and said, "Come on, you two. You can continue this squabble after we've had a surroundin'."

They walked across the street to the café. A crowd was still gathered around the bank. Smoke supposed that the surviving teller was running things for now.

The café was doing a brisk business since it was the middle of the day, and most of the people in there were talking excitedly about the attempted bank robbery and the resulting shoot-out.

Smoke ignored the curious looks the townspeople cast at him and his companions. He had long since gotten used to being gawked at, especially when some trouble had broken out and he'd been in the middle of it.

The three of them sat at a table covered with a blue-checked cloth and ordered meals consisting of roast beef, potatoes, greens, biscuits, and deep dish apple pie.

"And keep the coffee comin'," Preacher told the smiling waitress, who promised to do so.

"How's Sally doing?" Matt asked while they were waiting for their food.

"She's fine," Smoke said. "Anxious to see you fellas again, I expect."

Preacher said, "How about them hands of your'n?"

"Cal and Pearlie?" Smoke grinned. "As quarrelsome as ever. They wouldn't know what to do if they weren't squabbling."

In that respect, Smoke's foreman Pearlie and the young ranch hand Calvin Woods reminded him of a couple of other hombres, namely Preacher and Matt.

"We saw something interesting while we were riding up here," Matt said. "Did you know there's a wagon train headed in this direction, Smoke?"

The grin on Smoke's face was replaced by a puzzled expression.

"This is the first I've heard of it," he said.

"I saw dozens of wagon trains when I was a younger man," Preacher said. "Maybe a hundred or more. Traveled with a few of 'em, too. Them pilgrims wasn't always the smartest folks when it came to gettin' along on the frontier, but they was determined to build new lives for themselves, I'll give 'em that much. Shoot, I guess ever'body was a greenhorn once."

Matt said, "I thought you didn't like all the immigrants who moved west. You said they civilized places too much and changed everything from the way it was back in the Shining Times."

"Well, that's true," Preacher said. "They did, and I ain't over-fond of that so-called civilization they brung with 'em. But you can't stop things from changin'. It'll happen while you ain't even lookin'."

Smoke asked, "You didn't talk to the people with the wagon train, did you?"

"Nope," Preacher said. "We just waved at 'em and went on our way."

Matt said, "Why do you ask, Smoke?"

With a shrug, Smoke replied, "I was just curious where they're bound, that's all. I'm not aware of any land around here being opened recently for settlement."

Some of the Sugarloaf stock grazed on open range, but Smoke knew that concept was dying out in the West. More and more land was being claimed officially, instead of just being there for anybody who wanted to use it. The day was coming, he knew, when cattlemen would have to file claims for the range they were using and fence it in. He didn't like the thought of it, but like Preacher said, things changed whether a fella wanted them to or not.

"I wouldn't worry about that wagon train," Matt

said. "Chances are it's headed for somewhere north of here. Wyoming, maybe, or even Montana."

"You're probably right," Smoke said. He saw the waitress carrying a tray loaded down with food toward their table and put the subject out of his thoughts with the casual comment, "Anyway, those immigrants don't have anything to do with us."

Chapter Four

"How much further is it, Friedrich?" the woman on the wagon seat asked the man who rode alongside the vehicle on a fine black stallion. "Will we reach this place Wyoming soon?"

Baron Friedrich von Hoffman smiled tolerantly at his young cousin Erica. Some of the American states were larger than their entire homeland, and Erica had trouble understanding the vast distances involved in traveling across this country.

"It will be another week at least, probably more, before we arrive at our destination," von Hoffman told her. "We're still in the American state called Colorado."

Erica shook her head in dismay. She was a beautiful young woman in her early twenties, with long, straight blond hair so pale it was almost white. At the moment, her hair was gathered into a thick braid that hung down her back under the sunbonnet she wore. She was dressed like an American immigrant woman, and von Hoffman knew that she didn't like it.

At least the men were able to dress more like they would have back in Germany if they were to go out hunting on their estates, in boots and riding breeches and plain shirts. Von Hoffman had a broad-brimmed brown hat on his head, and an American repeating rifle was in the saddle sheath under his right thigh.

No one would ever mistake him for a cowboy, but he didn't look completely out of place here.

The baron had the tall, lean, rangy body of an aristocrat who had trained with the saber at Heidelberg. He had served in the Prussian army and was an excellent shot with both rifle and handgun. In his mid-thirties, he had a dark, hawklike face. A neatly trimmed mustache adorned his upper lip.

He was the unquestioned leader of this wagon train. Having visited the United States many times in the past on hunting expeditions, he had decided that he would dispense with the services of a guide and wagonmaster and take charge of the journey himself.

So far, that had worked out quite well. He had brought the wagons from Missouri across Kansas to Colorado and then had turned north to Wyoming. Admittedly, it was difficult to get lost. As long as he kept the rearing spires of the Rocky Mountains on his left hand, the wagons would be heading in the right direction.

The baron felt a definite responsibility toward the people he was leading. Among them were other members of the Prussian nobility, his friends and relatives who were counting on him to establish a new homeland for them. The rest were commoners, but for the most part they were members of families that had worked for his family and the families of the other aristocrats for generations. The others were businessmen who had supported unpopular political positions, as had von Hoffman, and who had the money to escape from almost certain retribution at the hands of those who were now in power.

All in all, it was a group that had the potential to become highly successful and extremely important in the mostly untamed land to which they were going, von Hoffman thought. He would take over the Rafter 9 ranch and build it into the most lucrative cattle operation in the state of Wyoming. Most of the others would form the foundation for the new town he would establish near the ranch. There were a few hamlets scattered across the region, but no major settlements. The town would fill a need not only for von Hoffman's plans but also for the other settlers in the area.

"I wish we would get there," Erica went on. "This new land is so far from our home."

"This new land will *be* our home," von Hoffman said firmly. "Never forget that, Erica. Wyoming is where we will live from now on, and we will be happy there."

Because there was no other alternative, he thought. They could not go back to Germany. To do that would be tantamount to signing his own death warrant. His political stands had made some powerful enemies. He worried that even coming this far, all the way to America, would not be enough to keep the men who wanted him dead from coming after him. Although they wouldn't come themselves, of course. . . .

Rich, powerful men usually sent others to do their killing for them.

The man sitting beside Erica and handling the lead wagon's team said, "Baron, I see a rider coming."

Von Hoffman looked across the rolling prairie in front of them toward the foothills and mountains that rose in the distance and spotted the man on horseback. He seemed familiar, and after a moment von Hoffman nodded in recognition.

"It's Dieter," he said. "I sent him ahead to scout our route. I'm sure he's bringing back news about the best way for us to go."

Dieter Schumann was an ambitious young man, the son of an old von Hoffman family retainer. During the ocean voyage across the Atlantic and in the months since then, he had taught himself English by reading American dime novels. Because of that, he expected everything in the United States to be the same as the wild and woolly fictional

West he had read about. It had come as a severe disappointment to him when there hadn't been any gunfighters, outlaws, or savage Indians waiting for them on the docks of New York.

Things had improved, at least in Dieter's opinion, when the wagon train set out from Kansas City. At least they were moving into a world that bore some resemblance to the one he'd read about. He had seen some Indians, although they were all peaceful, and some men wore guns and looked like they knew how to use them.

Von Hoffman signaled a halt and waited for Dieter to ride in. The young man came loping up on his horse a few minutes later. He had a broad, friendly peasant's face under the ridiculously high-crowned cowboy hat he wore. His shirt was decorated with fringe, and a gunbelt with intricate designs worked into the leather was strapped around his waist. He carried a pearl-handled revolver in the holster attached to the belt. The outfit had cost him nearly all the money he had saved up and brought with him from Germany.

"Well, Dieter, what did you find?" von Hoffman asked.

"The trail runs into those hills," Dieter replied, turning in his saddle to point. "It won't be difficult to follow, Baron. But I saw quite a few cattle grazing in the hills as well. I think perhaps the land belongs to someone, probably the same man who owns the cattle. Perhaps we should seek to determine this and request his permission to cross his range."

"Nonsense," von Hoffman said. "We will do no harm. There is plenty of water and grass for our animals. The man's stock will never miss what our beasts consume."

"You're right, of course, Your Excellency. I was merely concerned that some gun-totin' rannihans might take offense at our presence."

That mixture of formality and dime novel Western vernacular was the way Dieter talked now, and von Hoffman found it grating at times. He also didn't like the way the young man looked at Erica when he thought no one was watching.

There was nothing lecherous about Dieter's gazes. Instead, they were the longing, calf-eyed looks of a young man desperately in love with a young woman who was unattainable.

And most definitely, Erica was unattainable for the likes of Dieter Schumann. She was noble-born; he was a commoner. The only thing he could ever do for her was serve her. If he kept looking at her like that, von Hoffman would have to do something to put a stop to it. He hoped it wouldn't come to that, because despite Dieter's bizarre affectations, he had proven to be a capable scout and outrider.

Von Hoffman waved the wagons into motion again. Dieter turned his horse and fell in alongside the lead wagon. He doffed his hat and nodded politely to Erica.

"Fraulein von Hoffman," he said. "The afternoon light treats you well. Or perhaps it is you who makes the light seem so radiant."

Erica smiled.

"That's a lovely thing to say, Herr Schumann," she told him.

Dieter was about to say something else, a compliment, no doubt, but before he could speak, von Hoffman said, "Ride ahead again, Schumann. Locate a suitable place for us to camp for the night."

"Of course, Baron." He clapped his hat back on his head and added to Erica, "I'll be seein' you, ma'am."

Erica was smiling as Dieter rode away. Von Hoffman's eyes narrowed slightly as he looked at her. She enjoyed having the young man play up to her like that, he thought. Perhaps it would be wise if he spoke to her, too.

Dieter's horse was a leggy buckskin. It carried him easily away from the wagon train and into the foothills. As he rode, he reached down and checked the gun at his hip, making sure it rode loosely in its holster, so he could get it out quickly if need be.

This was America, after all. One never knew when one would run smack-dab into a desperado bent on robbery or a savage Comanche after scalps.

Of course, an adventure such as that would liven things up, Dieter told himself. So far the trip had been, well, boring. There had been some nice scenery, but nothing nearly as impressive as there was to be found back in Germany. Every day was the same, the ox-drawn wagons rolling at their slow, steady pace across the plains. At least now their route was starting to pass through more rugged country. The hills and mountains would make travel more difficult, but still they would provide a welcome break from the monotony.

Dieter began looking for a good place to camp when he had ridden only a short distance into the hills. The afternoon was well advanced, and it would still take the wagons a while to come this far.

It didn't take him long to find a broad, level stretch of ground beside a tiny creek that flowed down from the higher elevations to twist its way through the hills and finally out onto the plains in a meandering path. This was the perfect spot, Dieter thought as he looked it over. Plenty of grass and water, just as the baron had predicted.

But as Dieter had warned him, there were also cattle grazing here, probably fifty or sixty of them. Dieter tried to count them but kept losing track and finally gave up. The cows would probably move on when the wagons showed up, he thought, but perhaps it would be better if they weren't even here when the baron and the others arrived. He had never herded cattle from horseback before, although he had sometimes worked as a herdsman back in Germany. That job had been carried out on foot.

How difficult could it be? Dieter was a good rider.

He sent his horse toward the cattle and took his hat off. When he got closer, he waved the hat and shouted at the beasts. As he expected, they began walking away from the creek, not getting in any hurry about it.

Dieter rode back and forth, bunching the cattle up and hazing them ahead of him toward some trees. He would push them up there, he thought, and then when the wagons arrived, the open land beside the stream would be unoccupied, just waiting for the immigrants to make camp.

The cattle began to enter the trees. Dieter didn't know how far these woods extended or what was on the other side of them, but that wasn't really his concern. He just wanted to impress Baron von Hoffman by showing some initiative.

And the baron's cousin, Fraulein von Hoffman, as well, of course, although Dieter was reluctant to admit that even to himself.

"Ah, Erica," he said with a sigh, now that there was no one around to hear him. "*Mein liebchen . . .*"

"Hold it right there, mister!" a voice barked behind him.

Startled, Dieter jerked on the buckskin's reins. The horse turned sharply. As Dieter swung around, he caught a glimpse of another man on horseback sitting in the trees and pointing a rifle at him.

"Don't reach for that gun!" the stranger warned.

It was too late. Dieter's hand slapped against the pearl-handled butt of the holstered Colt, just like in the dime novels, and before he knew what he was doing, he had pulled out the revolver and was trying to lift it.

The stranger's rifle cracked sharply, the report echoing from foothill to foothill.

Chapter Five

With snow-capped mountains looming nearby, rolling hills covered with pines, valleys dotted with aspens, and broad, grassy meadows next to icy, spring-fed, fast-flowing streams, the ranch called Sugarloaf was the prettiest place Smoke Jensen had ever seen. Every day of his life, he counted himself lucky to live here.

Of course, the fact that he lived here with a beautiful, intelligent, courageous, and loving woman probably had something to do with how fortunate he considered himself.

Sally Jensen was a schoolteacher by training. That was what she'd been doing when Smoke met her in Idaho. She had given up that job when she married him and they established the ranch in Colorado, except for brief stints filling in whenever the school in Big Rock didn't have a regular teacher. She didn't miss it. Her marriage to Smoke and their life together on the ranch filled her days quite satisfactorily.

She enjoyed having company, though, Smoke knew, and seeing some new faces, even if they were old familiar faces in their way. She was standing on the porch when Smoke, Matt, and Preacher rode up later that afternoon.

By the time Smoke dismounted, Sally had come down the steps. She put a hand on his arm for a second, then turned to Preacher and hugged the old mountain man.

"Preacher, it's so good to see you again," she said.

"And it's mighty good to be here," he said, patting her on the back a little awkwardly. Open displays of affection always embarrassed the old-timer, but he didn't mind too much when they involved being hugged by a pretty gal.

Sally certainly fit that description with her sparkling eyes and long, thick brown hair. She hugged Matt, too, and said, "I'm glad the two of you were able to make it here today. I have a big supper planned."

"I'm glad they got here when they did, too," Smoke said. "I reckon Preacher probably saved my life . . . again."

Sally's eyes widened slightly.

"Saved your life?" she repeated. "Smoke, what in the world happened? Was there some sort of trouble in town?"

"I'm afraid so," he said with a solemn expression on his rugged face now. "A gang of owlhoots tried to rob the bank. The bank president was killed, along with Mitch Byrd, one of the tellers. And Elaine Harris was wounded in the shooting, as well."

Sally lifted a hand to her mouth as she made a noise of horror and sympathy.

"Oh, no! That's terrible, Smoke. How badly is Mrs. Harris hurt? Is she going to be all right?"

"Doc Simpson thinks she'll live, but she may not ever be a hundred percent again."

"That poor woman. I'll have to take the buckboard and go into town tomorrow to visit her. And to pay my respects to Mr. Byrd's wife, of course. I didn't know the new bank president very well."

"Nobody around here did, since he hadn't been in town for long," Smoke said.

Sally's features hardened with anger.

"What about the outlaws?" she asked. "What happened to them?"

"One of them's locked up in Monte's jail with a bullet hole in his leg." Smoke shrugged. "The rest of 'em are at the undertaker's, I reckon. I don't think there's been time to plant them yet."

"Good," Sally said with a note of savagery in her voice. She hated lawbreakers every bit as much as Smoke did, and had as little patience with them. To her way of thinking, justice needed to be both swift and effective, and it usually was whenever Smoke was involved. She looked at Matt and Preacher and went on, "I suppose you two were in the middle of the ruckus, too?"

"We got there just as it was getting over with," Matt said.

"Just in time for me to blow the head off one of

the varmints with my old Sharps," Preacher added with a bloodthirsty grin.

Sally shuddered, and Matt explained, "The fella was about to set off both barrels of a sawed-off shotgun at Smoke and Sheriff Carson."

"Is Monte all right?" Sally asked quickly.

"He's fine," Smoke assured her. "The trouble's over."

"Well, I'm sorry about the townspeople who died," Sally said, "but I'm sure it would have been a lot worse if you hadn't been there. Let's try to think about more pleasant things instead. If you men want to sit out here on the porch and enjoy what's left of the afternoon, I'll bring out a pitcher of lemonade."

Preacher licked his lips for a second, as if he would have preferred something a mite more potent than lemonade, but he said, "That sounds mighty nice, Sally gal."

"We'll do that as soon as we've tended to the horses," Smoke said.

While they were taking care of their mounts, Pearlie rode in. Sugarloaf's foreman was a tall, lanky cowboy with a drooping mustache and graying dark hair. Like Monte Carson he had been a hired gun at one time in his life. Also like Monte, he had started off as one of Smoke's enemies but had become a staunch friend and ally instead. Smoke relied heavily on him to keep the ranch running smoothly and to supervise the crew of half a dozen cowboys who worked there.

Pearlie swung down from his saddle and shook hands with Matt and Preacher.

"It's mighty fine to see you fellas again," he declared. "Been too long since you visited."

"We feel the same way," Matt told him.

"Where's Cal?" Smoke asked. Pearlie and Cal were fast friends despite the fondness for arguing, and they often rode the range together.

"I sent him over to check that east pasture along Snake Creek," Pearlie said. The stream had gotten its name because of the way it twisted back and forth. "Saw some wolf sign over there a day or two ago, so I figured it'd be a good idea to keep a little closer eye on the stock. We start losin' many cows, we'll have to get up a hunt."

Smoke nodded. Usually the wolves stayed up higher in the mountains, but they roamed down into the lower elevations from time to time.

Pearlie unsaddled his mount and turned the horse into the corral with the others. The four men walked toward the house, where Sally was setting a tray containing a pitcher of lemonade and three glasses on a small table on the porch, next to several rocking chairs.

"I didn't know you'd come in, Pearlie," she said as they reached the steps. "I'll fetch another glass."

"I'm much obliged, Miss Sally," Pearlie said as he took off his battered old hat and held it in front of him. Like all the other men who worked on Sugarloaf, he treated Sally like she was a queen.

Sally had just turned toward the door of the ranch

house when the sound of a shot drifted through the late afternoon air. She paused and looked toward the east, just like the four men were doing. The shot had come from quite a distance away, but it sounded like it was in that direction.

"Cal's over yonder," Smoke said quietly.

"Yeah, but there was only the one shot," Pearlie said. "If he was in trouble, he would have fired more than that. Chances are, he spotted one of those dang lobos and took a shot at it."

After a moment, Smoke nodded.

"I think you're right," he said. "We'll go ahead and have our lemonade. Cal's perfectly capable of taking care of himself."

But despite the confidence he felt in the young cowboy, Smoke caught himself glancing off to the east as he sat there with the others and sipped lemonade.

He would be mighty glad when Cal came riding in, just so he could be sure that the youngster was all right.

Spooked by the shot, the buckskin reared sharply as the bullet whistled over Dieter's head. He felt himself slipping and let out an alarmed yell as he grabbed for a better hold. The effort failed, and he toppled backwards out of the saddle, landing with stunning force on the ground. The impact knocked the breath from his lungs and the gun from his hand.

Which meant that the man with the rifle would now kill him, he thought.

And he would never see Erica von Hoffman again. He would die without ever having told her how he felt about her.

Instead of shooting him, the stranger merely pointed the rifle at him and said, "Stay where you are, mister. The next shot won't be a warning."

Dieter didn't move except to gasp for breath and drag air into his lungs. When he could speak again, he said, "*Danke* . . . I mean thank you . . . for not killing me."

"Who are you?" his captor demanded.

"My name is . . . Dieter Schumann." An explanation for what was going on here occurred to him. "You are . . . the hombre who owns this spread?"

"Me?" The idea drew a curt laugh from the rifleman. "Not hardly, but I work for him. This is Sugarloaf range, and I ride for Smoke Jensen."

Dieter could see now that the man was too young to own a ranch, possibly not even twenty years old yet. But despite his youth, he seemed very calm and deadly as he pointed the rifle. Dieter recognized the weapon as one of the repeating rifles called a Winchester.

"Would it be all right . . . if I sat up?" he asked.

The young man considered the request for a second, then nodded.

"Don't try anything funny, though. I'll drill you if you do, I swear."

Dieter struggled to a sitting position and continued catching his breath. His voice was stronger as he said, "I will not try anything funny, I assure you. I am not that sort of galoot."

"Yeah, well, you got me wonderin' just what sort of galoot you are, Peter."

"Dieter."

"Dieter," the young cowboy repeated. "Don't reckon I've ever met anybody with that name before." He paused, then added, "I'm Cal. Calvin Woods."

"I am pleased to meet you, Calvin. As long as you do not ventilate me."

Cal studied Dieter for another moment before shaking his head in amazement.

"I got to admit, you're about the oddest rustler I ever did see."

"Rustler!" Dieter exclaimed in surprise. "I am no rustler!"

Cal inclined his head toward the cattle.

"Those are Sugarloaf cows you were chousin' along, and as far as I know, you don't work for Smoke. To my way of thinkin', that makes you a rustler."

"I was not stealing the cattle," Dieter insisted. "I was merely moving them."

"And why would you do that?"

"To clear this meadow so that the wagon train to which I belong might camp here."

Cal frowned and said, "Wagon train?"

"Yes. Led by Baron Friedrich von Hoffman."

Dieter hesitated. "I warned the baron there might be trouble if we did not seek permission first."

"Yeah, it's always a good idea to ask before you go traipsin' across somebody's range or movin' his stock," Cal agreed. "Stand up and back off, well away from that gun you dropped."

"I mean no trouble, I give you my word."

"Just do it," Cal ordered with a slight jerk of the Winchester's barrel.

Dieter did as he was told, keeping his arms half-lifted and his hands in plain sight as he backed away from the Colt. Cal managed to dismount without the rifle ever wavering out of line. The young cowboy picked up the fallen revolver and tucked it behind his belt.

"Now you can get back on your horse," Cal said.

"You are going to allow me to return to the wagon train?"

"Shoot, no," Cal said. "I'm takin' you to see Smoke. Maybe he can figure out what to do with you, because I sure as blazes can't."

Chapter Six

Cal was still on Smoke's mind when he spotted the riders coming toward the ranch headquarters. The fact that they were riding single file down a distant hill gave Smoke his first clue as to what was going on. As the riders came closer he was able to tell that the second man held a rifle. That confirmed Smoke's hunch.

Somebody was bringing in a prisoner, and considering the direction the riders were coming from, it was likely that one of them was Cal.

But the question remained, was Cal the captor in this situation . . . or the captive?

"Riders comin'," Preacher announced. The old-timer still had eyes like a hawk.

"Yeah, I saw them, too," Matt said.

Smoke set his empty lemonade glass aside and got to his feet.

"I think one of them is Cal," he said.

"Likely is," Pearlie agreed. "Which one?"

"It looks like they're headed straight here," Smoke said, "so I reckon we'll find out in a little while."

Sally came out of the house, unaware of what was going on.

"Supper will be ready—" She stopped short as she saw Smoke standing tensely at the porch railing. She couldn't help but notice that the other three men were alert, too. "What's wrong?"

"There are a couple of men riding in," Smoke explained. "One of them is holding a gun on the other. We figure Cal is one of them, but we don't know if he's the one in trouble. Why don't you go back inside, Sally?"

She drew in a deep breath that caused her breasts to lift and her nostrils to flare.

"I'll go back inside, all right," she said. "To fetch my own Winchester."

"That's not necessary," Smoke said. "There are four of us and only two of them, at most. We've got 'em outnumbered."

Sally looked reluctant to retreat into the house, but she said, "Don't let anything happen to Calvin."

"We won't," Smoke said.

He hoped he could keep that promise.

By the time the riders came close enough for the men on the porch to make out who was who, Sally had gone back into the house and all four men were waiting tensely at the railing. Smoke felt a wave of relief go through him as he recognized Cal riding behind the other man, who was a stranger. Cal had his rifle pointed in the general direction of the hombre's back.

A smile broke across Cal's face as he saw Matt and Preacher standing on the porch.

"Howdy, fellas!" he called to them. "Smoke told us you were supposed to show up today. I'm glad you did."

"Good to see you, too, younker," Preacher said. "What in the sam hill is that you got there?"

"I'm not quite sure," Cal replied. "He's some sort of foreigner, and he claims he comes from a wagon train."

Matt and Preacher glanced at each other, then at Smoke.

"Told you we saw a wagon train," Matt said.

Smoke nodded.

"You sure did."

He moved to the steps and went down them. As he approached the two newcomers, he saw that the stranger was young, probably only a few years older than Cal. He had dark blond hair and a face that might have been friendly if it wasn't so nervous. The big hat and fringed shirt made him look like the fake cowboys Smoke had seen back East hanging around Wild West shows. Drugstore cowboys, somebody had called them.

"Why are you pointing that rifle at him, Cal?" Smoke asked.

"I caught him driving some of our stock out of the pasture over by Snake Creek," Cal explained. "I thought he was a rustler, so I got the drop on him. He slapped leather anyway, and I had to put a warning shot over his head. His horse threw him and made him drop his gun." Cal shrugged. "That's about the size of it. Oh, yeah, he says his name is Dieter."

"Dieter Schumann," the young man said. "I sincerely apologize for causing a . . . a ruckus."

Smoke heard traces of an accent in Dieter's voice and recognized it. He had met a number of people from Germany and had actually traveled to that country himself once, while he and Sally were touring Europe.

"You're Prussian, aren't you?" Smoke asked.

Dieter looked surprised but pleased.

"Ja. Sprechen sie Deutsche?"

"Just enough to know you asked me if I speak your native lingo," Smoke said. "And I'm afraid I don't."

"No matter," Dieter said. "I speak very fine English. You are the man who owns this ranch?"

"That's right. Smoke Jensen's my name."

"I am honored to meet you, Herr Jensen. May I dismount?"

Smoke glanced at Cal.

"You've got his gun?"

Cal tapped the butt of the Colt stuck behind his belt and nodded.

"Right here, Smoke. I didn't search him, though. He might have a hideout gun."

"I assure you, I am unarmed," Dieter said.

Smoke nodded and said, "Light and set, then. We believe in hospitality here on Sugarloaf. But we believe in being careful, too, so don't get any ideas."

Dieter swung down from the saddle. He didn't appear to represent any sort of threat, so Smoke went on, "I think you can put your rifle away, Cal. Why don't you go tend to your horse, and Dieter's, too, if you don't mind."

Cal slid his Winchester back into its saddle boot.

"Sure, Smoke," he said. He held out his hand, and Dieter gave him the buckskin's reins. Cal headed for the barn and the corral, leading the visitor's horse.

Sally came out onto the porch carrying another glass. Obviously, she had been listening to the conversation from just inside the door.

"There's a little lemonade left, Mr. Schumann, if you'd like some," she said.

Dieter snatched his hat off and bowed from the waist.

"That sounds wonderful, *fraulein*," he said.

"It's *frau*," Sally told him. "I'm Mrs. Jensen, Smoke's wife."

"It is an honor and a pleasure."

"Don't get any ideas about kissin' the back of her hand," Preacher warned. "She's the spunky sort. Liable to punch you if you do."

"Don't listen to him, Mr. Schumann," Sally said with a smile. "Visitors are always welcome on Sugarloaf . . . if they're not looking for trouble."

"Such an idea is the farthest thing from my intention, I assure you."

Dieter came up onto the porch. Smoke and the others watched him closely, but he appeared as harmless as he claimed to be. He sat down in one of the rocking chairs and swallowed nervously as the four frontiersmen surrounded him.

"Oh, back off and let the poor man breathe," Sally said as she poured the last of the lemonade into the clean glass. She handed it to him and went on, "Here you are, Mr. Schumann."

"I'm much obliged, ma'am." Dieter took a long swallow of the cool, tart liquid. When he lowered the glass, he licked his lips and said, "That's larrupin' good."

"Where'd you say you were from?" Matt asked with a frown.

"Germany. Prussia, to be precise."

"What's this about a wagon train?" Smoke asked.

"Baron Friedrich von Hoffman is our leader," Dieter answered. "He is taking a large group of settlers to the American state called Wyoming. The baron has bought a ranch there and intends to establish a town as well."

"Sounds like a fella with big plans," Preacher commented.

Dieter took another drink of lemonade and nodded eagerly.

"Oh, yes, very much so. He intends to be another sort of baron as well. A cattle baron!"

Smoke said, "Where are these wagons now?"

"Coming up the trail that runs east of the mountains. It curves through these hills on its way north."

"That's right," Smoke said. "But we've never had a wagon train come through here before. The ones bound for Wyoming, Idaho, and Oregon usually take a more northerly route across Kansas and Nebraska. Your wagonmaster shouldn't have brought you this far south. Nothing wrong with the trail, but it's a longer way around. It'll take you at least a couple of weeks longer than it would have if you'd gone the other way."

Dieter looked uncomfortable as he said, "My apologies, Herr Jensen. The baron did not engage the services of a guide or wagonmaster. He said that he has visited America enough times and is familiar enough with the Western frontier that he could lead us and determine our route himself."

"Oh," Preacher said. "A greenhorn know-it-all furriner."

Dieter set his glass aside on the table.

"Them's fightin' words," he said.

"Take it easy," Smoke said. "Preacher doesn't mean anything by it."

Preacher snorted.

"That's what this old mossyhorn is called, by the way," Smoke went on. "As for the rest of us, this is Matt Jensen, my brother, and my foreman Pearlie. The young fella who brought you in is Calvin Woods."

Dieter nodded and said, "Yes, Calvin introduced himself to me. I am pleased to make the acquaintance of the rest of you rannies."

Matt laughed.

"You're an unusual sort of fella, Dieter," he said.

"Thank you," Dieter said with a smile. He turned back to Smoke. "My apologies for trespassing on your range, Herr Jensen. I swear, I was not trying to rustle your cattle."

"I believe you. And call me Smoke."

"If you would like, Smoke, I will return to the wagons and inform the baron that we are not allowed to travel through this area. The wagons may have already reached the boundaries of your range, but they can turn around and go back the way they came until we are able to circle around the hills."

"Smoke . . ." Sally said, and he knew what she was getting at. She didn't want them to be inhospitable.

Smoke said to Dieter, "There's no need for you folks to do that. That would just add more time to your trip, and it's already going to take you longer to get to Wyoming than it ought to. I don't mind you passing through, although it would have been nice if this baron of yours would have looked me up and asked me about it first."

Dieter came to his feet and bowed again.

"You are a true gentleman, Herr Jensen . . . I mean, Smoke."

Preacher said, "Better be careful with that bowin', boy. You'll throw your back out. We don't much hold with it in these parts, anyway. This is America, where folks don't have to bow to each other. Every man's as good as the next one."

"This is what I have heard, Mr. Preacher. Coming from the old country as I do, such a concept is . . . difficult to grasp."

"Just Preacher," the old mountain man growled. "No mister."

Sally said, "You'll stay and have supper with us, won't you, Dieter?"

The young man shook his head regretfully.

"I cannot. I must return to the wagons, report to the baron, and assist in setting up camp. With your permission, of course, Smoke."

"You've got it," Smoke said. "But I'm coming with you. I want to meet this baron of yours."

"So do I," Matt said. "I'm not sure I've ever met a baron."

Preacher grunted and said, "I have. They ain't nothin' special."

Sally asked, "Does Baron von Hoffman have a family?"

"A cousin," Dieter said. "She is his only close relative."

"Smoke, I can hold off on getting supper ready for a while," Sally said. "If you're going out to the wagon train, why don't you ask the baron and his cousin if they'll come and eat with us?"

"That's a good idea," Smoke said. "And you, too, Dieter."

The young man's eyes widened.

"I could not—" he began.

"Sure you can," Smoke said. "Like Preacher told you, you're in America. We do things a mite differently here."

"I understand that, but I'm not sure the baron will."

"One way to find out." Smoke nodded toward the corral. "Let's go saddle some horses."

Chapter Seven

"Dieter should have been back by now," Erica said.

Von Hoffman heard the worried tone in his cousin's voice and was annoyed by it.

Not as annoyed as he was by Dieter's failure to reappear, though. He had been counting on the young man to guide them to a suitable campground. When Dieter hadn't come back, von Hoffman had called a temporary halt to wait for him.

The wagons had been stopped for a while now, however, and still there was no sign of Dieter Schumann.

Something had happened to him, von Hoffman thought. Perhaps he had finally run into outlaws or savages or one of the other frontier perils he seemed so eager to see.

"We can't just sit here and wait for darkness to overtake us," von Hoffman said as he paced back and forth next to the lead wagon, having dismounted to let his stallion rest for a few minutes. "This is not a good place to camp. There's grass for the animals, but no water."

"Perhaps we should continue on," Erica suggested from where she sat on the wagon seat. The driver had gotten down earlier to put some water from one of the barrels into a bucket so the oxen could drink. "Dieter said the trail was easy to follow."

Von Hoffman scowled but didn't say anything. Young Schumann might think the trail was obvious, but the baron was having trouble seeing it, although he wouldn't have admitted that to anyone else. He didn't relish the idea of wasting time, but he certainly didn't want to get them lost, either.

"Help me down, please, Friedrich," Erica went on. "I would like to stretch my limbs while we're stopped." She smiled ruefully. "And this seat is hardly what one would call comfortable."

"Of course," von Hoffman said. He stepped over to the wagon to assist his cousin. A moment later, Erica's feet were on the ground.

She glanced along the line of wagons and suddenly frowned. Von Hoffman noticed the expression and asked, "What's wrong?"

"Frau Schiller is coming," Erica said.

The baron looked toward the rear of the wagon train and saw that she was right. Greta Schiller was walking toward them with a determined stride. Her lovely face wore a frown of concern.

At any other time, von Hoffman wouldn't have minded talking to the beautiful redheaded widow.

He knew that Greta might well have designs on him, and he didn't discourage her interest. A man would have to be a fool to do that. With her thick auburn hair, her richly curved body, her sensuous lips, and her provocative green eyes, Greta Schiller was as tasty a morsel as von Hoffman had ever seen in his life.

She was also the widow of an old friend of his, so decorum demanded that he treat her with respect when what he really wanted to do was tumble her into a comfortable bed and have his way with her. Greta's bold gazes sometimes made him think that was exactly what she wanted, too.

But right now he had much more important things on his mind than finding the right time and place to bed a randy widow.

She came up to him and Erica and murmured, "Baron."

"My dear Frau Schiller," von Hoffman said. "What can I do for you?"

"Some of us are wondering when the wagons will resume their journey. Evening is not far away now."

He felt a surge of irritation. Did she think he was blind? He could see for himself how low in the sky the sun was.

"And you were appointed to speak for the group?" he asked coolly.

She shrugged, which made her proud breasts do intriguing things under her dress.

"I volunteered," she said. A smile curved her lips. "I hope that I have not presumed on our friendship,

Friedrich. I thought that since you and my late husband were so close . . ."

"Of course," von Hoffman said. "You have every right to speak to me. But as for your question . . . We're waiting for the Schumann boy to return. He was searching for a suitable location for us to camp."

"Dieter is not a boy, Friedrich," Erica put in. "And I think something must have happened to him. He may be hurt. We should go ahead, so we can look for him."

Von Hoffman hated being challenged that way. Erica was perhaps the only person alive whom he would allow to speak to him in that manner.

What was most irritating was the fact that she was right. It made no sense to just sit here. He knew the direction Dieter had gone. Perhaps the boy *was* hurt. Von Hoffman wasn't particularly concerned about Dieter's health, but he wanted to know what had happened.

He smiled at Greta and said, "Tell the others to prepare to get started again. We will resume our journey right away."

"Thank you, Your Excellency." Greta spoke in a tone of respect, but there was a coquettish gleam in her eyes.

Soon, von Hoffman told himself. Soon he would have to find out just exactly how far she was prepared to go.

Within minutes the wagons were rolling again. Von Hoffman rode in front of the first wagon, leading the way. Two hills rose in front of him, but the area between them was nice and wide and that seemed to be the way the trail should go. He headed for the gap, and everyone followed him.

Naturally.

He was the baron, after all. He sat straight and proud in the saddle and led his people between the hills. He turned to give them a confident smile and show them what a splendid leader he was.

That was when he heard something buzz past his ear like a giant insect, and a split second later, the crack of shot sounded from the hill to his right.

That must have been a signal, because suddenly guns began to roar on both sides of the wagon train.

Smoke told Pearlie and Cal to stay at the ranch headquarters. He and Dieter Schumann rode east from there, accompanied by Matt and Preacher.

"Tell me more about this Baron von Hoffman," Smoke asked the young man from Germany.

"The baron is a fine man," Dieter declared without hesitation. "I have never seen a more accomplished swordsman, or a better shot, or a more honorable gentleman. He served with valor and distinction in the army and was wounded in the war against the French."

"You know," Preacher said, "I never could keep track of who was fightin' who over yonder in the old country. Seemed like I'd go to St. Louis and hear folks talkin' about how some place was fightin' some other place, and then the next time I went, those two bunches had thrown in together to fight against some other entirely different folks. You know what I mean?"

Dieter said, "Allegiances do seem to shift quite a bit. Politics are very important in my homeland."

Preacher leaned over in the saddle and spat.

"Politics!" he said. "A bunch of vultures tryin' to feather their own nests and devil take the hindmost, from what I've seen of it. And most of 'em are partnered up with out-and-out crooks, like that blasted Indian Ring."

Dieter shook his head.

"I know nothing of this about which you speak."

"It's not important right now," Smoke told him. "And all those European allegiances you were talking about don't matter anymore, Dieter. You're in America now. The country got started because people came here to lead new lives, and they're still doing that."

"Yes," Dieter said with a nod. "New lives."

"For example," Matt said, "we don't have barons over here. Now that you're in America, you don't have to bow and scrape to this von Hoffman hombre."

"My family has served the von Hoffman family for generations," Dieter protested. "It is the way of things."

"It's the way things used to be," Matt argued. "Not anymore. Sure, you can work for him if you want to, but if you don't, there's nothing stopping you from going and doing something else."

"But . . . what would I do?"

"Anything you want to. Drive a stagecoach, prospect for gold, start your own ranch if you want to."

"My own ranch . . ." Dieter said as a faraway look appeared in his eyes. "It is something to dream about. If only . . ."

"There are no 'if onlies' here. If you want it bad enough, you can do it."

Dieter sighed and shook his head.

"Not this. Even if I had my own ranch, I would need something else to make it complete." He paused. "Someone else."

Matt grinned.

"A girl, eh? Does she know how you feel about her?"

"No," Dieter answered instantly. "I could never tell her!"

"Why not?"

"Because she . . . she is not for the likes of me."

"You're talking about someone of noble birth? And you can't approach her because you're just a common man?"

"That's right," Dieter said.

Matt leaned over in the saddle and poked a finger against Dieter's shoulder.

"Well, let me tell you something, amigo," he said. "In this country, a man's only as common as he wants to be. If you want to be an uncommon man, what you've got to do is reach out and grab whatever it is you're after—"

Matt might have continued with his advice, but at that moment all four men reined in abruptly as the sound of gunfire filled the warm, late afternoon air. It came from somewhere ahead of them, and it sounded like the battle wasn't far off.

"Come on!" Smoke said as he leaned forward in the saddle and heeled his horse into a gallop.

Chapter Eight

The baron wheeled his horse sharply as Erica screamed. Von Hoffman saw the stricken driver slumping against her as blood pumped from the bullet hole in his chest.

"Get inside the wagon!" von Hoffman shouted at his cousin as he jerked his rifle from its sheath and sent his horse plunging alongside the wagon. "Stay down!"

He knew that the bed of the big, canvas-covered wagon was filled with crates and bags and pieces of furniture, and Erica would be as safe there as anywhere. He paused until he saw her scrambling through the gap in the canvas before he galloped along the line of wagons, shouting for his people to take cover.

He heard more bullets whipping through the air nearby as rifles continued to crack on both of the hills flanking the wagon train's route. This was not the first time von Hoffman had been under enemy fire. He knew that if he kept his head and stayed calm, he would have a better chance of surviving this ambush. He planned to take cover under one of the wagons as soon as he could.

But first he had to make sure his people were safe. He rode all the way to the back of the wagon train and saw the immigrants scrambling to get inside or under the heavy vehicles. The thick boards that formed the bodies of the wagons would stop most bullets, he thought.

Several of the oxen bellowed in pain as they were wounded. The outriders who accompanied the wagon train were fighting back as best they could, galloping back and forth and firing up toward the pine-covered slopes. Von Hoffman knew that wasn't going to do much good—it would be pure luck if the defenders hit anything—but at least they were putting up some resistance.

"Take cover!" he shouted to them. "Take cover and make your shots count!"

It was time to follow his own advice, he thought as another slug sizzled past his ear. He had kept moving so the attackers would have a harder time drawing a bead on him, but now he needed to seek shelter.

He whirled his horse to head for the lead wagon again, so he would be closer to his cousin, but as he did, the stallion screamed in pain and reared upright to lash angrily at the air with his hooves. Von Hoffman caught a glimpse of the bloody furrow on the horse's shoulder where a bullet had grazed him.

Normally, Baron von Hoffman was an excellent rider and would have been able to stay in the saddle no matter what, but this crisis took him by surprise. He felt himself slipping and grabbed for the saddlehorn, but he was too late. He toppled off the horse and crashed to the ground.

That made him an easier target for the ambushers. Grit stung his eyes as a bullet kicked up dirt only inches from his face. Still clutching his rifle, he rolled desperately for the cover of the nearest wagon. He barely avoided being stepped on by his panic-stricken mount.

Von Hoffman lunged underneath the wagon as a bullet rang off one of the iron-tired wheels. He crawled to the center of the space and lay there for a few moments trying to catch his breath. The fall from his horse had knocked the air out of his lungs.

His pulse was pounding heavily, too, but it slowed somewhat as he lay there. Anger burned fiercely inside him. He was sure that some of his people were wounded, perhaps even dead. He wanted to strike back at the men who had done this.

The question of who they were nagged at von Hoffman's brain. It was possible the wagon train had been attacked by outlaws who had lain in wait to rob the immigrants, the sort of bloodthirsty desperadoes Dieter Schumann read about in his precious dime novels. Just because they were used in fiction didn't mean they couldn't exist in real life as well.

Or perhaps the wagons were under attack by

hostile Indians, although to the best of the baron's knowledge, all the tribes in this area were currently at peace with the white men. This might be a band of renegades. After all, less than a decade earlier the famous Colonel Custer and his men had been wiped out by a huge force of savages.

But even though those possibilities went through his head, von Hoffman knew what the most likely explanation for this ambush had to be.

His enemies from the old country had caught up to him, or rather, killers hired by those enemies to settle all the old political scores.

So, when you looked at it that way, von Hoffman thought grimly, this was his fault.

He crawled over behind one of the wagon wheels and stuck the barrel of his Winchester through a gap between spokes. His eyes searched the hillside he could see from here, and after a moment he spotted a puff of powder smoke from behind a tree. The smoke gave away the location of one of the hidden riflemen.

Von Hoffman nestled his cheek against the smooth wood of the rifle's stock, squinted over the sights, and drew a bead on the spot. He waited patiently, and after a moment he caught a glimpse of a man's hat.

The baron squeezed the trigger.

The Winchester cracked as it bucked against his shoulder. He was an excellent marksman. A split second later, a man tumbled out from behind the tree the baron had been watching. The man sprawled on the hillside and didn't move, and von Hoffman knew he had drilled the ambusher through the head. It was a fine shot, especially considering the range and the angle.

He shifted the Winchester's barrel and searched for another target. This fight was just getting started.

The baron hoped that not too many of his people would die before it was over.

As Smoke, Matt, Preacher, and Dieter galloped toward the sound of shots, Smoke caught a glimpse of white between the hills known as East and West Kiowa Peaks. He pointed it out to the others and called, "Wagons?"

"Looks like it to me!" Matt answered. "Come on!"

He didn't have to urge the other men. They all leaned forward in their saddles and pounded toward the hills at top speed.

As they came closer, Smoke saw that his guess was right. A long line of several dozen wagons had entered the gap, and now the immigrants appeared to be pinned down by rifle fire from both hills. He pointed to the eastern peak and said, "Matt, you and Preacher see if you can roust out some of the varmints on that side! Dieter and I will head west!"

"Got it!" Matt replied. He and the old mountain man veered their horses toward the east.

Smoke angled west and looked over to make sure Dieter was coming with him. The young man urged his horse ahead, doing his best to keep up with

Smoke. Dieter looked a little scared, and Smoke figured this would be his first real gun battle.

"Herr Jensen!" Dieter called. "I am unarmed!"

Smoke grimaced. He had forgotten that Cal had taken Dieter's pistol and hadn't given it back. He couldn't lead the youngster into the middle of this ruckus when Dieter didn't have any way to fight.

"Can you handle a rifle?" Smoke asked.

"I have shot a Winchester a few times!"

Smoke pulled his rifle from the saddle boot and brought his horse close enough to Dieter's mount that he could pass the weapon over to the young man.

"Here you go! It's got fifteen rounds in it! You'll have to work the lever between shots!"

"I understand!" Dieter said over the pounding hoofbeats.

Smoke pulled slightly ahead again to lead the way. He had circled far enough to the west that he and Dieter were able to start up the back side of the hill. Smoke's horse was fresher and took the slope easier. Dieter began to fall back. Smoke waved for the young man to follow him and kept going. Delay might mean that more innocent people would be killed.

As Smoke neared the top of the hill, he reined in and swung down from the saddle to go ahead on foot. His Colt was in his hand as soon as his boots hit the ground.

There was a good chance the bushwhackers had left their horses somewhere up here in the trees, along with some men to keep an eye on the animals. Smoke didn't want to blunder right into them, so he moved forward with caution.

A racket in the brush behind him made him look over his shoulder. Dieter had sort of caught up and had dismounted, too. Now the young man was stomping forward through the brush, trying to catch up even more. Smoke motioned for him to slow down and take it easier . . . and quieter.

Dieter did so. His eyes were so big now they looked like they were going to jump right out of their sockets. Smoke decided it might be better to wait for him, so he paused until Dieter came up and joined him at the hill's crest.

The sound of shots from lower down the slope filled the air. Smoke said, "Stay with me, and if you have to shoot, don't waste any time, but don't rush it, either. Make sure the rifle's pointing at one of them and not me before you pull the trigger."

"*Jawohl,*" Dieter said with a nervous, eager nod. "I mean, yes, Smoke. I understand. Who are these men?"

"I don't have any idea, but they're shooting at your wagon train. That's enough for me."

"For me, too," Dieter declared. "Let us ventilate some of the mangy polecats."

"Yeah, we'll do that," Smoke said. He was going to have to ask Dieter how come he talked that way . . . if they both lived through this fight, of course.

They began stalking down the slope. From the corner of his eye, Smoke spotted movement through the trees and underbrush and motioned for Dieter to follow him as he moved to the left. A moment later Smoke saw the movement again and recognized it as several horses moving around nervously. He pointed out the animals to Dieter, who nodded.

Putting his mouth close to the young man's ear, Smoke said, "There'll be at least two of the bushwhackers with the horses, maybe more. They won't expect anybody to be coming up behind them, so we ought to be able to get the drop on them. If they put up a fight, though, don't hesitate to shoot."

"I won't, Herr Jensen . . . I mean, Smoke. I will do what I have to."

"That's all I can ask of any man," Smoke said with a grim smile. "Come on."

Chapter Nine

On the far slope of the eastern hill, Matt and Preacher brought their horses to a halt and swung down from their saddles.

"Split up?" Matt suggested.

"I don't need no nursemaid, if that's what you're askin'," Preacher replied with a snort.

Matt grinned.

"It wasn't, but I reckon I can take care of myself, too," he said. "Good luck. Be careful, Preacher."

The old-timer snorted again. He wore a pair of holstered Colts and as he drew both guns, he said, "I got all the luck I need right here, and careful men die in their beds. I'll be damned if I want that!"

He started off into the trees, and in little more than the blink of an eye, he was gone, completely vanished from sight. Matt recalled Smoke telling him that in Preacher's younger days, some of the Indians had called him Ghost Killer, because he could glide into their camps like a phantom, slit the throats of some of his enemies, and slip back out again without anybody knowing he had been there until the bodies were discovered.

Age hadn't robbed the old man of much of his stealth.

Matt could move pretty silently himself when he needed to, although he wasn't as skilled at it as Preacher. He made his way through the trees until he heard some horses blowing and stamping. He knew he was close to the spot where the bushwhackers had left their mounts.

Crouching, he held his Colt in one hand and parted the brush with the other. Through the gap he made he was able to see several horses. A man passed through his line of sight as well. The hombre was roughly dressed in range clothes, and dark beard stubble covered his hard-planed jaw. He looked like the sort of hardcase that was much too common on the frontier, a man who was capable of ruthless, brutal violence if the price was right . . . and that price probably wouldn't be too high, either.

Matt edged forward as the man went out of sight. He wanted to get an idea of how many of them were close by before he made his move.

He wasn't expecting the sudden crackle of brush as a man pushed through it and nearly tripped over him.

"Son of a—" the man yelled as he stumbled and tried to catch his balance. He seemed to be taken as much by surprise as Matt was. He clawed at the holstered gun on his hip.

Matt leaped back, but as he did so, one foot caught on an exposed tree root. He fell backwards and landed on his rump. His left hand went behind him to steady him as he raised his Colt. He fired as soon as the other man's gun cleared leather.

The .44 slug punched into the man's chest and knocked him down. Matt leaped to his feet and bulled through the brush, breaking into the clearing where the bushwhackers' horses were tied just as two more men spun toward him. They had been lighting quirlies. The cigarettes dropped from their mouths as they split up, making Matt choose between them.

He went for the one on the right first, triggering two swift shots that sent the man spinning off his feet. That gave the man on the left enough time to unlimber his Colt, and the gun boomed as Matt whirled toward him. Matt heard the wind-rip of the bullet's passage beside his ear as his revolver roared and bucked again in his hand.

The third man staggered and dropped his gun, blood gushing from his bullet-torn neck. He clapped his hands over the wound, but that didn't do any good. The crimson flood just washed over his fingers. The man made a grotesque strangling noise that might have been him trying to curse Matt with his last breath, then he pitched forward on his face.

Matt stood there tensely, waiting to see if anybody else was going to show up in response to the gunfire. The horses were spooked by the shots and the sharp tang of gunsmoke in the air, not to mention the cop-

pery scent of freshly spilled blood, but their reins
had been tied securely to the trees and they couldn't
pull loose. After a minute they began to settle down.

None of the other ambushers farther down the
slope seemed to be paying any attention to the shots
from up here. That came as no surprise to Matt,
considering how much gunfire filled the air already.
He opened his Colt's cylinder and thumbed in three
fresh rounds from the loops on his shell belt to replace the ones he had fired. As he snapped the
cylinder closed, he began moving down the slope in
search of more bushwhackers.

Preacher was already considerably lower on the
hillside than Matt. A big fight like this was nothing
new for the old-timer. When he first came west, the
vast frontier was full of enemies. Kill one, and a
dozen more took his place. So Preacher was used to
the odds being against him.

He liked it that way.

These gunmen today weren't all that much of a
challenge, though. Guided by the continuing crack
of rifle fire, he came up behind a man who knelt in
some rocks, shooting at the wagons in the gap
below. Preacher holstered both Colts and drew his
Bowie knife instead.

The varmint never knew what hit him as nearly a
foot of cold, razor-sharp steel buried itself in his
back. The deadly keen tip of the knife pierced his

heart and killed him. He let out a surprised whimper as he died.

Preacher pulled the knife free, wiped the blood from the blade on the dead man's shirt, and began looking for new prey to stalk.

He wasn't long in finding it, but there were two of the bushwhackers this time, using a pair of thick-trunked pines about ten feet apart for cover. One man's Winchester ran dry, and he half-turned to reload it. When he did, he saw the old man in buckskins standing there.

"Avery!" he yelled as he dropped the empty rifle and reached for his revolver. The other man whirled around in alarm and swung his rifle toward Preacher.

Preacher's hands came up, both of them filled with his revolvers. The twin Colts blasted at the same instant. The man to Preacher's left was driven back against the tree trunk by the slug's impact. The one on the right doubled over, shot through the belly. Both of them collapsed.

That made three of the varmints done for, Preacher thought. He wondered idly how many more bushwhackers were on this hill. He hoped he wouldn't run out of them too soon. This was a better fight than the one against the bank robbers in Big Rock earlier that afternoon, but it still wasn't a patch on some of the epic battles he had taken part in during the old days.

The worrisome thing was that the light was starting to fade. The sun would be setting soon, and when it did the shadows on this wooded hillside would grow thick in a hurry. That wouldn't bother Preacher—he had eyes like a cat—but it might make things more difficult for Smoke and Matt.

Not that he had to be overly concerned about those two, he reminded himself. They had been in too many battles to count. Maybe they hadn't always come through unscathed, but they were still alive and the bad hombres they had come up against were dead. No, Smoke and Matt could handle themselves just fine.

Preacher followed the sound of shooting until he came upon three more men clustered behind some trees. His Colts were in his hands and he was about to open fire on them when they paused in their attack on the wagon train and started talking to each other.

The words didn't really make any sense to Preacher, but he knew he had heard some of that language before. And the men's accents were similar to Dieter Schumann's voice. They were speaking German, Preacher realized.

That wasn't surprising. There was a whole wagon train full of German folks down there, and these varmints were shooting at them. Of course there was a connection.

But the bushwhackers could have been common, everyday outlaws. Knowing that they weren't might come in handy later on, Preacher thought, because this might not be the last attack on those immigrants.

He was looking forward to sitting down and

talking this over with Smoke and Matt when he got the chance.

Until then . . .

"Hey, you Dutch-talkin' varmints!" Preacher called as he stepped into the open. "*Sprechen* some o' this!"

He waited until the men turned before he opened fire. Shots rolled from his Colts in a wave of gun-thunder. The men didn't go down easily, even with slugs from Preacher's revolvers smashing into them. They got off several shots in return. The broad-brimmed felt hat sailed off the old-timer's head. Another bullet plucked at the fringe on his sleeve.

One of the bushwhackers finally crumpled under the leaden onslaught, then another, and finally Preacher drilled the last of the hombres in the forehead and made him collapse like a puppet with its strings cut.

Preacher pouched one of the irons and got busy reloading the other Colt. He did that mostly by feel, because he was keeping a close eye on the fallen gunmen, in case one or more of them was still alive. Unlike the other bushwhackers he had seen, these three were wearing town clothes, tweed suits and bowler hats. That jibed with his realization that they weren't from around these parts.

When both guns had full cylinders again, Preacher checked the bodies and made sure the men were dead. One of the hombres was short and beefy, with a red face and clean-shaven jowls. The other two had been taller and sported close-cropped beards.

He wondered if these men were behind the attack on the wagon train. They could have paid the other men to bushwhack the immigrants. That thought led him to search the bodies. He found their wallets and tucked them away inside his buckskin shirt. He would look over their contents later, when he was back with Smoke and Matt.

That done, he started down the slope again, but he hadn't gone very far when he heard men coming toward him, crashing through the undergrowth as they hurried up the hill.

From the sound of it, they were giving up the ambush and lighting a shuck out of here. Preacher wasn't surprised. It took a craven coward to bushwhack folks in the first place. The people with the wagon train seemed to be putting up a fight, and after a while, hired gunmen would get tired of that and decide to cut their losses and run.

Preacher found himself a nice sturdy tree and got ready. Both Colts had full cylinders, which meant he had twelve shots without reloading, and he intended to make good use of each and every one of them.

"Come on, you sons o' bitches," the old mountain man muttered as he waited. "The ball's about to open, and it's gonna be one hell of a fandango!"

Chapter Ten

Over on the other hill, Smoke and Dieter circled the bushwhackers' horses, following the sound of voices. Smoke smelled tobacco and knew the guards had lit quirlies. That told him they weren't nervous. They didn't think they had anything to fear because they had the easy job, watching the horses while the rest of the men ambushed the wagon train.

They were about to find out how wrong they were.

Colt leveled, Smoke stepped around the horses and saw the two gunmen standing there. He said sharply, "Hold it! Don't go for your guns!"

They ignored the order. The two men whirled and jerked their pistols from leather.

"Now, Dieter!" Smoke said. His gun roared as the whipcrack of a shot from the rifle wielded by the young Prussian split the air as well.

In the blink of an eye, Smoke had put two slugs in the chest of one of the gunmen. He pivoted slightly, ready to bring down the other one, but the man had already dropped his gun and took a stumbling step to the side. He fell to his knees and sprawled on the ground as his strength deserted him, along with the life's blood welling from his chest.

Smoke looked over at his companion as Dieter lowered the Winchester. The youngster's face was pale and drawn, but he seemed composed enough.

"Is the man dead?" Dieter asked.

"More than likely," Smoke said.

"I have never killed a man before. I never even shot at anyone before."

"I won't say it's something you ever get over, but it helps to know that he would have killed you without blinking an eye. And the people he's working with may have already killed some of your friends down there."

Smoke wouldn't have thought it was possible, but an even more pronounced pallor came over Dieter's face. Smoke knew the young man was thinking about the girl he had feelings for, the one he had never told that he loved her.

Best to channel that fear into action. Smoke said, "Let's go. There are more of them farther down."

After making sure the two gunmen were dead, they left the bodies lying there next to the skittish horses and started down the slope. A hundred yards farther on, they came up behind a man using one of the pines for cover as he fired a rifle at the wagons down in the gap.

Dieter raised Smoke's Winchester and pointed it

at the man's back, but Smoke rested his free hand on the rifle barrel and pushed it back down.

"Might be a good idea to take a prisoner if we can," Smoke whispered. "That baron of yours might want to ask him some questions."

Dieter nodded in agreement. Smoke motioned for him to stay where he was, then moved closer to the man. Preacher had taught Smoke how to be quiet when Smoke was just a young man, and while he wasn't quite as good at it as the old mountain man, there wasn't much difference between them.

The bushwhacker didn't even know Smoke was there. Smoke reversed his gun, raised it above his head, and brought the butt crashing down on the back of the man's skull. The man dropped his rifle and sagged forward against the tree. His arms clutched at the rough bark for a second before he lost consciousness. Out cold, he slid down the trunk to the ground.

Smoke holstered his Colt and bent down to jerk the man's belt from its loops. He used the belt to lash the man's hands together behind his back. He wasn't gentle about it, either. The way he saw it, would-be murderers didn't deserve any special consideration.

When he was finished with that, he drew his knife and used it to cut strips from the man's shirt. With those, he tied the man's ankles together.

"That way he can't get up and run off," Smoke explained to Dieter. "He'll still be here when we get back, unless one of his friends comes along and turns him loose."

"Should I stay here and guard him?" Dieter asked.

Smoke shook his head.

"No, you come with me. From the sounds of it, the odds are still pretty heavy against us."

That was true. A lot of guns were still going off on the hillsides.

And those folks down there with the wagons were still under heavy fire. They were bound to have taken some casualties by now.

Baron von Hoffman had been firing up at the slopes for what seemed like forever, although it was probably more like a quarter of an hour. He crawled back and forth underneath the wagon so he could send shots at both hills.

He never should have brought the wagons through the gap, he told himself bitterly. Looking back on it now, he could see that this was a perfect spot for an ambush, and he had led his people right into it.

He should have known it was going to happen sooner or later. He had opposed some powerful men back in Germany and come very close to up-setting all their plans. Even though he had failed and they had proven successful in their efforts, they weren't the sort of men to forgive such defiance.

Being well aware of that, he had made hasty plans to leave the country, taking his allies and servants with him. A year earlier, he had made arrangements to buy the failed ranch in Wyoming, knowing that sometime in the future he might need such a place for sanctuary. He had hoped that would be enough to spare them any trouble. . . .

But deep down, he had known that it wouldn't be.

However, the voyage to America had gone smoothly, and once he and his group were in this country, they hadn't encountered any problems. They had traveled by train to Kansas City, where the baron had bought wagons and supplies for the trip to Wyoming.

They could have taken the train all the way to Cheyenne, but he thought that setting out by wagon from Kansas City might help throw any pursuit off their trail. It was slower, of course, but to his way of thinking they wouldn't be as easy to follow.

Clearly, he had been wrong. The lack of trouble had lulled him into complacency, and all the while his enemies were making arrangements of their own, hiring men to get ahead of him and set the trap that had now closed. . . .

Those thoughts were eating at von Hoffman's brain like acid when he felt something drip onto the back of his hand. He looked down and saw the splash of blood on his skin.

Lifting his head, he looked above him. The blood had seeped through a crack in the floorboards of the wagon bed. That meant there had to be a lot of blood up there, which probably meant someone was dead.

Von Hoffman cursed bitterly, wiped his hand on the grass, and crawled to the side so the blood wouldn't continue to drip on him. He was sick inside. Anger boiled up in his belly. He wanted to scramble out from under the vehicle, leap to his feet, and charge the ambushers, shrieking out his rage as he emptied his rifle at them.

If he did that, the only thing he would accomplish would be to get himself killed even more quickly. He was a Prussian nobleman, he told himself. He ruled his emotions, not the other way around. He drew a deep breath and brought himself under control.

It seemed to him that there were fewer shots coming from the slopes now. The attackers couldn't be giving up. They still had the upper hand. They could keep the wagons pinned here until dark, and then they could come swarming down from the hills like Cossacks to overrun the defenders. It wouldn't be long until that happened, and for the life of him, the baron couldn't see any way to stop it.

Then he lifted his head again as he heard a sudden outbreak of shots from the eastern hill. This wasn't rifle fire, though. It sounded like several handguns going off as fast as someone could fire them.

Something was going on up there, von Hoffman thought with a frown. Something he hadn't expected.

* * *

After killing the three men with the horses, Matt had followed the sound of shots to two more bushwhackers and gunned them down as well when they ignored his command to drop their rifles. He was thinking that it might be a good idea to take a prisoner so they could question the man and maybe find out what this attack was all about. But he could only do that if one of the varmints cooperated and didn't make Matt kill him.

One thing was certain. In a situation like this where the odds were stacked so heavily in favor of the other side, a fella couldn't afford to get fancy. Any time Matt had to shoot, he was going to shoot to kill.

He was moving through the brush when a gun suddenly blazed at him from the left. One of the bushwhackers must have figured out that there was an enemy stalking them. Matt hit the dirt, but he didn't return the fire. He didn't want to waste bullets, and he also didn't want to give away his exact position.

Instead he waited, breathing shallowly.

After a few moments, he heard branches rustle. He tipped the barrel of his Colt in that direction. A rifle emerged from the brush first, followed by the man holding it.

The man stopped short when he saw Matt lying there. He tried to lower the Winchester so he could get a shot off, but before he could pull the trigger, Matt's revolver roared and a slug ripped through the bushwhacker's thigh, shattering the bone and dropping him to the ground. The man howled in pain and rolled around, clutching at his wounded leg.

Matt started to his feet, thinking that he might be able to take a prisoner after all, but as he did, the man he had just shot put the pain of his broken leg aside and grabbed the gun on his hip. Matt crouched and fired as the man's Colt came up. Flame gouted from the muzzles of both guns.

The bushwhacker's slug missed, but Matt's didn't. It plowed into the man's brain, leaving a red-rimmed black hole in his forehead. His head jerked back, then forward, and then his face hit the ground as he died.

Well, he wouldn't be taking that hombre prisoner, Matt thought, despite just winging him at first.

No sooner had that thought gone through his head than he heard a huge commotion about fifty yards to his right. Shot after shot blasted out, so close together it was hard to tell them apart, and interspersed with the dull booms of a pair of revolvers came the wicked cracks of rifle fire. A *lot* of rifles.

"Preacher," Matt breathed.

Chapter Eleven

Eight men came up the hill toward Preacher. He heard one of them saying something about getting the horses before it got dark, and another said that as soon as it *was* dark, they could ride down there into the gap and finish off the job.

"A lot of them are just women and kids, so they won't give us any trouble," the hired killer said. "And Klaus told us the men are nothing but farmers and shopkeepers. We don't have to worry about them, either."

Preacher stepped out from behind the tree, pointed his guns at them, and said, "You can worry about me instead, you no-account snake."

The men had rifles in their hands, but it took them a second to swing the weapons up. In that blink of an eye, each of Preacher's guns had already roared twice. Four shots that cut down three of the men and wounded another.

And Preacher kept shooting.

The bushwhackers were fighting back by now, and the storm of lead raging around his head forced Preacher to duck behind the tree again. Chunks of bark and splinters of pine flew in the air as slugs chewed into the trunk.

Preacher thrust his right-hand gun around the tree and fired again, then weaved to his left and snapped a shot around that side. Another man was down, blood and brains leaking from the hole in his head. Another stumbled back and forth, shrieking in pain as he clutched at his belly where one of Preacher's slugs had torn through his entrails.

That left three of the bushwhackers on their feet, and they had thrown themselves behind trees, too. The hammer of Preacher's right-hand gun clicked on an empty chamber, and a second later the left-hand gun did the same.

"He's empty!" one of the men called to the others. "Rush him before he can reload!"

That would have been a bad mistake on their part if he'd had a spare gun, Preacher thought . . . but he didn't.

That didn't make any never-mind to him. He still had his Bowie. Those old boys were about to think they had cornered themselves a grizzly bear.

Before that could happen, Matt burst out of the woods behind them and yelled, "Hey!"

The bushwhackers spun toward him, but Matt's guns were already spitting fire and lead. The barrage of bullets knocked two of the men off their feet, but the third one was able to get his Winchester going and cranked off three swift shots that made Matt dive to the side to avoid being ventilated.

Preacher figured Matt would have taken care of the buzzard anyway, but there was no point in taking a chance. The old mountain man drew his Bowie knife from its fringed sheath as he stepped out from behind the tree.

His arm flashed back and then forward, and the knife flew across the intervening space to bury its heavy blade in the would-be killer's back. The man let out a cry of pain, dropped his rifle, and stumbled forward a couple of steps as he tried to reach behind him and pull the knife from his back.

He failed. His legs went out from under him and he pitched forward in a limp sprawl.

Matt climbed to his feet and said, "I would have gotten him in a second."

"I know, I know," Preacher said. He strode forward to retrieve his knife. "Just savin' you some bullets."

"Are there any more of them around?"

Preacher cocked his head to listen.

"I don't hear no more shots comin' from over here. You reckon we got 'em all?"

"Sounds like it," Matt agreed. "We'd better take a look around, though."

Preacher grunted.

"After we make sure all of these varmints are dead."

"That goes without saying," Matt said.

"If it goes without sayin', why'd you just say it?"

Matt grinned, shook his head, and said, "Come on."

It didn't take long for them to confirm that all the men whose bodies were scattered around the slope were dead. As they began moving quietly among the trees in search of more bushwhackers, Matt said, "I don't suppose you left any of the ones you ran into alive, did you?"

"Wasn't time for that," Preacher said. "How about you?"

"Well, I tried to take one of them prisoner, but he wasn't having any of it."

"I ain't surprised. All the ones I seen were hard-cases. Low-down hired gun-wolves." Preacher paused. "Except for three of 'em."

Matt looked over at the old-timer with interest.

"What about those three?" he asked.

"They was city fellas, and furriners, at that. They spoke that Dutch jabber, like young Dieter. And I heard one of those gunnies say somethin' about a man called Klaus. I reckon he might've been the one who hired 'em to ambush the wagon train."

"You think this Klaus was one of the men you killed?"

"Don't know," Preacher said. He tapped his shirt where he had stowed the wallets of the dead foreigners. "But I got their bona fides right here. We can have a look at 'em later, once we're sure the fight's over."

Another flurry of shots came from the other hill. From the sound of them, they weren't directed at the wagons anymore.

Matt looked across the gap and said, "Smoke's bound to be in the middle of that ruckus."

"He usually is," Preacher agreed.

Smoke had heard the furious outbreak of shooting on East Kiowa Peak a few minutes earlier, and he felt confident that Matt and Preacher were the cause of most of it. He knew that both members of his adopted family could take care of themselves, but despite that, they were outnumbered and he would be glad to see them again and know for certain that they were all right.

Of course, he and Dieter were outnumbered, too, and they got proof of that when several of the bushwhackers spotted them and opened fire.

Smoke grabbed Dieter's arm and dragged him down behind some rocks as bullets whined around them.

"Keep your head down," Smoke told the young man. "Those slugs can ricochet."

"Have they broken off their attack on the wagon train?" Dieter asked as he pressed himself to the ground.

"Seems that way. They're coming after us now."

"Good. At least they won't harm any more of my friends."

"I'm sure that gal's all right, Dieter," Smoke said as another slug spanged off a rock near his head. "She's probably forted up inside one of the wagons."

"I pray it is so."

Smoke heard men shouting, and the shots that had him and Dieter pinned down in the rocks increased even more.

"They're making a break for their horses," he said.

"You mean they are abandoning the attack?" Dieter asked.

"That's what it sounds like to me. They just want us to keep our heads down until they can get away."

"We must stop them!"

Dieter put his hands on the ground in preparation for pushing himself to his feet.

Smoke grabbed the young man's shoulder this time.

"Hold on, hold on," he said. "We've spooked them enough to make them light a shuck out of here. Considering the odds, that's a pretty good job of work."

"But we cannot allow them to get away!" Dieter protested. "They may have killed some of the people with the wagons."

"They probably did," Smoke agreed grimly. "But getting yourself killed won't change that."

"Justice must be done!"

That was an admirable goal, but Smoke was practical enough to know that it wasn't always possible. He and Dieter had killed several of the bushwhackers, and he figured Matt and Preacher had done for some of the others over on the eastern peak. That might have to count for settling the score in this case.

At least until Smoke could figure out who was responsible for this ambush. Then things might be different.

The shooting stopped, but Smoke still heard men forcing their way through the brush. He raised up enough to empty his Colt in that direction, but he figured he was just hurrying them on their way. Sure enough, as the echoes of his shots rolled across the hills, he heard the swift rataplan of hoofbeats climbing the hill.

"They are getting away," Dieter said with despair in his voice.

"Yeah, but now we can get down there to the wagons and see just how bad folks are hurt."

Dieter nodded.

"Yes. We must rattle our hocks."

They stood up and began climbing the hill, heading back toward the place where they had left their mounts. Along the way they passed the place where Smoke had left the tied-up bushwhacker. The man was gone. One of his companions must have come along and turned him loose, as Smoke had halfway expected would happen.

The horses were still there. Smoke and Dieter swung into their saddles and rode quickly down the far slope. When they reached the bottom of the hill, Smoke led the way around it toward the wagon train.

The wagons hadn't moved, Smoke saw as the big, canvas-covered vehicles came into view. The wagons weren't the only thing he saw. He spotted two riders coming from the direction of the other hill.

"Dieter, ride ahead and let your folks know that we're friends," Smoke said. "They're probably pretty jumpy after going through that ambush, and if they see strangers coming, they're liable to start shooting again. They ought to recognize you, though."

"That's a good idea," Dieter agreed. He heeled his mount into a gallop and headed toward the wagons.

Smoke lifted a hand to catch the attention of Matt and Preacher. He had been pretty sure from the start that they were the two riders he saw, and as he came closer he was able to confirm that. Relief went through him. It appeared that both of them were all right, although the sun was down now and the light was starting to fade, so Smoke couldn't be sure of that.

They angled across the gap to rendezvous with him. Matt called, "Smoke, are you hit?"

Smoke reined in as they joined him. He shook his head and said, "A few slugs came close, but none of them tagged me. How about you two? It sounded like you had a real war going on over there."

"That was mostly Preacher," Matt said with a grin.

"The boy's just peeved because I killed a heap more of those varmints than he did," the old mountain man said.

"But we're both all right," Matt added. "How about Dieter?"

"He did just fine," Smoke said. He nodded toward

the rider now coming toward them. "I sent him ahead to let the folks with the wagons know that we're friendly."

"Good idea," Preacher said. "Don't want a bunch of greenhorns gettin' trigger-happy."

Dieter brought his horse to a stop and took off his high-crowned hat. As he waved it over his head, he called, "Herr Jensen! Smoke! Come! You are welcome!"

Smoke lifted a hand to acknowledge the invitation, then said to his companions, "I reckon we get to go meet ourselves a baron."

Chapter Twelve

Now that the danger seemed to be over, the immigrants had emerged from cover and were milling around the wagons. Smoke, Matt, and Preacher headed for the lead wagon, where Dieter had gone after waving them in. Dieter had dismounted and stood beside the wagon now, talking to a tall man and a woman with fair hair under a thrown-back sunbonnet.

The tall man turned toward the three of them as they rode up. He carried himself with the stern, rigid bearing of a military man, an aristocrat . . . or both. Which, according to Dieter, Baron Friedrich von Hoffman was.

Dieter said, "Your Excellency, this is Herr Smoke Jensen, Herr Matt Jensen, and, uh, Herr Preacher. Gentlemen, His Excellency Baron Friedrich von Hoffman."

Von Hoffman extended his hand to Smoke.

"Herr Jensen," he said. "Young Schumann tells

me that we owe you a considerable debt of gratitude. Without the assistance of you and your companions, those 'bushwhackers,' as Schumann calls them, might have wiped us out."

"We were glad to pitch in and lend you folks a hand," Smoke said as he shook hands with the baron. Von Hoffman turned to Matt and Preacher and shook with them as well.

Then he gestured toward the young woman and introduced her.

"My cousin, Fraulein Erica von Hoffman."

All three men tugged on their hat brims, and Smoke said, "Ma'am. It's an honor."

He saw the way Dieter was looking at Erica von Hoffman, and he knew this was the young woman Dieter wanted to court. To the youngster's way of thinking, though, that was impossible because of who he was . . . and who she was.

Smoke didn't see things that way, but it was hard for a fella to get over the attitudes that had been drummed into him while he was growing up. That was certainly true in his own case, Smoke mused, since he had been raised to be bold and fiercely independent, as well as fair and forthright, and he liked to think he was still all of those things.

"Herr Jensen," Erica responded with a polite smile. As far as Smoke could tell, she had come through the attack without being wounded.

That wasn't true of everybody, though. He heard sobbing and wailing coming from elsewhere in the wagon train and knew those were the sounds of mourning over slain loved ones.

"You lost some folks, didn't you?" he asked von Hoffman.

The baron nodded curtly.

"Three men, one woman, and one child." Von Hoffman's voice was flat and hard, but Smoke thought he heard an undercurrent of pain and loss in it. "And perhaps a dozen more wounded, some of them seriously. Our casualties could have been much worse, but still I regret every one. Schumann tells me that you killed some of the men who attacked us?"

"That's right. Maybe as many as twenty, all told."

Von Hoffman's rather bushy eyebrows rose in surprise.

"The four of you killed twenty men?"

"More or less," Smoke said. "I reckon we can get a better count when we haul in the bodies tomorrow. The ones the scavengers haven't carried off by then, anyway."

"My God," von Hoffman murmured. "This really is a violent land, isn't it?"

"It's a land that's whatever an hombre makes of it," Smoke said.

"I assure you, I meant no offense, Herr Jensen. My own homeland has seen its share of blood being spilled."

Smoke figured it was time to change the subject.

"My ranch house isn't far from here," he said. "Dieter found you a good campground just ahead about half a mile. Why don't you get the wagons moving while you still have some light, and you can make camp up there. We'll show you the way. Then you and your cousin can come back to the house and have supper with us."

"We are honored by the invitation," von Hoffman said formally. "I should probably remain with my people, though, to make sure they are safe. The men who attacked us could return."

"That's not very likely," Smoke said, "but you can post some guards and I'll send some men over to help. Matt, how about you riding back to the ranch and telling Pearlie to send four men to the Snake Creek pasture?"

Matt nodded and reached for the dangling reins of his horse.

"I can do that," he said. He smiled and nodded politely to Erica again. "Fraulein von Hoffman, I'll see you back at the ranch."

"Yes, of course, Herr Jensen," she said. "I look forward to it."

Smoke heard something in her voice and saw a look on her face that told him she was mighty impressed with Matt. From the way Dieter was frowning, he had noticed Erica's reaction, too. Matt was a ruggedly handsome devil, Smoke supposed, and women had a habit of being impressed by him.

He hoped that wouldn't cause trouble between Matt and Dieter. They didn't need any more complications while these pilgrims from far away were on Sugarloaf range.

It took awhile to get the wagons rolling. Everyone in the group was still scared and upset, especially those who had had loved ones killed or wounded. Some of the oxen had been killed, too. They had to be unhitched from their traces, the wagons moved, and other oxen from the small herd being driven along with the wagon train hitched up in their places.

With all of that to take care of, dusk was settling down pretty thickly over the landscape by the time the wagon train reached the broad, open pasture next to the creek.

At least the immigrants had plenty of experience pulling the wagons into a circle and setting up camp. They went about those chores efficiently, although an air of stunned sorrow still hung over the entire group.

While that was going on, Pearlie arrived with three of the ranch hands, all of them well armed.

"Matt told me you wanted me to send over four men, but I figured I'd come myself," Smoke's foreman explained. "I'll take charge of settin' up guard shifts and make sure there's a good man on each of 'em."

Smoke clapped a hand on his shoulder and said,

"Thanks, Pearlie. These folks have been through a lot today. They'll need somebody giving them a hand."

"We'll take good care of 'em, don't worry about that."

Smoke wasn't worried. Pearlie was a good man, one of the best.

He took Pearlie over to von Hoffman and introduced him to the baron, assuring him that Pearlie would see to it the camp was well guarded.

"We can head for the ranch house now," Smoke went on.

"As soon as I freshen up and change," von Hoffman said.

"We don't stand on ceremony out here, Baron," Smoke said. "You're fine just the way you are."

"With the smell of gunpowder clinging to my clothes?" Von Hoffman smiled thinly and shook his head. "But then, the smell is quite common on the frontier, isn't it?"

Smoke might have taken offense, but he didn't think von Hoffman was trying to be insulting. The hombre just wasn't used to watching what he said around folks. Where he came from, he could say whatever he wanted and nobody would ever dare to complain about it.

The frontier would knock that attitude out of von Hoffman sooner or later, Smoke thought. He said, "I'd worry more about what my wife will say if the food she fixed gets too cold."

Erica said, "Frau Jensen does not even know that guests are coming, does she? Won't she be upset?"

"Not Sally," Smoke said. "It takes a lot to throw her for a loop. Anyway, it was her idea, so she's expecting you." He looked over at Dieter and added, "Come on, Dieter, you're invited, too."

Dieter's eyes widened as he glanced at von Hoffman and Erica. The baron's eyes narrowed in disapproval.

"Oh, no, I . . . I could not . . ." Dieter began.

Preacher said, "Sure you could," and slapped Dieter on the back with enough boisterous force to make the young man stumble forward a step. "This is America. You can do anything you want."

"If it wasn't for you bringing Matt, Preacher, and me back here, that ambush might've turned out even worse than it did," Smoke pointed out.

Maybe that was his way of getting back at von Hoffman for that powder-smoke comment. He didn't know. But it wouldn't hurt for the baron to start figuring out that things were different here on the frontier.

Erica turned to Dieter and said, "Yes, you should come along. We are all in your debt, aren't we, Friedrich?"

Von Hoffman didn't like that, either. But he forced a thin smile onto his face, nodded, and said, "Of course. Come with us, Schumann."

Under those circumstances, Dieter couldn't very well refuse. He swallowed hard and said, "Thank you, Your Excellency." He turned to Smoke. "And thank you, too, Herr Jensen."

"Smoke, remember?" He put a hand on Dieter's

shoulder. "Get your horse and let's go. Can you handle a saddle mount, Miss von Hoffman?"

"Of course," Erica said. "I went riding often on Friedrich's estate. It was quite wonderful."

"I'm sure it was."

Smoke couldn't help but wonder why von Hoffman had come to America in the first place and brought all these folks with him. The man had a title, an estate, and evidently plenty of money if he'd been able to afford to outfit this wagon train and buy a ranch in Wyoming. Why leave all that behind and come all this way to a new country?

Maybe it had something to do with today's attack on the wagon train, Smoke mused. It wasn't really any of his business, but he was still curious.

And in a way it *was* his business. These pilgrims were on Sugarloaf range, and von Hoffman and Erica would soon be sitting down at his table. That made them his guests, all of them, and Smoke didn't like it when somebody tried to murder his guests while they were on his land. He didn't cotton to it at all.

So even though von Hoffman might refuse to talk about it, Smoke decided he was going to try to find out what was going on here. Maybe there was something he could do to help.

Chapter Thirteen

It was full dark by the time the group of riders came up to the Sugarloaf ranch house, but that didn't matter. Smoke knew every foot of his range and had no trouble leading the others back to his home.

Sally heard the horses coming, as he'd expected she would. She stepped into the doorway. Matt sat in one of the chairs on the porch. He had it tipped back, and one booted foot rested on the porch railing to balance him. Cal stood in the open door of the bunkhouse, his shoulder leaned against the jamb in a casual pose.

But it was all a pose, Smoke knew. Until they were sure everything was still all right, they would be watchful, alert for trouble. That sort of caution was ingrained in all of them.

When Sally saw Smoke, a smile of welcome spread across her lovely face. She wouldn't have to reach for the Winchester that was leaning against the wall just inside the door after all.

Matt stood up and moved to the steps as the five riders reined in. Cal came from the bunkhouse as they dismounted, calling for one of the other hands to come with him.

"We'll take care of the horses, Smoke," Cal said as he reached for the reins.

"Thanks, Cal," Smoke said with a nod.

"Your servants call you by your first name?" von Hoffman asked as Cal and the other man led the horses toward the corral.

"Cal's not a servant," Smoke said. "He works for me, but he's a friend, too. And a top hand, despite his age."

Von Hoffman looked puzzled, but he didn't say anything else about that. Instead he took his hat off as Sally came down the steps to greet them.

"This is my wife, Sally Jensen," Smoke introduced her. "Baron Friedrich von Hoffman and his cousin Miss Erica von Hoffman. And you know Dieter."

"Of course," Sally said. She put out her hand to von Hoffman, and the baron shook it American-style, although he looked a little uncomfortable doing so. She went on, "Welcome to Sugarloaf."

"You honor us, madam," he said. "Our apologies for intruding on your home."

"Oh, it's no intrusion," she assured him. "When Smoke rode out to see you folks, I told him to bring you back with him for supper. It's the least we can do for guests on our range." Her expression grew more solemn. "But Matt tells me there was some trouble. . . ."

The baron nodded.

"Yes, we were attacked. Some of our people were . . . killed."

"I'm so sorry," Sally said. "There's a little cemetery here on the ranch, or the one at the church in Big Rock. We'll help you see to it that they're laid to rest properly."

"You have my gratitude for that, madam."

"Right now, why don't you come inside and we'll eat? Things always look a little better after a good meal."

Soon they were all gathered around the long table in the dining room. The crew had eaten earlier, so there was plenty of room for everyone. The atmosphere was subdued because of the tragic deaths of the people with the wagon train, but the food was excellent and seemed to lift the spirits of von Hoffman, Erica, and Dieter.

Erica had managed to sit next to Matt, which probably lifted her spirits as well, Smoke thought. Erica kept casting glances at Matt, Dieter kept looking at her, and Matt, although he probably wasn't oblivious to what was going on, acted like he was trying to be.

After supper, Sally shooed the men out onto the porch.

"I'll clean up in here," she said.

"Let me help you," Erica offered.

"Oh, no, that's all right. You're a guest."

"I insist," Erica said.

With a smile, Sally said, "In that case, all right,

and thanks. We'll get to it as soon as these men get out of our way."

"I reckon that's our cue, gentlemen," Smoke said.

He made sure that von Hoffman and Dieter took two of the rocking chairs. He and Preacher sat down in the other two, and Matt perched a hip on the railing.

Smoke didn't waste any time getting down to business.

"Baron, do you have any idea why those men ambushed you today?"

Von Hoffman hesitated before replying, "I assume they were thieves. Outlaws who wanted to loot our wagons."

Preacher snorted and said, "What you mean is that Klaus sent 'em."

Von Hoffman sat forward sharply and muttered something in German under his breath.

"Klaus," he repeated. "Where did you hear that name?"

"One of those varmints mentioned it just before hell busted loose again," Preacher explained. "I thought maybe Klaus was one of the foreign fellas I swapped lead with a little before that."

"There were foreigners among them? You saw them?"

"I killed 'em," Preacher said. "They was tryin' to ventilate me."

Smoke said, "You didn't tell me anything about this, Preacher."

"Hadn't got around to it yet," the old mountain

man said. "Figured it'd be better to wait until we were all together and could hash it out."

"Tell me, please," von Hoffman said. "These men, what did they look like?"

"Well, one was short and kind of fat. He had a piggy face. The other two were taller and skinnier and had little beards." Preacher reached under his shirt. "I got their wallets."

In the light that spilled through the windows and open door, the men gathered around Preacher to examine the contents of the wallets. They found a considerable amount of money, in both American greenbacks and German currency, but no identification papers.

The baron sat down in the rocker again.

"From the descriptions Herr Preacher gave us, I do not know those men," he said. "They were associates of Klaus, perhaps, but not him."

"Maybe you'd better tell us who this hombre Klaus is," Smoke suggested, "and what he looks like, too, in case we happen to cross trails with him."

"You do not want to 'cross trails,' as you put it, with Klaus Berger. He is an evil man. A killer. He handles . . . certain tasks . . . for some powerful men in Germany who are now my enemies."

"You mean he's a hired gun," Matt said.

"Worse than that. Guns, knives, even bombs. If his employers want someone dead, Klaus finds a way to make that happen."

"Well, then, why in tarnation ain't he locked up?"

Preacher asked. "Or better yet, how come he ain't been strung up to a nice tall tree by now?"

"Because, as I said, the men he works for are very powerful. They wield a great deal of political influence."

Preacher leaned forward in his chair to spit off the porch. That summed up his feelings about politics.

"So there are some fellas in Germany with a grudge against you, Baron," Smoke said.

Von Hoffman nodded.

"That is correct. I thought that by leaving the country when I did, I might escape their vengeance. Clearly, I was wrong. They simply took their time about sending someone after me."

"The bushwhackers we saw looked like hired guns," Matt said. "These enemies of yours could afford to hire a small army of killers like that?"

"Without a doubt," von Hoffman answered instantly. "Money is no object to them. It is merely a tool in their quest to get what they really want . . . power."

Smoke said, "How is killing you and your people over here in America going to help them halfway around the world in Germany?"

"I challenged them. I stood in the way of their plans. I was almost able to put together a coalition in the government that would have opposed them. But once it fell apart . . ." Von Hoffman shrugged. "I knew then that I had to leave and take everyone I cared for, everyone who had supported my efforts, with me. Otherwise none of them would be safe. They want to make an example of me, you see. They want to demonstrate just how powerful they really are, so that no one will dare to oppose them again."

"Sounds to me like somebody needs to teach the no-good varmints a lesson," Preacher said.

"Someone does." Von Hoffman shook his head. "But it will not be me. All I want now is to protect my people and establish a new home for them."

"In Wyoming," Smoke said.

"Yes. I bought a ranch there. The Rafter Nine, it's called. Not far from the Medicine Bow Mountains."

Smoke nodded and said, "I know the area. It's still a good ways from here. This fella Klaus will have time to make another try for you, assuming he can hire more gunmen to replace the ones we killed today."

"There are always more gunmen," Matt said. "They won't be hard to find."

"I think you're right." Smoke turned to von Hoffman again. "It sounds to me like you're in for more trouble, Baron, unless you think Klaus will give up."

"And risk having his employers turn on him?" Von Hoffman shook his head. "Never. Besides, he enjoys killing too much to do that. He is a monster."

"Then you got trouble just waitin' for you," Preacher said.

"I know, but what can I do? We cannot turn around and go back. We must go on. How much longer do you think it will take us to reach our destination, Herr Jensen?"

"At least a week," Smoke said. "Maybe longer."

"We can only hope that it will take Klaus longer than that to assemble another force to move against us. If we can reach the ranch, we can defend it. As long as they don't catch us on the trail again, we will prevail."

"Yeah, you'd have a better chance of that," Smoke agreed. "You never did tell us what Klaus looks like."

"Like a corpse," von Hoffman said. "He is the palest man I have ever seen, and gaunt as if he has been in his coffin for a long time. His hair is long and almost as pale as his skin."

"An albino?" Matt asked.

Von Hoffman shook his head.

"No, I don't believe so. His eyes are very dark, almost black, as if they leached all the color out of the rest of him and concentrated it there. I've seen him only a few times, but once you lay eyes on him, you never forget him. You just wish you could."

"Sounds like an hombre to avoid, all right." Smoke turned to Dieter. "You're mighty quiet tonight."

"What?" The young man sounded surprised that someone had spoken to him.

"What do you think about all this?"

"Why, I . . . I don't think anything of it. Such things are for the baron to deal with."

Preacher said, "The rest of you folks were gettin' shot at, too, and you're liable to get shot at again. I reckon that gives you a right to speak up."

"Well, I . . ." Clearly, Dieter was at a loss for words.

Finally, he said, "I will do everything in my power to defend the baron from his enemies."

"Of course," von Hoffman said. "My people are loyal to me."

The baron was going to need more than loyalty from his people, Smoke thought. It was still a long way to the Medicine Bow Mountains in Wyoming, and the chance that Klaus Berger wouldn't be able to mount another attack before they got there seemed pretty slim to Smoke.

No, what Baron von Hoffman and the immigrants traveling with him really needed was a hand from some hombres who knew the country and knew what they were doing.

Luckily for the baron, Smoke knew three men who fit that description. Two of them were Matt and Preacher.

And he was the other.

Chapter Fourteen

That night while he and Sally were lying in bed, Smoke said, "I was thinking that maybe Matt and Preacher and I would ride along with the baron's wagon train for a while, just to make sure they get started to Wyoming all right."

She turned toward him and said, "That's not what you were thinking at all. The three of you are going to go all the way to Wyoming with them and see to it that they get set up all right on that ranch the baron bought."

Smoke chuckled.

"That's what you think, is it?" he asked.

"Well? Are you going to deny it?"

For a moment, Smoke didn't reply. Then he shook his head and said, "That's sort of the way I figured things might turn out, all right."

"Of course they will. Smoke Jensen isn't the sort of man who does things halfway. You never have been and you never will be. That's one of the things

I love about you." She moved closer to him and reached out to touch him. "For example, if you were to make love to your wife tonight, you wouldn't want to do a bad job of it, now would you?"

"I've never considered making love to you a job," Smoke pointed out.

"You know what I mean." He felt her warm breath on his skin. "You'd want to make love to me as thoroughly and effectively as you possibly could. No going halfway and then stopping."

"No," Smoke said huskily as passion rose in him, the passion that Sally had always been able to fan into a brightly burning flame. "I sure wouldn't just go halfway."

"Prove it," she urged.

So he did.

The next morning over breakfast, Smoke talked to Preacher and Matt about his idea. The two of them had escorted Baron von Hoffman, Erica, and Dieter back to the wagon train camp the night before.

"You ain't suggestin' anything I ain't already thought of," Preacher said. "That bunch of greenhorns has got no business tryin' to go all the way to Wyomin' by themselves."

"They've made it most of the way so far," Matt pointed out.

Smoke said, "That's probably because it's taken this long for Klaus Berger to gather his forces and set up that ambush. They may have given him the slip for a while by leaving from Kansas City, like the baron said."

"But he's bound to come after 'em again," Preacher added.

"I'm not arguing with you," Matt said. "I think it would be a good idea for us to go along, too. I just wasn't sure how Sally would feel about it."

She came into the dining room from the kitchen carrying a fresh pot of coffee in time to hear Matt's comment.

"Smoke already talked to me about this," she said as she added hot coffee to their cups. "I wasn't the least bit surprised. Do you honestly think I expected the three of you to sit around and have a nice, peaceful visit when you could go galloping off on some adventure?"

"If you're worried—" Smoke began.

"I'm *always* worried," Sally said. "That would just be a way of life for any woman who was married to Smoke Jensen. I mean, think about it. You ride into Big Rock yesterday morning on a nice, simple errand—meeting Matt and Preacher—and seven men try to rob the bank and shoot up the town. You didn't have to go meet them. They know the way here. But you went anyway, just to see them sooner, and wound up in the middle of a gun battle. Things like that are *always* going to happen, Smoke. That's just the way life is around you." She poured coffee for herself and sat down. "But the advantages of being married to you outweigh the disadvantages. Definitely."

Smoke cleared his throat and said to Matt and Preacher, "Sally doesn't mind."

"Yeah, I get that idea," Matt said with a smile. "Well, it sounds good to me. I don't have to be anywhere, so I might as well go to Wyoming."

"Same here," Preacher said. "You know me . . . I'll go anywhere there's a chance of a good scrap."

Smoke nodded.

"That's what I thought you'd say, both of you. We'll ride over to the baron's camp after breakfast and tell him."

Matt asked, "What if he doesn't want us to come along? He strikes me as a pretty proud man. He may not want to admit that he can't take care of those folks who are with him."

"Then he'd be plumb foolish," Preacher said.

Smoke leaned back in his chair and sipped his coffee.

"It's possible von Hoffman could react that way," he admitted. "If he does, we'll try to talk some sense into his head. If he's still stubborn about it"—Smoke's broad shoulders rose and fell in a shrug—"he can't very well stop us from taking a ride up Wyoming way on our own, now can he?"

Matt's smile widened into a grin.

"I don't rightly see how," he said. "But I hope it doesn't come to that. I wouldn't mind getting to know that cousin of the baron's a little better."

"You tarnal idjit!" Preacher snapped. "Don't you know that gal's the one ol' Dieter was moonin' over?"

"Sure I do. But when it comes to romance, it's every man for himself. If Dieter wants Erica, he needs to speak up. Maybe he'll realize that if he sees that somebody else is interested in her."

That made Smoke wonder if Matt really felt any interest in Erica, other than admiring her beauty, or if he was just trying to goad Dieter into sticking up for himself and telling her how he felt. That was a strategy ripe with the potential for trouble. . . .

But everybody involved was a grown-up, and they could sort things out for themselves, Smoke decided.

However, at moments such as this, he was very glad that he was happily married and didn't have to worry about such nonsense.

Before Smoke, Matt, and Preacher could leave the ranch, Pearlie rode in from the wagon camp.

"I left the other three fellas over there to keep an eye on things," the foreman explained. "I told the baron I'd bring back our ranch wagon and take the folks who were killed into town, to the undertaker's."

"That's a good idea," Smoke said. "So the wagon train's going to stay camped there for a few days?"

"Yep. The families of the folks who were killed want 'em buried in the church cemetery, so that's what they're gonna do."

Smoke nodded and said, "All right. When you

get back from town, Pearlie, I've got another chore for you."

"Gatherin' up the bodies of them dead gunnies?" Pearlie asked grimly.

"I'm afraid so. I'd say just leave them where they fell, but I don't want them rotting on my range."

Pearlie frowned in thought as he nodded.

"I know a nice deep gully where we can put 'em and maybe cave in the side," he said. "That'd sure beat diggin' a hole big enough for the whole bunch."

"Do whatever you need to do," Smoke told the foreman. "We're going to see the baron now."

"Gonna offer to go along and help 'em get to Wyoming?"

Smoke laughed.

"Does everybody know what I'm going to do before I know it myself?"

"Well, you got to remember, we been around you for a long time. And none of us have ever seen you run from trouble, not once. More likely to be the other way around."

Smoke couldn't deny that. He told Pearlie not to worry too much about the ranch chores today and to concentrate on helping the immigrants and cleaning up after the gun battle. Then he, Matt, and Preacher saddled their horses and rode toward the wagon camp.

As they approached, Smoke saw quite a few people moving around the wagons. They were still grieving over the ones they had lost, but work still had to be done. It was good to keep busy, too. That helped with the sorrow by reminding folks that someday things would return to normal.

Baron von Hoffman strode out to meet them and lifted a hand in greeting.

"Good morning, gentlemen," he said.

"Any more trouble last night?" Smoke asked, even though he knew there hadn't been. If there had, Pearlie would have told him about it.

Von Hoffman shook his head and said, "No, the night passed peacefully. I was about to come see you, Herr Jensen, and request permission to remain camped here on your land for another day or two."

Smoke swung down from the saddle and nodded.

"That's fine, Baron," he said. "Pearlie told me that the folks you lost are going to be buried in the cemetery in town."

"If the church will have them," von Hoffman said.

"I'm sure that won't be a problem. You can get them laid to rest this afternoon. But after that, feel free to stay as long as you'd like."

"We will not abuse your hospitality, Herr Jensen."

Smoke smiled and waved a hand at their surroundings.

"There's plenty of grass and water for everybody," he said. "I don't see how you could abuse our hospitality if you tried." He paused. "There's something else we came over here to talk to you about, Baron."

"You must call me Friedrich."

Offering to put himself on familiar terms with a

commoner probably cost him an effort, Smoke thought. He just smiled and nodded, though.

"Sure, if you'll call me Smoke."

"What was the other matter you wished to discuss?"

"Matt and Preacher and I have talked it over," Smoke said, "and we want to go to Wyoming with you."

Von Hoffman frowned in surprise.

"But this is your home, is it not?"

"We're not going to stay," Smoke explained.

Preacher spoke up, saying, "Speak for yourself. My home's wherever I hang my hat. I might just decide to settle down up yonder in the Medicine Bows."

That would never happen, and Smoke knew it. As long as Preacher was able, he would be on the move, and despite his age he didn't really show any signs of slowing down or becoming any less fiddlefooted.

"The same goes for me," Matt added, smiling. "I might want to put down roots."

"You would be welcome, of course," the baron said. "But the real reason you make this offer is because you think Klaus Berger and his gunmen will attack us again, is that not true?"

Smoke shrugged and said, "There's a good chance of it. We figure if he comes after you, you might need a hand."

"Of course. But, to be blunt, what do you get out of offering to assist us?"

"The chance to ventilate some more of those low-down buzzards!" Preacher said.

Smoke smiled and said, "That's one thing about

the frontier, Friedrich . . . most of the time folks will help out just because it's the right thing to do."

He could see emotions warring inside the baron as von Hoffman weighed the offer. Pride was uppermost. He wasn't the sort of man to admit that he needed help.

But he was worried about the people who had come to America with him, Smoke knew, and he was also realistic enough to be aware that their chances of reaching Wyoming safely would be higher with Smoke, Matt, and Preacher along.

Before von Hoffman could reach a decision, Erica climbed out of the lead wagon and came over to them, looking happy to see them. She went straight to Matt and said, "Good morning, Herr Jensen. What brings you to our camp?"

The baron answered before Matt could.

"These three gentlemen have offered to accompany us to our destination and help keep us safe along the way."

"Why, that's wonderful!" Erica exclaimed, smiling brightly up at Matt. "You told them how grateful we will be for their help, didn't you, Friedrich?"

"I haven't told them anything yet," von Hoffman said with an indulgent smile. "But under the circumstances, how can I refuse?" He turned to Smoke, Matt, and Preacher. "I accept your offer, gentlemen. Welcome to our group of humble pilgrims."

He extended his hand.

There was nothing humble about Baron Friedrich von Hoffman, Smoke thought, but he gripped the man's hand and was glad that von Hoffman had agreed to the proposal.

"Looks like we're off to Wyomin'," Preacher said, "and devil take the hindmost!"

"Not the devil," von Hoffman said, his face growing solemn. "Rather Klaus Berger. But in every way that counts, they are practically one and the same. . . ."

BOOK TWO

Chapter Fifteen

The combined funeral that afternoon for the five victims of the ambush was a solemn occasion, as funerals always are. Especially tragic was the death of the young boy struck down by bushwhack lead, leaving his parents gripped by sorrow and loss.

Smoke and Sally, along with Matt, Preacher, and the entire crew from Sugarloaf, attended the service. Afterward, Pearlie, Cal, and the other punchers returned to the ranch while Smoke drove the buckboard he and Sally had brought to town back to the wagon camp. Matt and Preacher rode alongside.

Sally and Erica sat on chairs brought out from one of the wagons while the men stood and discussed their plans.

"I see no need to wait," von Hoffman said. "I think we should start for Wyoming first thing in the morning."

Smoke said, "That's all right with me as long as Matt and Preacher agree."

"It don't make me no never-mind when we go," Preacher said. "I'm pert-near as free as the wind."

"So am I," Matt added. "I reckon we'll be ready, Baron."

"Excellent," von Hoffman said. "I will have my people ready to roll the wagons at dawn."

"We'll be there," Smoke promised.

"In the meantime," Sally said, "won't you and Erica join us for supper again tonight?"

Von Hoffman smiled and said, "I appreciate your gracious offer, Frau Jensen, but there is a great deal to do between now and tomorrow morning. I want to take advantage of this opportunity to check all the wagons and make sure they are in the best condition possible."

"That's a good idea," Smoke said. "You've still got a ways to go before you get to Wyoming, and you don't want any breakdowns if you can avoid them."

Once the decision when to leave was made, Smoke, Sally, Matt, and Preacher headed back to the ranch house. Being drifters, Matt and Preacher always traveled light, and whenever Smoke hit the trail, he did, too. So packing for the trip wouldn't take long.

Smoke had other things to take care of, though. He might be away for as long as a month, so he wanted to make sure that he and Sally said a proper good-bye.

Maybe more than once.

* * *

The next morning, in the gray light of approaching dawn, she kissed him good-bye as he stood by his horse holding the reins in one hand while his other arm was around her waist, holding her closely against him.

"Be careful," Sally whispered as she broke the kiss. "I know it doesn't do much good to say that, but . . ."

"I'm always as careful as I can be," Smoke said, "because I know I've got you to come home to."

"Are you sure you shouldn't take Pearlie and Cal with you?"

Smoke shook his head.

"I'm counting on those two to keep things running smoothly here on Sugarloaf. It shouldn't be much of a problem since we don't have anything big coming up, but you never know."

"And I don't want you worrying about what's going on here when you should be thinking about keeping those immigrants safe, as well as you and Matt and Preacher." Sally smiled. "We'll be fine here. Don't even think about us while you're gone."

"Now, I don't think *that's* going to happen," Smoke said as he returned her smile.

"Sun'll be up 'fore you know it," Preacher called impatiently from where he and Matt were already sitting on their horses.

"Don't you have any romance left in your soul?" Matt asked with a grin.

"Boy, I've forgotten more about womenfolks than you'll ever know," Preacher responded.

"Well, I believe you've forgotten it, anyway."

Matt held the reins of a loaded pack horse. They

were taking along their own supplies, so they wouldn't cut into the provisions that the baron's people had brought. Although if it became necessary, all three of them could easily live off the land for a while.

"I'm coming," Smoke said. He bent his head to give Sally one more quick, sweet kiss, then let her go and swung up into the saddle. As he lifted a hand in farewell, he told her, "I'll be back in a few weeks."

"I'll be waiting," she said.

This was hardly the first time he had ridden away from his wife and his home, Smoke thought as he turned his horse and went to join Matt and Preacher. Responsibilities to family and friends had taken him all over the frontier and plunged him into some of the wildest adventures any man could ever have.

At times his own thirst for excitement had done the same thing. But when the moment came to leave, it was never easy, even though it was his own choice to do so. The grim possibility that he might never see Sally again was always in the back of his mind. He had lost his first wife and their son that way, years earlier.

But a man couldn't live always waiting for something bad to happen. It wouldn't take long for that to drive a fella plumb loco. It was better to think that something good was going to happen, that he was going to accomplish great things and make a difference in the world. When a man set out with that attitude, that was usually what happened.

Fate sometimes had other plans, though, and Smoke couldn't completely forget that, either.

He pushed those thoughts out of his mind and concentrated on what a beautiful early summer day it was going to be. At this elevation, the mornings were always cool, and today was no exception. The air was crisp and clean, and the eastern sky had streaks of gold and pale blue in it as sunrise approached. The birds were already singing.

By the time the three men reached the wagon camp beside Snake Creek, the blue had climbed higher into the sky and the eastern horizon was bathed in reddish-gold light.

Preacher said, "Gonna be a pretty day."

"I think you're right," Smoke said.

Baron von Hoffman and Dieter Schumann galloped out to meet them. The baron raised a hand as he used the other to bring his horse to a halt.

"Good morning!" he said. "Are we ready to depart?"

"That's for you to say, Baron, not us," Smoke replied.

"The three of us are rarin' to go whenever you are," Preacher added.

"The wagons are ready to roll," von Hoffman declared. "Young Schumann has been serving as our scout. Would you prefer to ride with him?"

"Matt, why don't you take the point with Dieter?" Smoke suggested. "Preacher and I will take the flanks."

"As long as you don't stick me in the drag, I don't care where else you want me to ride," Preacher said. "I'm too old to breathin' that much dust."

"This isn't a cattle drive," Matt pointed out. "There won't be that much dust."

"There'll be some," Preacher insisted. "There always is when you got this many critters movin'."

"Well, it doesn't matter today," Smoke said, "because you can take the right flank, and I'll take the left."

Preacher nodded and said, "Sounds good to me."

He heeled his horse into motion and rode toward the right side of the wagons that had formed up into a long, northward-facing column.

"And I'm fine with taking the point," Matt said as he handed the reins of the pack horse to Smoke. "Come on, Dieter."

Smoke noticed that as the two of them rode past the lead wagon, both young men glanced in that direction. Matt even waved at somebody.

Likely Erica von Hoffman was sitting on the seat of that wagon, Smoke thought. He hoped he hadn't made a mistake by suggesting that Matt and Dieter work together as scouts. He'd thought it would be a good chance for them to get to know each other and maybe, just maybe, clear the air a little between them.

Either that, or their mutual interest in Erica von Hoffman would make their pairing like putting together a lit match and a fuse attached to a stick of dynamite.

* * *

Matt and Dieter rode across the shallow, rocky bed of Snake Creek. Their horses' hooves splashed water in the air, the droplets gleaming golden in the dawn light. Neither man said anything for several minutes as they headed north, until Matt finally commented, "Pretty morning, isn't it?"

"A beautiful morning," Dieter agreed. "As pretty as a speckled pup."

Matt grinned over at him.

"You know, no offense here, Dieter, but you don't talk like any other German I've ever met."

"Have you met very many Germans?" Dieter asked.

"Not really, but a few. Some of them barely spoke English, and some of them spoke it pretty well. But none of them came out with some of the things you say."

"But this is how people talk on your American frontier, is it not?"

"Well, sort of. Where'd you learn it?"

"From your American literature. Ned Buntline, Colonel Prentiss Ingraham, John B. Boothe, Frank Reade . . . wonderful authors such as those."

It was all Matt could do not to throw his head back and hoot with laughter.

"You mean those fellas who write dime novels, don't you?"

"I believe that is what their publications are called," Dieter said. "American literature."

"Well, they're American," Matt said. "I'm not so

sure about the literature part. You realize a lot of those fellas just make things up, don't you? They live back East and don't know much about what really goes on out here on the frontier. And what they don't know, they just make up out of their own heads. Like that steam-powered mechanical man I read about in one of those Frank Reade books. You don't think such things really exist, do you, Dieter?"

"No, I knew that story was just a figment of the imagination," Dieter admitted. "But surely there are gunfighters and outlaws and savage Indians like in the other books."

Matt shrugged.

"I reckon so, but even there, you'll find differences in the way they really are and the way they're portrayed in those books. Smoke, for example. Smoke's one of the fastest, deadliest gunfighters there ever was. But you wouldn't know it to see him sitting at the dinner table with Sally or joshin' around with Pearlie and Cal, now would you?"

"Not really," Dieter said.

"But you saw what he can do when he's pushed into it, like in that fight with those bushwhackers day before yesterday."

"Yes. Exactly. Then he looked like a figure from a dime novel, truly."

"That's the way it is," Matt said. "A man's made up of many parts. A gunfighter doesn't just swagger around all the time looking for folks to shoot.

Sometimes he's quiet, sometimes he's scared, sometimes he's lonely."

"What about you, Matt?" Dieter asked. "Are you a gunfighter?"

"I'm a pretty fair hand with a Colt. Not as good as Smoke, but there are only a few men who are or ever will be. It's like he was born to the gun."

"And those quiet, scared, lonely times . . . you have known them?"

Matt nodded and said, "More than I like to think about."

Dieter didn't say anything else for a few minutes. Then he said, "I think you are a fine hombre, Matt. I wish we could be friends. Amigos."

"Why can't we?"

"You know the reason as well as I do," Dieter said. "You must have seen the way Fraulein von Hoffman looks at you."

"And you want her to look at you that way."

"Yes," Dieter said with a nod. "Even though it is hopeless, that is my wish."

"Nothing's ever hopeless," Matt told him. "But your job just got harder, because I don't intend to back off and give you a clear trail."

"Nor would I expect you to," Dieter said stiffly. "Fraulein von Hoffman is the most beautiful young woman in the world. A man would have to be a fool to refuse her interest. And you do not strike me as a fool, Matt Jensen."

"I don't reckon you are, either. But right now,

we've got a job to do, and that's scouting trail for that wagon train. Are you willing to put everything else aside except that?"

"Of course," Dieter answered without hesitation. "But as you Americans say, this is not over, eh?"

"That's right," Matt agreed. "It's not over."

Chapter Sixteen

Snake Creek flowed fast, but it was shallow enough and the stream bed was firm enough that the wagons had no trouble fording it. Smoke had tied the pack horse onto the rear of the last wagon in line, and he spent the next hour riding back and forth across the creek, making sure that none of the vehicles ran into any trouble.

He had told von Hoffman to wait until everybody was across before starting up again. Once all the wagons were north of the creek, Smoke rode along the column until he caught sight of the baron up ahead. He took off his hat and waved it over his head in a signal to von Hoffman, who called out commands to the drivers of the first few wagons in line and waved for them to start moving. Once again the big wheels began to turn.

Smoke rode about a hundred yards out on the left flank of the wagon train. Preacher took up a similar position to the right. The baron was in the lead, riding directly in front of the first wagon. Matt and Dieter were out of sight, somewhere up ahead.

As he rode, Smoke's eyes were constantly on the move as well, searching the wooded hillsides and the broad, open pastures. He knew that gullies cut across some of those pastures, and they were deep enough that ambushers could hide in them. Also, there was plenty of cover on the slopes to conceal riflemen, but at least the hills were a little more scattered north of the creek. There weren't any places quite as perfect for an ambush as the gap into which von Hoffman had led the wagons two days earlier.

Smoke watched especially for sunlight glinting off of something. Even the most skilled bushwhacker sometimes allowed a stray sunbeam to bounce off his rifle barrel, or even a belt buckle or one of the silver conchos on a hat band. Anything that didn't belong was cause for concern.

He didn't see anything out of the ordinary, but he kept looking. A man who grew complacent and let his guard down when he might be riding into trouble could wind up dead in a hurry. Smoke didn't intend to let that happen to him, not with the beautiful wife and the ranch he had to come home to.

He had taken on the responsibility of helping these pilgrims reach their destination safely, too, and he didn't want to let them down.

By midday, the wagons had covered several miles, and the trail was starting to curve back to the east, toward the plains. Smoke knew that was going to happen. Even though this wasn't a main wagon trail, enough people came through here that two reasons had been discovered for the westerly bow, both of them having to do with Snake Creek. It was a good source of water, and it was much easier to ford where it ran through the foothills. Farther out on the prairie, the stream widened and became a series of muddy sandbars and stagnant pools and sinkholes. A wagon that tried to cross it out there was liable to bog down in a hurry. So it was faster and easier to detour through the foothills and the edge of Sugarloaf range. Smoke never minded, as long as people didn't hang around and try to cause trouble.

The baron called a halt to rest the oxen and the horses, and while the wagons were stopped, Matt and Dieter rode in.

"Everything looks good ahead," Matt reported. "The trail's clear, and once the wagons are back out on the flats, they ought to be able to make pretty good time."

"Splendid," von Hoffman said. "Do you agree, Schumann?"

"Yes, Your Excellency," Dieter responded. "Herr Jensen is correct."

The baron nodded.

"Very well. We'll rest here for an hour, then resume our journey."

People built several small cooking fires to prepare hot meals. Smoke, Matt, and Preacher were used to making do with jerky for a noon meal when they were on the trail, but these folks weren't like that. Even in the middle of nowhere, they still liked their creature comforts, Smoke thought. But he supposed there was no point in living on jerky if you didn't have to.

Erica came over to where Smoke, Matt, and Preacher were rubbing down their horses and said, "Our cook will have dinner ready shortly. The three of you are welcome to join us, of course."

"You brought a dadgum cook along?" Preacher asked in amazement.

"Certainly," Erica said. "Who else would prepare our meals?"

Preacher opened his mouth to say something else, but Smoke caught the old mountain man's eye and shook his head. There was no point in it. Life on the frontier would teach these pampered aristocrats a few things. It was just a matter of time.

"We're much obliged to you, ma'am," he said, "but we brought our own supplies."

"Nonsense," Erica said. "I insist, and so does Friedrich."

Matt said, "We don't want to hurt these folks' feelings, Smoke." He turned to Erica and went on with a grin, "We'd be honored to join you, fraulein."

She smiled back at him and offered him her arm.

"Come with me, then," she invited.

Matt linked arms with her and the two of them walked toward the lead wagon. Smoke glanced around, wondering where Dieter was and if the young man had seen what just happened. A second later, he spotted Dieter on the far side of the wagons, watching with a frown on his face.

Preacher saw the same thing. The old-timer said, "Sure as shootin', there's gonna be a blow-up 'tween them two 'fore we get to Wyomin', Smoke."

"I wouldn't be a bit surprised," Smoke said.

Matt's prediction about their pace proved to be accurate. Once the wagons reached the plains, they were able to go somewhat faster, although the combination of plodding oxen and heavily loaded wagons was never going to make for much speed.

The rest of the day passed peacefully, and the wagon train had covered as much ground as anyone could have hoped for, Smoke thought. He said as much to Baron von Hoffman that evening beside the large campfire in the center of the circle formed by the wagons.

"Keep this up and you'll reach the Medicine Bows in another week or ten days," Smoke said.

"And then our journey will be over," the baron said. Smoke heard the weariness in his voice. The travelers had come a long way, and every step of the journey, von Hoffman had carried the weight of their safety, as well as the knowledge that it was his actions that might have put them in danger.

"Do you ever regret what you did, Baron? Back there in Germany, I mean. Getting on the wrong side of those men Klaus Berger works for?"

Von Hoffman shook his head.

"My efforts may have failed, but someone had to oppose them," he said. "They would have led the

country into war after war, bankrupting us and
causing needless deaths. The long war against France
has already drained my homeland. As a Prussian, I
have been taught the art of war since I was only a
child. It is what I was bred for. But there comes a
time . . ." His voice trailed off and he shook his
head. "To answer your question, Herr Jensen, no, I
do not regret my actions. I regret only that they
failed to accomplish their goal."

"Well, I reckon a man's got to do what he thinks
is right. That's all the world can ask of us."

Von Hoffman smiled thinly.

"No. Sometimes it asks more. Sometime the
world demands . . . everything."

Smoke wasn't sure what the baron meant by that,
but he didn't press the issue. Instead, he went to
look up Matt and find out how the day's scouting
had gone with Dieter.

He found Preacher first and asked the old mountain man, "Have you seen Matt?"

Preacher jerked a thumb toward one of the
wagons.

"He was headed over yonder to talk to that girl, I
reckon."

Smoke grunted. Matt was going to pursue his at-
traction to Erica von Hoffman, regardless of what
Dieter thought. Smoke couldn't blame him for that
or tell him that he shouldn't, but still, the situation
held the potential for trouble.

Maybe more than the potential, he thought as he
approached the baron's wagon and saw Matt and

Erica sitting side by side on the wagon tongue. They were pretty close to each other, and they had their heads together talking quietly.

Dieter was walking toward them from the other direction. He was closer, too, and would get there before Smoke would.

Maybe it was better this way, Smoke told himself. Get things out in the open right away so it wouldn't be looming over the wagon train all the way to Wyoming.

"You must be getting bored, listening to me talk about myself this way," Matt said.

Erica shook her head and said, "No, no, it is fascinating, Herr Jensen. I mean, Matt." He had told her to use his first name, and she seemed to be getting used to it. "You have had so many colorful adventures."

"Not nearly as many as Smoke and Preacher. Why, Preacher's been out here on the frontier more than sixty years. When he went west, there weren't more than a few dozen white men who had ever laid eyes on the Rocky Mountains. *He's* the one who's really got some stories. It was pretty wild when Smoke came out here, too, right after the war. You wouldn't believe it to look at him now, but there was a time when Smoke was an outlaw—"

Erica stopped him by resting a hand on his arm.

"It is your stories I am interested in, Matt." She lowered her voice a little. "It is *you* I am interested in."

Some of the flickering firelight reached there, enough to paint Erica's face with a rosy glow that made her even prettier, although before he had seen it with his own eyes Matt wouldn't have thought that was possible. She was only a few inches from him, close enough for him to feel the warmth of her breath, and it would have been the easiest thing in the world for him to lean even closer and press his lips to hers. . . .

"Good evening, Fraulein von Hoffman."

Erica jumped slightly as the man's voice addressed her. She pulled back from Matt and looked up.

"Oh. Dieter, you startled me."

Dieter had taken his high-crowned hat off. He held it in front of him with one hand. He said, "My apologies, fraulein. I did not mean any harm."

"No, no, of course not. You are a perfectly harmless young man."

Dieter's mouth tightened. He looked like he didn't appreciate being called harmless, Matt thought, although it was likely he would take it, coming from Erica as it did.

And it wasn't strictly true that Dieter was harmless, Matt reminded himself. According to Smoke, Dieter had killed at least one of those bushwhackers during the battle a couple of days earlier.

"What can I do for you, Dieter?" Erica went on.

"I need to speak to Herr Jensen. About our scouting plans for tomorrow."

"I figure we'll ride out ahead of the wagon train and see what's there," Matt drawled. "Are those good enough plans for you, Dieter?"

Dieter took a deep breath.

"I would still like to speak with you, Matt."

"In a little while, when I'm done talking to Fraulein von Hoffman."

"No," Dieter insisted. "Now."

Irritation welled up inside Matt. He knew good and well Dieter just wanted to get him away from Erica, so that he couldn't sit here talking with her . . . or whatever else he might do with her.

At first, seeing that Erica was taken with him, Matt had thought that if he played up to her a little, the competition might bring Dieter out of his self-imposed shell.

The more time he spent with the lovely young blonde, though, the more Matt realized that he was genuinely attracted to her. He liked talking to her, and he was sure he would enjoy kissing her, as well. So maybe it was time for him to stop worrying about Dieter, he had decided, and let the young German deal with his own problems.

Which was exactly what Dieter was trying to do, Matt supposed. But that didn't mean he had to co-operate.

"We'll talk later," he said.

"I must insist," Dieter said.

Erica asked, "Dieter, what's gotten into you? You seem angry."

"Insist all you want to," Matt said, "I'm not going anywhere."

"I think you are," Dieter said to Matt, ignoring Erica's question.

Even though he was well aware of how childish it sounded, Matt said, "And who's going to make me?"

Dieter drew in another deep breath.

"I am, you no-good ranny!" he cried, and as the words left his mouth he dropped his hat and stepped forward, swinging a punch at Matt's head.

Chapter Seventeen

Smoke grimaced and started moving faster as he saw the unmistakable signs of confrontation between Matt and Dieter. Both young men were holding themselves stiffly, and Smoke could almost see the anger building around them.

He didn't get there in time. Dieter threw his punch at Matt first.

Unfortunately for Dieter, Matt was an experienced brawler and had no trouble pulling his head back so that Dieter's looping blow passed harmlessly in front of his face. Instinct brought Matt to his feet and sent his left fist crashing into Dieter's midsection. The force of the blow made Dieter double over and put him in perfect position for the right fist that Matt brought around to catch him on the jaw with stunning force. Erica cried out in alarm as the punch landed.

The impact sent Dieter reeling backwards. He probably would have fallen if Smoke hadn't been there to catch him. Smoke grabbed Dieter under the arms and held him up.

Matt stalked toward them with his fists still doubled.

"Back off, Matt!" Smoke snapped.

"He threw the first punch!"

"I know he did, but I also know he's not any match for you."

That was probably the wrong thing to say, Smoke realized as soon as the words were out of his mouth. Dieter lct out a desperate sob and tore loose from Smoke's grip. Normally he wouldn't have been able to break Smoke's hold on him, but Smoke wasn't expecting the young man to have any fight left in him.

Obviously he had underestimated Dieter. With a bellowing roar of anger, Dieter threw himself forward and tackled Matt around the waist.

Matt was slightly taller and heavier, but Dieter came at him like a runaway freight train. The collision as Dieter buried his shoulder in Matt's belly lifted Matt off his feet and drove him backwards. He came crashing down on his back with Dieter on top of him.

Smoke could tell the hard landing knocked the breath out of Matt's lungs. Dieter took advantage of the opportunity to start flailing wild punches at Matt's head. At the same time, he dug a knee into Matt's stomach.

Erica was on her feet now, too. She danced around the two men, crying, "Dieter, no! Stop! Stop this!"

Some of the other immigrants ran toward the source of the commotion. They shouted to each other, and Smoke figured it was the German equivalent of a bunch of onlookers yelling, "Fight! Fight!"

Dieter's luck wasn't going to last long. Matt would recover in a matter of seconds, and when he did, he might be mad enough to really hurt the youngster. So Smoke moved closer to the struggling figures, waited a few seconds for an opening, and then reached down to wrap his arms around Dieter's torso and haul the young man off of Matt.

Dieter yelled something in his native tongue, too. Smoke growled in his ear, "Settle down, boy. If you're trying to get yourself killed, why don't you wait for another attack by the baron's enemies?"

"Let me go!" Dieter shouted.

Matt had climbed to his feet. He stood there in the firelight with his chest heaving as he caught his breath. When he could speak again, he said, "Yeah, let him go, Smoke, if he's bound and determined to have it out!"

Preacher had arrived on the scene of the fracas, too. He moved in front of Matt and rested a hand on the young man's chest.

"Hold your horses," the old mountain man said. "You know Dieter ain't no match for you, Matt."

"He's the one who started it," Matt said hotly. "He's brave enough to take a swing at me, but he's too much of a coward to say what's really on his mind!"

"That is not true!" Dieter yelled.

"Then why don't you tell everybody what this is really about?" Matt challenged him. "Why don't you tell Erica how you really feel about her instead of trying to come between her and me?"

Dieter had been struggling futilely to get loose from Smoke's grip. At Matt's words, he stopped fighting. In fact, he sagged in Smoke's arms like all the starch had gone out of him.

Erica stepped toward them. Her eyes were wide with surprise. She half-lifted a hand and said, "Dieter, what . . . what is Matt talking about?"

Quietly, with his mouth next to Dieter's ear, Smoke whispered, "If you're ever going to grow a spine, boy, this is the time."

For a second he didn't think Dieter was going to react. Then, slowly, the young man started to stand straighter. He squared his shoulders, looked at Erica, and in a voice that trembled only slightly, he said, "It is true, Fraulein von Hoffman. I am very . . . fond of you. With your permission, I would like to court—"

"Schumann!"

The outraged roar came from behind Smoke. He let go of Dieter and turned to see the baron standing there. Von Hoffman's face was dark with anger as he glowered at Dieter. Obviously fearing his wrath, most of the immigrants who had gathered around to watch the fight began to draw back. None of them wanted to attract the baron's attention to them when he was this angry.

Von Hoffman strode forward and put his face right in Dieter's.

"Did I hear you say you wanted to court my cousin?" he demanded. "She is of noble birth, you fool!"

Dieter started to babble.

"I know, Your Excellency. I . . . I am sorry. . . ."

His voice trailed off, and once again he made a visible effort to steel himself.

"No," he said. "I am not sorry. I have no wish to offend you, Baron, but I am very attracted to your cousin Fraulein von Hoffman—"

That was as far as he got before the baron's left hand came up and cracked across his face in a back-handed blow that sent Dieter staggering. Erica cried out in horror.

"Friedrich, no!"

Von Hoffman raised his other hand and started after Dieter, clearly intending to give him a bare-handed thrashing. Smoke knew Dieter probably wouldn't fight back. The way he had been raised would make him just stand there and take whatever punishment the baron dealt out.

Smoke hadn't been raised that way. He took a swift step, and his hand closed around von Hoffman's wrist before another blow could fall.

"That's enough," Smoke said in a flat, hard voice.

Von Hoffman's head jerked toward him. The baron's mouth twisted in a furious snarl.

"You dare lay hands—"

"This is America, Baron," Smoke said, cutting

into the man's bluster. "A man dares whatever he thinks he can back up."

For a second their angry gazes dueled at close range. Then, tight-lipped, the baron said, "Release me. I will not strike the boy again."

"Good." Smoke let go of von Hoffman's wrist and took a step back, but he was ready to move again if he needed to. "He doesn't deserve a beating just because he likes a girl."

"My cousin is not just a girl," von Hoffman snapped. He cast a scathing glance at Dieter. "She is an aristocrat, noble by birth. He is nothing!"

"He's a good man, and he's been doing a good job for you as a scout. That's worth a lot."

"Not enough." Von Hoffman's flinty tone made it clear that he would never be convinced otherwise.

"Please," Dieter said. "I . . . I have caused enough of a ruckus. With your permission, Your Excellency, I wish to . . . withdraw what I said before."

"You will not press your courtship of my cousin?"

"No, Your Excellency."

Smoke saw the way Erica's face fell at that. She had just found out that Dieter liked her—and she probably should have realized that before now, Smoke thought—and just like that he was taking it all back. That had to be quite a blow to her pride. She stepped toward him and said, "Dieter, if I had known—"

"Enough," von Hoffman said sharply. "Erica, go inside the wagon."

"But Friedrich—"

"Inside the wagon," the baron repeated. His attitude softened enough for him to add, "Please."

"V-very well." Looking stunned and unsure of herself, Erica backed toward the wagon. She glanced at Matt, then quickly looked away. She turned and climbed into the wagon.

Von Hoffman glared at the bystanders who were left. He swung an arm curtly and said, "The matter is closed! Go on about your business."

The small crowd dispersed almost instantly, leaving von Hoffman standing there with Smoke, Matt, Preacher, and Dieter.

Von Hoffman addressed the young man again, saying, "My affection for your late father is the only thing that prevents me from taking sterner measures with you, Schumann. From now on, keep your distance from my cousin."

"Of course, Your Excellency," Dieter said without lifting his downcast eyes.

Von Hoffman turned to Smoke.

"As for you, Herr Jensen . . ."

"Yeah?" Smoke asked softly, but in a tone that packed considerable menace.

Von Hoffman took a deep breath and said, "I realize that your ways and mine are very different. I understand as well that we are in your country, not mine. Therefore I hereby tender you my apology for losing my temper."

"That's all right, Baron." Smoke was damned if

he was going to address any man as *Your Excellency.* "I reckon it takes a while to get used to the way things are done in a new place."

Von Hoffman smiled thinly.

"Indeed." He turned to Matt. "I hope you took no offense at anything I said, Herr Jensen."

"Why, because I'm one of those filthy commoners who's not good enough to talk to your cousin, too?"

"Take it easy, Matt," Smoke advised.

Matt shrugged and said, "I don't want trouble with you, Baron, but the way I see it, it's up to Miss Erica to decide who she wants to talk to and spend time with. That's the way we do things here."

"Yes, of course," von Hoffman said. His jaw was clenched tightly enough that a little muscle jumped slightly in it. "But I am her guardian and have only her best interests at heart. You must understand that."

Smoke gave Matt a stern look, and Matt shrugged again.

"Sure. I reckon I can respect that. Just like I respect your cousin, and I'll continue to do so."

"I suppose that will have to do for now," von Hoffman said.

"Yeah, I suppose it will."

"I'll bid you all good night, then. We have many more miles to cover tomorrow." Von Hoffman started to turn away but paused. "That is, if you are still coming with us."

"We said we would," Smoke told him.

"Ain't none of us in the habit of goin' against our word," Preacher added.

"Just as I expected." The baron nodded to them. "Good night."

He went to his wagon and climbed inside. Smoke, Matt, and Preacher watched as he jerked the canvas flap closed.

"Don't go giving me some lecture, Smoke," Matt said. "I had every right to talk to the girl."

"Sure you did. And so did Dieter. The sooner these folks accept the fact that they're not in the old country anymore, the better."

"Speakin' of which," Preacher said, "where in tar-nation did Dieter go?"

Puzzled, Smoke turned and looked around the camp.

Dieter was nowhere in sight.

Chapter Eighteen

He had never known torment such as this. Better that wild Indians had captured him and burned him at the stake, he thought. That would not have been as painful as being forced to grovel in front of the woman he loved.

He had tried to stand up to the baron, Dieter thought as he walked blindly across the grassy plains. The wagons were several hundred yards behind him, and he continued putting more distance between himself and the scene of his shame.

Eventually he would have to stop, turn around, and go back. He knew that. But right now he couldn't stand to be there. He couldn't bear the misery of having Erica look at him and know what a pathetic excuse for a man he really was.

He should have told her how he felt about her long before now, he thought. The outcome wouldn't have been any different, of course—he still would have been forced to crawl before the baron's wrath, no matter when he broached the subject—but at least he wouldn't have had everything weighing on him for so long.

On the other hand, by letting Erica believe that he was simply her friend, he had been able to enjoy being around her, to talk to her and see her smile and hear her laugh. That had to be worth something. It was worth a great deal, he told himself.

But it never would have been enough. He always would have wanted more. More than he could have . . .

He stopped and looked up at the millions of stars floating in the ebony sky. Those stars had witnessed his humiliation, too, but they said nothing. They simply hung there, cold and silent, casting their silvery illumination over the prairie.

After a moment Dieter fell to his knees. He bent forward and covered his face with his hands. The enormity of what had happened threatened to overwhelm him. Once the wagon train reached Wyoming, he couldn't stay there with the other settlers. He couldn't bear the thought of being around Erica for the rest of his life, knowing how much he wanted her but knowing as well that he could never have her. He would have to go somewhere else, he decided. He would become a drifter, a saddle tramp. . . .

He was kneeling there like that when he heard

the faint jingle of a bit chain, somewhere far off in the darkness.

The sound didn't penetrate Dieter's consciousness at first. But when it was followed by a hoofbeat, then another and another, he realized what he was hearing.

Someone was out there in the darkness, moving at a deliberate pace toward the wagon camp.

Outlaws! Indians! Assassins hired by the baron's political enemies!

All those thoughts flashed through Dieter's mind, temporarily banishing his emotional turmoil. It was possible, of course, that those unknown night riders had nothing to do with the wagon train, but he barely considered that idea before he discarded it. His instincts told him that the strangers represented a threat to the group.

That meant they represented a threat to Erica as well, and even though he had been humiliated in front of her and could never hope to win her over, he couldn't let anything happen to her, either. Not if he could prevent it.

He dropped to his belly and lay absolutely still and silent, listening intently as the men approached. He didn't want them to realize he was there.

The hoofbeats came closer, along with the jingling of bit chains and the creak of saddle leather. Dieter started to worry that the men were going to ride right over him, but then the noises stopped. After a moment he decided that the riders had reined in, coming to a halt several yards away from him. He was lying in fairly tall grass, so it was unlikely they would spot him.

They were close enough to see the campfire from here. In fact, on these plains a good-sized fire was visible for a long distance. Maybe they weren't going to attack the camp after all. Maybe they weren't even going to come any closer to it than they already were. He began to hope that they had nothing to do with the baron's party of immigrants.

That hope was dashed when one of the men spoke in a low, guttural voice. The words were in German.

"This should be a good place," the man said. "The wind is behind us."

"I wish it was blowing a little harder," another man replied, also in German. His voice was higher pitched but had a grating, unpleasant quality to it. "I worry that it will not carry the flames quickly enough."

Flames, Dieter thought. Flames!

These men intended to start a fire.

Dieter had read about prairie fires in his dime novels. They were terrible things. High-leaping flames raced across the landscape, destroying everything in their path, and there was nothing that could be done to stop them.

Dieter lifted his head slightly, just enough to feel the breeze that stirred the grass around him. Like the second man said, the wind wasn't blowing very hard, but there was enough wind to fan the flames and drive them on toward the wagon camp. Even though the fire wouldn't spread very fast, it would be impossible to get the oxen hitched to the wagons in time to save the vehicles. The flames would overtake the slow-moving beasts.

Some of the immigrants might be able to escape, but everything they owned would be destroyed. Not only that, but they would be stuck out here in the middle of nowhere, too, easy prey for these human vultures who sat their saddles so near to him.

"All right," the man with the grating, high-pitched voice said. "Get started."

The sharp reek of kerosene made Dieter's nose wrinkle. The first man ordered, "Soak those torches so they won't go out when you light them and throw them as you're riding."

So that was their plan. They would ride along pitching blazing, kerosene-soaked torches into the grass at various points, and that would create a long line of fire that would be impossible for the immigrants to escape. It was a cruel scheme, and when it succeeded, it would condemn the baron and all his people to either a fiery death or a fatal shot from a hired killer's gun.

As far as Dieter could see, there was only one way to stop them. It would probably cost his life, but he had no choice. His life would mean nothing if Erica was dead, anyway.

He pulled his pistol from its holster, gathered his courage, tensed his muscles, and suddenly sprang to his feet. A couple of the nearby horses neighed in surprise and shied away from him as his gun came up.

"Eat hot lead, you sons of bitches!" he yelled at the top of his lungs as he started pulling the trigger.

The shots blasted out from his revolver as he aimed at the shadowy, mounted figures. Men yelled in surprise and alarm, and one of them howled in pain. When Dieter heard that, he knew at least one of his bullets had found its target.

"Light the torches!"

That order came from the man with the grating voice. Dieter swung his gun in that direction and pulled the trigger again, hoping he could kill the leader. The gun bucked against his hand, but when he pulled the trigger again, the hammer fell on an empty chamber. He had emptied the cylinder without realizing it.

Which meant he was at their mercy. A sheet of muzzle flame split the darkness as several shots roared as one. Dieter felt the blow of a giant fist against his body. They were going to kill him now, he thought.

But the yelling and the shots must have alerted the camp, and Smoke and Matt and Preacher would stop these evil men. Dieter knew that. It was what he'd really been hoping for all along, not his own survival.

Now it was up to Smoke and the others, he thought as he fell. More shots thundered, practically on top of him, and that was the last thing he knew as oblivion claimed him.

* * *

Smoke and Preacher walked around the camp, and it took only a few minutes to confirm what Smoke suspected. Dieter wasn't there, but the horse he'd been riding was. Smoke didn't think any of the other horses were missing.

"Boy stomped off on foot," Preacher said. "He's just walkin' around out there tryin' to cool off after that scuffle with Matt and the chewin' out the baron gave him. I wouldn't worry too much about him."

"You're probably right," Smoke said. "Still, he might run into some kind of varmint out there in the dark."

"What? A prairie dog?" Preacher chuckled. "I reckon even ol' Dieter can handle that."

"I was thinking more of a snake, maybe even a panther or a bear."

"If there was a panther or a bear out there, which ain't very likely to start with, it heard this bunch comin' a long time ago and took off for the tall and uncut. Dieter'll be fine, Smoke."

Smoke nodded.

"You're right. I know you're right."

"But you want to go find him anyway."

"He was pretty upset. He's probably not thinking very clearly right now."

"No young fella in love ever does."

Preacher had a point there, Smoke supposed. But it didn't ease his worry.

"I think I'll go take a look around," he said.

"I'll come with you, if you're bound and determined to do it," Preacher offered. "You want me to get Matt?"

Smoke shook his head.

"I don't imagine he's very happy with Dieter right now. Let's let him cool off, too."

The two of them stepped over one of the wagon tongues and walked out about a hundred yards from the camp. From that point, they began walking in a large circle that would take them all around the wagons. If they didn't find Dieter doing that, they would go out farther and repeat the maneuver.

Smoke thought about calling Dieter's name, but he wasn't sure the young man would answer even if he heard them. What Dieter had gone through had to be pretty humiliating. He probably didn't want to face anybody right now.

Smoke and Preacher had made only part of a circuit of the camp when both men suddenly stopped short and listened.

"You hear it, too?" Preacher whispered after a moment.

"Yeah," Smoke replied. "Horses. Over to the right, coming toward the camp."

"More of Klaus's men?"

"Maybe Klaus himself," Smoke said as he dropped to a knee so he wouldn't be as visible. Preacher hunkered beside him.

Smoke forgot about Dieter for the moment. This was a more pressing problem and might represent a real danger to the immigrants. While it was possible the riders he and Preacher heard didn't have anything to do with the baron's party, Smoke didn't believe that for a second. That would be too much of a coincidence.

The faint hoofbeats stopped. Preacher whispered, "We gonna get closer?"

"Yeah," Smoke replied. He went down onto his belly.

Preacher stretched out beside him and said, "I'm gettin' a mite old to be crawlin' around like a snake."

"Just be careful you don't go crawling over any actual snakes," Smoke advised.

With the stealth that only years of experience and their own natural skill could provide, the two men crawled toward the riders. They couldn't move very fast because they had to be silent and they didn't want to stir the grass too much, but Smoke's gut told him they didn't need to waste any time, either.

Voices carried to them, even though the men were speaking quietly. Sound traveled well over these plains. At first Smoke thought he couldn't understand the men because he and Preacher weren't quite close enough to them yet, but then he realized they were speaking a foreign language.

German, to be precise.

Preacher heard the words, too, and breathed, "Germans. Got to be Klaus."

Smoke agreed, and he knew that Klaus wouldn't have anything good in mind for Baron von Hoffman and the rest of the immigrants.

Suddenly he smelled something. Taking a deeper whiff of the night air, he whispered, "That's kerosene!"

Preacher smelled it, too.

"The buzzards are gonna set fire to the prairie!"

A blaze like that was one of the most feared things on the frontier. The destructiveness of a prairie fire was terrible. If that was what was threatening the immigrants, there was no time for stealth anymore. Smoke and Preacher had to stop the hired killers any way they could.

But as they leaped to their feet, a shout rang out.

"Eat hot lead, you sons of bitches!"

"Dieter!" Smoke exclaimed.

Colt flame bloomed in the night as shots stabbed from gun muzzles. The blasts rolled across the plains like thunder.

Guns drawn, Smoke and Preacher charged toward the fight.

Chapter Nineteen

The men bent on starting the fire had their hands full with the unexpected attack from Dieter, so they didn't seem to notice two more men racing across the prairie toward them.

They noticed, though, when Smoke and Preacher came within handgun range and opened fire on the shadowy figures mounted on nervous horses.

Smoke heard a man shout, "Light the torches!"

A second later, flame flared up as one of the men managed to scratch a lucifer into life and hold it to the head of a torch wrapped in kerosene-soaked fabric. In the glare, Smoke caught sight of Dieter falling under an onslaught of shots.

There was no time to worry about the young man. Smoke had to stop that man from throwing his torch into the tall grass.

He squeezed off another shot and saw the torch bearer reel in the saddle. The blazing torch slipped from his hand, but instead of wheeling through the air away from the group, it fell under the hooves of the horses as they danced around.

That spooked the horses even more. Several of them bolted and inadvertently trampled right over the torch.

Preacher had both Colts out. He had seen Dieter fall, too, and raced to the youngster's side. Planting one foot on either side of the young man, he fired both guns and drove the marauders away from him.

Smoke dashed to where the torch had fallen. The grass was burning in several places, but it was shorter here and he was able to stomp out the flames. The torch itself still burned, but it was dying down now because it had rolled through the dirt.

Muzzle flashes continued to split the night. Smoke returned the shots, aiming by instinct as much as anything else.

Someone yelled a command in harsh, high-pitched German. Men wheeled their horses and sent them galloping over the prairie. In the darkness, it was probably impossible to tell how many men they were facing. They might have stayed and made a fight of it if they had known that only two men opposed them.

But as it was, they did what hired killers always did when they met more resistance than they expected.

They cut their losses and ran.

Smoke sent another shot after them to hurry them on their way. So did Preacher.

Unfortunately, the would-be killers did more than flee. As they rode, several of the men managed to light their torches and fling the kerosene-soaked brands behind them. The grass caught fire and flames began to shoot up in several places.

"Dadblast it!" Preacher yelled. "Now we got more trouble!"

That was certainly true. It was going to be difficult if not impossible to stomp out these fires, unlike the one Smoke had caused the horses to put out.

"Preacher, get back to the camp!" Smoke said. "Tell Matt and the baron to grab some blankets and soak them in water and get out here!"

"What about Dieter?" Preacher asked.

"I'll see to him," Smoke snapped.

He holstered his gun and ran over to the young man while Preacher headed for the camp as fast as his long legs would carry him. Smoke bent, grabbed hold of Dieter, and hoisted the young man onto his shoulder. He could tell that Dieter's shirt was wet with blood but didn't know how badly the youngster was wounded. There was no time now to check.

Smoke had carried Dieter only a few yards when hoofbeats pounded in front of him and a rider loomed up and swept past them. In the light from the moon and stars, Smoke recognized Matt riding bareback. Something trailed from one of Matt's hands.

Smoke turned to watch as Matt reached the closest of the fires. Matt flung himself off the horse and began slapping at the flames with the thing he was carrying. Smoke knew then that Matt hadn't needed any instructions. He must have seen the glare when the first torch was lit and taken action immediately, soaking a blanket and jumping on a horse to get out here as fast as he could. Matt had enough experience to know how dangerous even the slightest wayward spark could be on the prairie.

Hearing more horses coming, Smoke moved quickly to the side to get out of their way. Several riders raced past, also trailing wet blankets behind them. They spread out and started fighting the fires.

Smoke hoofed it on toward the wagons. Dieter's weight was no problem for his great strength. He hoped the young man was still alive.

The whole camp was in a state of alarm by now. As Smoke trotted up to the wagons, several people met him and willing hands reached out to take Dieter.

"Be careful with him!" Smoke warned. "He's been shot!"

He heard a horrified exclamation and looked over to see Erica von Hoffman standing there with one trembling hand raised to her mouth.

"Why don't you see how bad he's hurt?" Smoke suggested in a firm voice.

That urgency got through to her. She nodded and followed the men who were carrying Dieter, telling them, "Take him to my wagon! Quickly!"

Smoke looked around for Preacher. When he spotted the old mountain man, he went over to him. Preacher looked winded.

"Matt rode past me . . . 'fore I got here," Preacher explained as he bent over and rested his hands on his thighs. "Then the baron and some other fellas . . . followed him."

Smoke nodded.

"I saw them. Matt didn't waste any time getting out there. I reckon he saw the first torch being lit and knew something bad was about to happen."

"The boy's right smart," Preacher agreed. The old-timer seemed to have most of his breath back now.

The two of them turned to look out at the plains where the men were still battling the scattered wild-fires. Silhouetted against the flames, figures dashed back and forth, slapping at them with the blankets. Even if the blankets weren't very wet by now, they could still be used to put out small fires.

"Reckon we better go help 'em?" Preacher asked.

"I think they're about to get the fires under control," Smoke said. "But it wouldn't hurt if we went out to stand guard just in case Klaus and his men came back."

"Good thinkin'," Preacher agreed. They went to get their rifles and then strode out onto the prairie.

All but two of the fires had been snuffed out by the time Smoke and Preacher had covered the two hundred yards. Matt saw them coming and stepped back while Baron von Hoffman and several men from the wagon train finished the job. As Smoke and Preacher came up to him, Matt asked, "Are you fellas all right?"

"We're fine," Smoke told him. "How about you?"

"I'm a mite singed here and there," Matt replied with a smile, "but I'll live."

"Hope the same thing's true of Dieter," Preacher said.

Matt's face instantly turned worried.

"Dieter? How was he mixed up in this?"

"He may have saved the wagon train," Smoke said. "I'm not sure Preacher and I were close enough to have stopped Klaus and his men from starting a whole line of fires, instead of just a few blazes scattered here and there."

The baron was close enough to overhear Smoke's comments. He stalked over to the three men and asked, "This was Klaus Berger's doing?"

"That's what I figure," Smoke said. "We heard men talking in German. Either Klaus was with them, or he set the whole thing up."

"I told you he is a monster. A man would have to be in order to use flames against innocent people."

"You'd better check and make sure all the embers are out," Smoke advised. "Preacher and I will stand guard while you're doing that. You don't want any of those little fires flaring up again."

Von Hoffman nodded in agreement and said, "Of course." He issued orders, and he and the men who had come out to fight the fires with him spent several minutes making sure even the smallest glowing ember was put out completely.

Eventually the men gathered up their horses and started walking back to the camp. As Matt led his mount, he said, "I want to check on Dieter. How in the world did he know what was going on, anyway?"

"I don't know," Smoke said. "Preacher and I

figured he was out walking around, trying to cool off after that ruckus with you, and we went to look for him. Before we could find him, we heard some riders coming, and then Dieter was right there among them, yelling and shooting at them. I reckon he must have heard them coming, too, and took cover until he found out what was going on."

"Then you're right," Matt said. "He probably did save the camp. I hope he's not hurt too bad." He paused. "I'm not going to apologize for what happened between him and me, though, or for being fond of Erica."

"Nobody's askin' you to," Preacher said.

They went straight to Erica's wagon. Quite a few people were gathered outside the vehicle. The crowd parted when they saw the baron striding toward them. Von Hoffman went to the lowered tailgate and climbed in, while Smoke, Matt, and Preacher waited tensely outside.

A few minutes later, von Hoffman reappeared and said, "Young Schumann is still alive, but he suffered two serious wounds and lost a considerable amount of blood. My personal physician is with him now."

So the baron had brought along his own sawbones, Smoke thought. He supposed von Hoffman had the money and influence to do something like that. So far, Smoke had met only a few of the immigrants, so there was no telling who else von Hoffman had brought with him.

Smoke said, "If there's anything we can do to help, Baron . . ."

Von Hoffman shook his head.

"It is out of our hands now, Herr Jensen. What I need is some advice on how to keep an attack like this from happening again."

"You've already been posting guards at night," Smoke said. "Maybe you should move them out farther away from the wagons. Maybe put a couple of men on horseback, too, circling the camp all the time. I can tell you this . . . if Klaus is determined enough, and it appears that he is, you're not going to be able to stop him from making another try for you. All you can do is be prepared and outfight him when it happens."

"You are telling me that more of my people will die before we reach Wyoming," von Hoffman said grimly.

Smoke nodded and said, "I think there's a mighty good chance of it."

Chapter Twenty

Dieter was still alive the next morning. Smoke climbed into the wagon and found Erica sitting on a short, three-legged stool next to one of the built-in bunks. Dieter lay on his side on that bunk, his torso swathed in bandages. Erica wiped his forehead with a damp cloth and frowned in concern as Smoke asked quietly, "How's he doing?"

"He has a fever," Erica replied in a hushed tone. "Dr. Gruber said it is from the shock of being shot. The doctor cleaned and bandaged the wounds and said there is nothing more he can do. The bullets went all the way through Dieter's body, so at least he did not have to operate to remove them."

"Well, I reckon that's good," Smoke said. "Has Dieter been awake?"

Erica shook her head.

"No. I suppose he is fortunate not to know what is happening to him. The doctor told me to keep him as cool as I can and make him comfortable, and

that's all that can be done. I wish there was more.
I wish—"

Erica's voice broke into a sob.

Dealing with crying women wasn't something
Smoke was particularly good at. He wished Sally was
here. She would know what to do.

But she was back at Sugarloaf, so he just gave
Erica's shoulder an awkward pat. He probably wasn't
supposed to do that, since he was a commoner and
she was an aristocrat, but he didn't particularly give
a hoot about such things. She was just a fellow
human being in pain as far as he was concerned.

"I'm sure you're doing all you can for him, and
I've got a hunch Dieter knows that and appreciates
it," he told her.

"I'm told that he saved the camp from Klaus
Berger," Erica said as she used the back of her free
hand to wipe away her tears while she continued
stroking Dieter's face with the damp cloth.

"I'd say that's true. He played a big part in it,
anyway. So did Matt and your cousin and some of
the other men."

"And you and Herr Preacher," Erica said. "The
woman who brought my breakfast was full of talk
about the gunfight with Berger and his men."

"We all did what we could," Smoke said.

"This makes twice you have saved our lives. How
many more times will someone try to wipe us out
before we reach our destination?"

"I can't answer that, but I can tell you that we'll be
ready for whatever they try next," Smoke promised.

Erica nodded and said, "I hope Dieter lives to see Wyoming. He talked about it so much."

"I hope he does, too."

There was nothing else Smoke could say, so he left the wagon. Men were hitching up the teams now, getting the big, canvas-covered vehicles ready to roll.

Smoke was checking the saddle on his horse when a woman came up behind him and said, "Herr Jensen?"

Smoke looked around and was impressed by what he saw. The fact that he was happily married didn't render him blind, nor did it keep him from recognizing beauty when he saw it. The woman who stood there with her sunbonnet pushed back from thick, wavy masses of auburn hair was beautiful, no doubt about that.

"I'm Smoke Jensen," he said in reply to her question.

The smile she gave him in return was brilliant.

"Oh, I know that," she said. "I merely wished to thank you for what you did last night. If not for what you and your friends did, surely those evil men would have wiped us all out." The woman extended a hand. "My name is Greta Schiller."

Smoke took her hand, even as he noted the wedding ring on her other hand.

"I'm pleased to meet you, Frau Schiller. I reckon your husband must be one of the baron's friends?"

"He was," Greta replied, with emphasis on the second word. "I'm a widow."

"I'm sorry to hear that," Smoke told her honestly.

"Life sometimes deals harshly with us all. But it also constantly presents us with new opportunities."

She still had hold of his hand. Her fingers were cool and smooth and soft, and strong enough that he couldn't slip his hand out of her grasp without being obvious about it. So he said, "That sounds like something my wife would say."

"You are married, then?"

"Yes, ma'am."

"Wait, of course, I knew that." She finally let go of his hand. "Friedrich and Erica went to dine at your ranch house."

"That's right."

"It's your brother who is unmarried . . . and quite taken with our little Erica. I remember now."

Smoke didn't particularly want to discuss the troublesome triangle involving Matt, Erica, and Dieter, and he didn't really want to prolong this conversation with Greta Schiller, either. Despite her beauty, there was something . . . predatory . . . about her. He didn't think it was fair to blame that on her being a widow, but she certainly gave off the impression that she might be searching for a new husband.

She could do her looking elsewhere as far as Smoke was concerned. He was a one-woman man, and had been ever since he had met Sally up in Idaho, in a town he had wound up almost wiping off the map.

He put his left hand to the brim of his hat and

said, "If you'll excuse me, ma'am, I need to make sure this horse of mine is ready to travel."

"Of course. We'll be leaving soon, won't we?"

"Yes, ma'am."

"I feel much safer knowing that you and your brother and your . . . father, is it?"

"Preacher's like a father to me and has been for a lot of years," Smoke said, "but he's not blood kin."

"Well, I feel safer with the three of you coming along with us, I was about to say." She gave him that brilliant smile again. "Good day, Herr Jensen."

Greta moved off along the line of wagons. Smoke was glad to see her go.

Preacher came over to him a few minutes later and asked, "Who was that redheaded gal talkin' to you?"

"Her name's Greta Schiller," Smoke explained. "Her late husband was one of the baron's friends."

"Late, eh?" Preacher said. "That means she's a widow woman now. You know what folks say about widow women, Smoke."

"Yeah, I know what they say about crotchety old codgers, too," Smoke replied with a chuckle. "That doesn't necessarily make any of it true."

Preacher drew himself up.

"So you think I'm a crotchety old codger, do you?"

"I didn't say that, now did I?"

"Maybe not." Preacher shrugged. "But I see what you're gettin' at. Still, I'd be a mite wary of that one, Smoke. My instincts tell me she might be trouble."

"And I know better than to argue with your instincts," Smoke murmured. "For what it's worth, Preacher, I agree with you. I think we need to keep an eye on Frau Greta Schiller."

"Just don't get too close while you're doin' it," Preacher advised.

That Smoke Jensen was a very handsome man, Greta thought as she walked toward her wagon. A year or two younger than her, perhaps, but that had never bothered her. Some of the best lovers she'd ever had were considerably younger than her. She had the experience, and they had the energy and enthusiasm of youth. It was a very potent combination.

She wasn't sure she had ever seen a man with such broad shoulders and brawny arms as Smoke. As she imagined what it would feel like to have those muscular arms of his close around her, a faint smile came to her lips. It would be good with him, she thought, so very good.

Such a shame that he was married, although Greta was confident that she could have had her way with him, given enough time.

And an even bigger shame that he would probably be dead, along with all the others, before that could come about.

"Frau Schiller?"

The thoughtful smile on her lips automatically turned into a seductive one as she looked around and saw the baron coming toward her.

"Good morning, Friedrich," she said.

"You are well this morning?" he asked stiffly. That was always the way he behaved around her. But she would get him to unbend eventually, she thought confidently. Her charms had always gotten her what she wanted sooner or later.

"Very well," she told him. "A bit nervous, though, because of what happened last night. I fear that those horrible men will try to attack us again."

"If they do, we will defeat them again," he said, as pompous as ever. He and Herman had been a good match, Greta thought, recalling what a stuffed shirt her late husband had been. It was no wonder that he and Friedrich von Hoffman had been close friends and political allies.

Von Hoffman did have one distinct advantage over Herman. He was much more appealing physically, especially compared to the portly, balding Herman Schiller. His hawklike features held a certain tinge of cruelty. Greta didn't mind that. Sometimes a little touch of cruelty just made the lovemaking that much more intense and satisfying.

"Did you need to speak to me about something, Friedrich?" she asked.

"Yes." He cleared his throat. "Please instruct your driver to place your wagon in line directly behind mine. I'd like to keep you nearer so that in case of more trouble, I can more easily insure your safety."

Finally! she thought. He was starting to come around at last. She had been sending him signs for weeks now, even since before their arrival in America. She'd begun to wonder if she was going to have to rip all her clothes off and throw herself at his feet before he got the idea.

She said, "Why, Friedrich, that is so thoughtful of you! I'll instruct Franz right away."

Von Hoffman cleared his throat again.

"Herman was one of my dearest friends," he said. "I would feel terrible if something happened to you, Frau Schiller . . . Greta."

Carefully, she kept the look of triumph off her face. The baron had taken the first step, and now, whether he knew it or not, he was lost.

She put her hand on his arm and squeezed lightly for a second, just enough for him to feel the warmth of her touch.

"Thank you," she whispered.

He nodded curtly, going all stiff again, and said, "Good day to you." Greta watched for a few seconds as he walked off, then went straight to her wagon where her driver, Franz, had finished hitching up the team of oxen.

She relayed the baron's order about taking the second place in line to the stolid servant, who nodded his understanding. Then she climbed into the wagon and pulled a small chest out from under the built-in bunk. She sat on the thin mattress and opened it.

Underneath the silk and lace of the garments packed inside the trunk, she felt the hard outlines of both the pistol and the sheathed dagger. She might not have to use either of them if Klaus Berger succeeded in his task, but she liked knowing that they were there if she needed them.

Herman had been such a fool. It had been so easy to slip the pills into his beer, the pills that Klaus had given her. That had eliminated the baron's staunchest ally. Von Hoffman would have been next, but Herman's death had frightened him into leaving the country so quickly that Klaus's employers had not had time to move against him. But when he was ready to leave Germany, he had asked her to come along, and there had never been any doubt about her answer.

Yes, the gun and the knife were there, but they were just tools.

She was truly the weapon of last resort for the baron's enemies.

Chapter Twenty-one

For several days the wagons rolled steadily north toward Wyoming, covering the ground at a nice pace now that they were on the plains again with the Rocky Mountains looming off to the left. Matt continued scouting ahead of the wagon train, with Smoke and Preacher serving as outriders. They were alert for any sign of trouble, and they made sure that the camps were well guarded at night.

Dieter was still alive. His fever had broken after a couple of days, thanks to luck and Erica's efforts to take care of him, and while he was still extremely weak, he was awake part of the time now and able to eat a little. Smoke was confident that the young man would start getting his strength back soon.

The first night that Dieter was coherent enough to know what was going on, Smoke sat in the baron's wagon with him and told him what had happened three nights earlier.

"I don't think there's any doubt you saved the wagon train," Smoke said.

Dieter shook his head.

"You and Preacher would have . . . stopped Berger and his men," he insisted.

"I don't know about that. When you stood up and started blazing away at them, you wrecked their plans and kept them from starting so many fires that we never could have put them all out." Smoke grinned. "It was like something out of one of those dime novels you read, the way you yelled at them to eat hot lead."

"I said that? I really . . . don't remember much . . . about what happened."

"You said it, all right," Smoke assured him. "And I think you ventilated several of the varmints, too. Nobody could have done any better than you did, Dieter."

"I was willing to die . . . to save Erica and the others."

"Erica's fine. She's been taking care of you since we brought you in."

A faint smile appeared on the young man's pale face.

"I know. When I first woke . . . I thought I was in heaven . . . because there was an angel looking down at me. . . ."

Smoke chuckled.

"You be sure and tell her that."

Dieter gave a tiny shake of his head and looked solemn and sorrowful.

"I cannot. It is not permitted. The baron would think—"

"Sooner or later you need to realize that what the baron thinks isn't as important as it used to be," Smoke broke in. "Like we keep telling you, Dieter, you're in America now. We don't have barons and counts and dukes and such-like."

"The baron will always be the baron," Dieter insisted, "no matter where he is."

Smoke didn't argue with the young man. Dieter would either come around to the American way of thinking, or he wouldn't. In the end, the choice was up to him.

"Matt and Preacher, they are all right?" Dieter asked after a couple of moments of silence.

"They're fine," Smoke told him. "None of us were hit while we were swapping bullets with Berger's bunch." He asked a question that had been nagging at him. "Did you overhear enough before the fight started to know if Klaus was with them?"

"No. There was a man giving orders . . . but no one used any names."

"I don't guess it really matters."

"One of the men I heard . . . I would know his voice again. It was high-pitched . . . but it had a sound to it . . . like a saw going through wood. I never heard anything . . . quite like it before. It was the sound of . . . evil."

Klaus Berger, Smoke thought. He would have bet a hat on it.

He patted Dieter on the shoulder and said,

"You've probably talked enough, son. You just rest now. And you can take it easy because you know you did good."

"Thank you, Herr Jensen . . . Smoke. That means a great deal . . . coming from a man such as yourself."

Dieter's eyes slipped closed. His bandaged chest rose and fell steadily as sleep claimed him. Smoke went to the back of the wagon and stepped down from the tailgate.

From the corner of his eye, he saw movement in the shadows just on the other side of the wagon. As he pivoted quickly and smoothly in that direction, his hand went to the butt of his Colt. Before he could draw the revolver, though, Matt said, "It's just us, Smoke."

He stepped out of the shadows with Erica beside him. Smoke didn't ask what they had been doing in the dark. He didn't want to know.

"How is Dieter?" Erica asked.

"He's asleep now," Smoke replied. "He talked for a little while, but I could tell he was getting pretty tired so I told him to go ahead and get some rest."

The young woman nodded.

"That's good. Rest is what he needs more than anything else now."

Smoke wasn't so sure about that. He thought maybe what Dieter needed the most was standing right in front of him. But that wasn't any of his business before and it still wasn't now.

"You could probably use some rest yourself,"

Smoke told Erica. "The way you've been taking care of him, you must be worn out."

"I'm tired," she admitted with a nod. "Good night, Matt."

She reached out and squeezed his arm. He patted her hand. His eyes followed her as she climbed into the wagon and disappeared behind the canvas flap.

"I'm glad that Dieter's doing better," Matt said. "For a while there, it looked like he might not make it."

"That's true," Smoke agreed. "Erica's a good nurse." He changed the subject by saying, "You want to take a turn on guard duty tonight?"

"Sure. I'll ride the circuit for a spell."

Smoke glanced at the night sky, his attention attracted by a flicker of lightning far in the distance.

"Better make sure you've got your slicker with you," he told Matt. "Looks like it might rain after a while."

Smoke's prediction turned out to be true. Rain it did, in buckets, accompanied by earth-shaking peals of thunder and blazing bolts of lightning so bright that when they struck, the night seemed like day.

The lightning was what made Matt and the other guards abandon their patrol around the wagon camp. On these plains, a man on horseback ran a real danger of being struck by one of the bolts, since his head was higher than most of his surroundings. Once lightning began striking in the vicinity, the riders headed for the wagons.

As Matt was unsaddling his horse, Smoke and Preacher came up to him. Both of them wore slickers and carried their Winchesters under the oilcloth garments.

"See anything out there before the storm started?" Smoke asked.

Matt shook his head and said, "Not a thing except a lot of empty prairie."

Smoke pointed to one of the wagons.

"That belongs to the blacksmith whose family has always worked for the von Hoffman family," he said. "He volunteered to let you bunk on the floor of his wagon tonight. I already put your war bag in there. Go get some dry clothes on and get some rest. Preacher and I and a few other men are standing guard here in the camp. Nobody's going to be able to start a prairie fire in this weather."

"That's the truth!" Matt agreed emphatically. "Thanks, Smoke."

Matt started toward the blacksmith's wagon, thinking that if they had gotten just the electrical storm, without the downpour, fire would have been a real danger again. A lot of forest fires and prairie fires alike had been started by lightning.

When he reached the wagon, he climbed onto the seat and rapped his knuckles on the frame.

"Howdy in there," he called, announcing himself before he pushed the canvas flap aside.

He had seen a light glowing through the wagon's canvas cover, so he wasn't surprised to see the vehicle's occupant sitting on the bunk reading a book by the glow from a lantern. The man lifted his eyes from the pages and said in heavily accented English, "Come in, Herr Jensen. *Wie gehts?* I mean, how are you?"

"Wet and tired," Matt replied with a smile. "You've got the advantage of me."

"Eh? Oh, you mean I know your name, but you do not know mine." The man stood up as much as he could inside the wagon and extended a big hand. "Rudolph Wolff, *mein herr.* A pleasure to meet you."

Rudolph Wolff wasn't very tall. He was built like a lot of blacksmiths, broad and powerful, with massive shoulders and brawny arms. At first glance he looked fierce, with a rumpled thatch of dark hair and a bristling beard, but he had a quick grin and a booming laugh, Matt discovered as they talked while he put on dry clothes. He felt an instinctive liking for the man.

Matt, Smoke, and Preacher had been sleeping under various wagons since joining the group of immigrants. That was fine as long as the weather was halfway decent. Matt had gotten many a good night's sleep on the ground.

But in a storm like this, when the ground turned to mud even underneath the wagons, it was nice to have a place to get out of the weather. Matt said as much to Wolff, thanking him for his hospitality, and the blacksmith replied, "I am glad to have you here,

Herr Jensen. You and your friends have done a great deal to help us."

"Well, we want to see you folks get to Wyoming and settle down to your new lives there," Matt explained. "The West needs fine new settlers like you, and it'll be a chance for all of you to live a whole new sort of life."

A frown appeared on Wolff's bearded face.

"I do not know if things will change all that much, whether we are in Wyoming or Germany," he said. "The baron will still be the baron."

That was the same attitude Dieter had, Matt thought, and hearing it from the blacksmith bothered him just as much as some of the things Dieter had said.

"There's no need for you to feel like that," he told Wolff. "In this country, you're no different from the baron. He may have more money, but he can't tell you what to do any more than any man you work for can."

The blacksmith grunted.

"So you say, Herr Jensen. But when we get there, and you and your friends go back to where you came from, nothing will change." Wolff suddenly looked nervous. "I should not be saying these things. You and the baron are friends as well—"

"Not so's you'd notice," Matt said. "Don't worry about me repeating anything you might say to me. As far as I'm concerned, that's nobody's business."

"I hope you are telling the truth. Otherwise, the baron may be angry with me."

"And you wouldn't like that?"

"Baron von Hoffman is a hard man," Wolff said. "He comes from a long line of men accustomed to being the absolute rulers of their domain. When something happens to displease him, or when someone opposes his will, he can act harshly at times."

"Well, you don't have to worry," Matt said again. "I'm not all that fond of the baron, either. I don't like the way he lords it over that cousin of his."

Wolff nodded in agreement.

"Fraulein von Hoffman is a lovely young woman, but she has no will of her own," he said. "The baron rules her with an iron hand, just as he does everyone else."

"If he tries to keep that up here, he's in for a rude awakening," Matt said. "Americans won't stand for it. They may put up with it for a while because they're good-hearted enough to give just about anybody the benefit of the doubt at first, but if somebody tries to push them around, sooner or later they'll dig in their heels and let the hombre know that they won't put up with it anymore. And if the varmint keeps trying to lord it over them anyway, well, he might just be in for a whippin'."

That brought a grin to Rudolph Wolff's face.

"This is a good thing to hear, Herr Jensen," he said. "I believe I may like it in your country after all—"

He might have said more, but at that moment, a series of booming sounds came from outside the wagon, and it wasn't thunder this time.

Or rather, it was gun-thunder.

Chapter Twenty-two

Rainwater ran in steady streams from the brim of Smoke's hat as he walked around the camp. He had spent plenty of wet nights on the trail, so it didn't particularly bother him. He had been on cattle drives where it seemed like it rained all the time, and back when he had been wanted unjustly by the law, he had been at the mercy of the elements on many occasions.

At least it wasn't cold tonight. A cold, steady rain truly was miserable.

The downpour also meant that campfires weren't possible, so everyone had had a cold supper and the only lights came from candles or oil lamps or kerosene lanterns inside the wagons. Most of the vehicles were dark, though. After a long day on the trail, people were worn out and ready to sleep.

Smoke, Preacher, and four other men walked their patrol around the wagons, spread out so they could cover the whole camp fairly well. Smoke knew that no one expected any trouble on a night such as this. . . .

And that just made him even more wary than usual. If he knew that the immigrants might let down their guard because of the storm, then Klaus Berger was probably aware of it, too. Smoke knew he didn't have to worry about Preacher, but he had tried to impress on the other sentries that they had to remain alert at all times.

Smoke had ventured about twenty yards outside the circle of wagons, walking along with the mud sucking at his boots, when his right foot struck something. The yielding nature of it warned him right away what it might be.

He took a quick step back and slid his rifle from under his slicker. Dropping into a crouch, he waited for lightning to strike again, and when it did a moment later, he saw just what he expected to see in the brief, flickering glare.

One of the guards lay on the ground, face turned to the sky so that the hard rain washed away the blood welling from the gaping wound in his neck. His throat had been cut so deeply it had almost decapitated him.

That meant his killer was probably inside the circle of wagons already.

Smoke turned and dashed toward the camp. He leaped over a wagon tongue, and as his boots splashed in the thick mud, he caught a flare of light in the corner of his eye. It came from underneath one of the wagons. Smoke whirled in that direction in time to see a man holding the match he had just struck to a length of fuse attached to a stick of dynamite.

Smoke brought the Winchester to his shoulder, aimed, and fired, all in one smooth, efficient motion. The man who had crawled under the wagon cried out in pain and surprise and dropped the dynamite. The fuse sputtered out as the explosive cylinder landed in a puddle of mud and rainwater.

The man was down but not out of the fight. He must have clawed a revolver from its holster, because muzzle flame stabbed from underneath the wagon where he lay. With the thunder and the heavy rain, Smoke couldn't hear the bullet and didn't know how close to him it had come, but he wasn't going to take a chance on the man getting off another shot.

He pumped two more rounds under the wagon as fast as he could work the rifle's lever.

As if those shots were a signal, more blasts rang out, competing with the thunder just as muzzle flashes competed with the lightning strikes. These shots came from outside the circle of wagons. Smoke figured that Klaus Berger's hired gunmen must have crept up on the camp under the cover of the storm.

Had more than one man snuck in with dynamite? Smoke didn't know, so he started running along the circled wagons, peering underneath all of them. When a gun went off practically in his face, he knew there was at least one more saboteur. He felt the heat of the bullet against his cheek as he dived off his feet. Rolling over in the mud, he stopped on his belly and fired under the wagon where the shot had originated. As lightning flashed again, he saw a man in a slicker going over backwards under the impact of the rifle slug.

But as darkness dropped down again, Smoke saw sparks shooting from a lit fuse. He came up on his knees, drove himself forward with his feet, and slid through the slick mud, winding up underneath the wagon where a stick of dynamite was wedged into the vehicle's undercarriage, out of the rain and the mud.

The fuse was burning fast, and only a couple inches of it were left.

With the same sort of speed that had made him one of the West's deadliest gunmen, Smoke reached up and plucked the dynamite loose. A flick of his wrist sent the cylinder spinning out from under the wagon. He threw it toward the open prairie, where Berger's men continued to fire at the wagons. The rain didn't have time to put out the fuse before the dynamite went off with a huge blast.

As the echoes of the explosion faded, Smoke heard someone screaming out there in the darkness. He hoped that the blast had caught some of Berger's men and not Preacher or one of the other guards.

He didn't have to worry about Preacher. He heard the old mountain man shouting, "Stay in your wagons! Keep your heads down! Fire at any muzzle flashes you see outside the camp!"

As usual, Preacher had kept his wits about him. At the sound of the first shots inside the camp, he had come running. Now he was here to help with the defense of the wagons.

Smoke crawled behind one of the wagon wheels. It would give him a little cover. In the glare of the next lightning strike, he saw several men running toward the camp and almost opened fire on them before he recognized them as the other three guards. They were caught in a bad spot and just wanted to get back to the wagons.

One man stumbled and clawed at his back, and Smoke knew he'd been shot. The lightning flash faded before Smoke could see the man fall.

It was like a scene from a nightmare with the thunder crashing and blending with the roar of guns, the lightning flickering, orange flashes of flame from gun muzzles, men shouting and cursing, women screaming in fear.

No, not a nightmare, Smoke amended. Like a painting by an artist who had gone mad.

But even surrounded by chaos, he kept his head and coolly fired again and again at the muzzle flashes he saw out on the plains. His own muzzle flashes drew the fire of Berger's men. Bullets thudded into the body of the wagon, whined off the iron rim of the wheel, and kicked up splashes of mud near him. He didn't let any of that keep him from fighting back.

"Smoke!"

That was Matt's voice. Smoke twisted his head to call back over his shoulder, "Under here!"

A moment later, Matt and Preacher both crawled under the wagon with him.

"Are you two all right?" Smoke asked them.

"Other than being soaked and covered with mud again, you mean?" Matt asked. "Yeah, I'm fine, but this isn't nearly as pleasant as sitting inside a dry wagon."

"Yeah, well, you nearly knocked me down and trampled me when you come jumpin' outta that wagon, you big lummox," Preacher said. "And if you ain't noticed, Smoke and me are soaked and covered with mud, too!"

"Better than having your throat cut, like the guard I found out there," Smoke said. "I figure Berger's men killed him, and then a couple of them slipped into camp with some dynamite."

"I thought that sounded like dynamite goin' off a minute ago," Preacher said. "Ain't any more of the hellish stuff around, is there?"

"I don't know for sure, but if there was, I think we would have heard it explode by now."

That was what Smoke was hoping, anyway. Blowing up two of the wagons would have been enough to throw the camp into a panic, and then it would have been easier for the hired killers to charge in under cover of the storm and wreak more havoc, maybe even wiping out the immigrants in the process.

Berger might not have enough men left to fight a straight-up battle against the baron's people, so he had to resort to things like dynamite and the attempt to set the prairie on fire to give him an advantage. Neither of those attacks had worked, thanks to Smoke, Matt, Preacher, Dieter, and a little bit of luck.

The immigrants were mounting a stiff defense now, pulling up the canvas on the outward-facing sides of the wagons and firing at Berger's force. Smoke, Matt, and Preacher continued shooting from under the wagon where they had taken cover, and their superb reflexes and natural gun skill enabled them to catch sight of a hired killer, target him, and bring him down before the flash from a lightning strike faded. They kept up this deadly counterattack for several minutes, until another bolt of electrical fire clawed down from the heavens and revealed a dozen or so riders on horseback fleeing across the prairie, putting distance between themselves and the wagon camp.

Preacher saw the same thing and let out an exultant whoop.

"The varmints are takin' off for the tall and uncut!" he exclaimed.

"Look at 'em lighting a shuck out of here!" Matt added.

"Let's make sure they don't dawdle," Smoke suggested as he finished reloading his Winchester and resumed firing in the direction the attackers were fleeing. Matt and Preacher joined in, sending a barrage of lead after the hired gunmen.

"I hope that dang Klaus fella is done for this time," Preacher said when they finally stopped firing.

"I wouldn't count on it," Smoke said. "Hombres like him usually seem to be able to dodge most bullets."

"Yeah, well, one of 'em's gonna have his name on it sooner or later," Preacher insisted.

Smoke hoped the old mountain man was right about that. If everything Baron von Hoffman had said about Klaus Berger was true, they would probably have to kill him to stop him.

Meanwhile, they needed to climb out from under this wagon and find out just how much damage Berger had done this time.

Chapter Twenty-three

Several men had been wounded in this latest battle, but only two had been killed—the guard whose throat had been cut and the one Smoke had seen shot in the back as the man tried to reach the safety of the wagons.

The lone dynamite blast had been far enough away from the wagons that it hadn't damaged any of the vehicles.

The two men who had tried to set off the dynamite underneath the wagons were both dead, as were three more men who had been left behind when the attackers fled. All five of them were typical hardcases, hired guns who would kill anybody if the price was right.

The two immigrants were given a proper burial, but the bodies of the gunmen were dumped in some tall grass and left for the wolves when the wagons pulled out the next morning.

The storm was over by dawn, which broke with a clearing sky and bright sun that sent the temperature climbing rapidly and made the still damp air muggy and miserable. Not only that, but the ground was a sea of mud. That made the going very slow, and people grew impatient and irritable.

By midday, the wagon train had covered only a little more than a mile. On several occasions, one of the wagons had bogged down and refused to budge, and a team from one of the other wagons had to be unhitched, then hitched up to the stuck vehicle along with its original team to pull it loose. This was a time-consuming ordeal.

So when Smoke and Preacher trotted in from their outrider positions, Smoke sought out Friedrich von Hoffman and told the baron, "It might be better just to call a halt for the day and let the ground dry out more before you start up again."

"That will mean wasting at least half a day," von Hoffman said with a frown.

"Yes, but what you're doing is wearing out those oxen, while not covering much ground," Smoke pointed out. "You'll be delayed more in the long run by pushing on now. Let the stock rest this afternoon, and maybe by tomorrow morning the ground won't be so muddy."

Von Hoffman thought it over for a moment, then nodded.

"What you say makes sense, Herr Jensen," he

admitted. "I will pass the word that we are stopping for the day and making camp."

"That'll give Matt and Preacher and me a chance to do a little hunting," Smoke said as he smiled. "I reckon we could all use some fresh meat."

"What sort of game is to be found out here?" von Hoffman asked.

"I thought you'd been on hunting expeditions before, Baron."

"I have, but it's been several years. I've been told that the buffalo are all gone now."

"No, they're not gone," Smoke said, "although most of the herds have drifted on down to the Texas Panhandle. The demand for hides isn't as high as it used to be, and since they finished the transcontinental railroad nobody hunts buffalo for meat anymore except the Indians. For a while there it looked like all the herds might be wiped out, but now I think the buffalo will survive." Smoke shook his head. "It'll never be like it once was, though."

That was sure the truth. The first time he had ventured across the plains of what was then called the Great American Desert, not long after the Civil War, he and his pa and Preacher had seen vast, seemingly limitless herds of buffalo, a veritable sea of the shaggy brown creatures that sometimes stretched from horizon to horizon.

He recalled making camp on a hillside overlooking a valley. The next morning, a buffalo herd began passing through that valley, filling it completely as the beasts moved from one grazing ground to another. By nightfall, the herd was still moving through the valley, and the exodus continued all night and on into the next day before the last stragglers finally cleared out. It had been one of the most amazing things Smoke had ever seen.

"I will come with you," the baron said now, breaking into that memory.

"What?" Smoke said.

"I will come with you on your hunt," von Hoffman said. "You'll find that I'm an excellent shot."

"I don't doubt that, Baron, but—"

"I need a fresh mount," von Hoffman went on as if he hadn't heard the beginning of Smoke's objection. "It won't take me long to have another horse saddled."

Smoke decided it wasn't worth the time and energy to argue with the baron. Anyway, von Hoffman might turn out to be a good hunter. He certainly seemed to believe he was.

While von Hoffman tended to getting a fresh horse, Smoke walked over to Matt and Preacher and said, "The baron went along with the idea of stopping and letting the ground dry out some before the wagon train moves on."

"It'll be a lot easier that way," Matt said.

"He thought it was a good idea for us to do some hunting, too." Smoke paused. "The thing is, he wants to come with us."

"The baron?" Preacher said. "That dang, stuffed shirt aristocrat? Goin' huntin' with us?"

"Yep," Smoke said.

"I don't reckon you told him he couldn't."

"Didn't seem worth the effort."

Preacher snorted.

"We'll see about that when he scares off all the game betwixt here and the Canadian border!"

Smoke didn't think it would be quite that bad, but he supposed they would have to wait and see.

Von Hoffman came over to them a few minutes later leading a leggy chestnut gelding. Smoke was an excellent judge of horseflesh, and the chestnut looked like a fine animal.

"Ready to go, gentlemen?" the baron asked.

Matt and Preacher still didn't look very happy about it, but Smoke nodded and said, "Yeah, we're ready."

The four men mounted up, and as they rode out of camp, they passed the wagon where Greta Schiller sat on the seat while her driver unhitched the team. She smiled at them, but the full force of the expression was directed at von Hoffman, Smoke thought.

The attractive widow seemed to have her sights set on the baron. That was just fine with Smoke. They would probably make a good match since they'd been acquainted with each other for quite a while and came from the same sort of background.

"I told some men to stand guard while we're gone," von Hoffman said.

"That's a good idea," Smoke said. "I don't think Berger is going to attack in broad daylight. We've whittled down his forces enough that he can't afford to come at you head-on right now. But you can't ever be sure what somebody else is going to do, especially a hired killer like Berger."

"I agree. We must still be careful."

"We won't get too far away from the camp. That way we can get back there in a hurry if we need to."

They rode north, which allowed them to scout the trail the wagon train would be taking when the journey to Wyoming resumed, while at the same time they were searching for game. After they had gone a mile or so, Smoke held up a hand to signal a halt.

The wagons were out of sight over the rolling hills behind them. As far as the four riders could tell from looking around, they might as well have been the only men for a hundred miles around.

Smoke pointed and said, "Some antelope over yonder."

"Yeah, I seen 'em, too," Preacher said, and Matt added a nod.

Von Hoffman stood up in his stirrups and craned his neck as he peered in the direction Smoke had pointed.

"Where?" he asked. "I don't see them."

"Look just to the right of that little bluff," Smoke said. "They're grazing there."

Von Hoffman reached into his saddlebags and pulled out a telescope. He opened the spyglass and peered through the lenses.

"You must have extraordinary vision, all of you," he said as he lowered the telescope a moment later. "The antelope are there, just as you said."

"Well, we wouldn't have no reason to lie about it," Preacher said testily.

"It's not a matter of vision as much as it is training your eyes to look over long distances," Smoke explained. "Out here it's usually good if you can see danger coming while it's still as far off as possible."

Von Hoffman nodded and said, "Yes, I understand," as he closed the telescope and put it away. "What do we do now? Approach them with stealth?"

"If you mean sneak up on 'em, that's it," Preacher said.

"We ought to be able to get pretty close," Smoke said. "The wind's blowing right to carry our scent away from them."

They heeled their horses into motion and rode toward the ridge near where the small herd of antelope was grazing. Smoke had known it was unlikely they would run across any buffalo, although he had a feeling that was what the baron would have preferred.

Antelope steaks were mighty good, though, and Smoke had figured there was a good chance they could find some of the fleet-footed creatures. That hunch was about to pay off, it appeared. If each of them could bring down an antelope, there would be plenty of fresh meat for the wagon train.

When they were a couple of hundred yards away from the herd, Smoke reined in.

"We'll take our shots here," he said. "You'll probably only get one, Baron. As soon as they hear our rifles, they'll take off, and there may not be time to try again."

"I understand," von Hoffman said. "And if you're worried that I'll miss, don't be. At this range, my aim will be true."

Preacher looked openly skeptical about that claim, but he didn't say anything and neither did Smoke or Matt. The four men swung down from their saddles and drew their Winchesters. The antelope were in range of the repeaters.

Von Hoffman worked the Winchester's lever to throw a cartridge into the firing chamber, then laid the barrel of his rifle across his saddle to steady the weapon while he took aim. Smoke, Matt, and Preacher did likewise with their horses. Quietly, each man announced which of the antelope he was targeting, so that none of them would accidentally aim at the same one.

"Everybody got your bead?" Smoke asked. When the other three answered in the affirmative, he said, "All right . . . steady now . . . we'll fire on three . . . one . . . two . . . *three!*"

The four rifles cracked, the reports coming so closely together that they sounded like one shot. Preacher and Matt immediately stepped away from their horses, jacked a second round into their rifles, and fired again at the swiftly running antelope, all of which had taken off at top speed. The two of them threw several rounds after the animals, but Smoke didn't see any more of the antelope fall or even falter.

"I must'a seen a thousand o' them varmints over the years, and I still can't get over how blamed fast they are!" Preacher exclaimed.

Smoke hadn't wasted any lead on a second shot. He lowered his Winchester and said, "Looks like we've got four of them down. That's good shooting, boys."

Indeed it was. At that range, it wouldn't have been surprising if one or two of the shots had missed. Instead it looked like all four of the hunters had been successful.

Or at least partially successful, Smoke saw as he and his companions mounted up and rode toward the ridge. Three of the antelope lay motionless in death, but one was still kicking and struggling to get up. It was only wounded.

Smoke knew which one it was, too. The baron was the man who had failed to make a clean kill.

From the dark, angry glower on his face, von Hoffman was aware of that, as well. He kicked his horse into a run and rode ahead of the others with his rifle still drawn.

Matt said, "Well, at least he's going to take care of it himself, instead of leaving it to us to do it for him like we're his servants."

"You don't like the ol' boy much, do you?" Preacher asked.

"I don't like the way everybody else in that wagon train is scared of him," Matt said. "You know there's got to be a reason for it, or they wouldn't all feel that way."

Von Hoffman rode up to the wounded antelope and aimed down at it from the saddle. The Winchester had to crack twice before the animal was finally out of its misery. The baron turned to look at Smoke, Matt, and Preacher with an unearned expression of triumph on his face.

By this time, however, the three frontiersmen had reined in and were looking up at the top of the bluff beyond von Hoffman. Several dozen riders in buckskins and feathers had appeared there with no warning, and now they sat on the backs of their ponies gazing down at the white men.

"Uh-oh," Preacher said. "We got comp'ny."

Chapter Twenty-four

"Cheyenne, you think?" Smoke asked. His voice was cool and steady.

"Could be," Preacher said. "Maybe Pawnee."

"There's a bunch of them, whoever they are," Matt added.

"Doesn't matter," Smoke said. "All the tribes in this area are at peace."

Preacher let out one of his characteristic snorts.

"Right now they are, as far as you know," he said. "That don't mean somethin' ain't happened to put 'em on the warpath." He paused, then went on, "That bunch don't appear to be painted for war, though. Reckon they probably just heard the shootin' and came to see what was goin' on."

"So as long as we all keep our heads—" Matt began.

"Includin' the baron," Preacher put in.

"We'll probably keep our hair," Matt finished.

"That would be my guess," Smoke said. "We'd better tell von Hoffman to stay calm—"

But it was too late for that. Seeing that they were looking past him at the bluff, the baron suddenly turned to peer up at the rim. Smoke couldn't see his face, but he could imagine that von Hoffman's eyes snapped wide open in fear and surprise.

The baron did the worst thing he could have done. He jerked his rifle to his shoulder and pulled the trigger.

Even as the whipcrack of the shot sounded, Smoke sent his horse plunging forward at top speed. He saw dirt fly from the face of the bluff, near the top, as von Hoffman's hurried shot missed the Indians. The baron worked his rifle's lever, but before he could fire again Smoke left his saddle in a diving tackle that sent him crashing into the man from behind. Von Hoffman's rifle flew from his hands as Smoke's weight drove him to the ground.

"Stay down, damn it!" Smoke ordered as he pushed himself up on one knee.

He didn't have to worry about that. The impact had knocked all the air out of von Hoffman's lungs, and all the baron could do was lie there gasping for breath, unable to move.

When Smoke looked up, he saw that several of the warriors had crowded forward to the very edge of the bluff. They pointed rifles down at him. Making sure that his hands were in plain sight, he raised his arms to show the Indians that he wasn't making any threatening moves.

A glance over his shoulder told him that Matt and Preacher were still mounted. They had drawn their rifles but didn't have the weapons pointed at the Indians.

"That blasted furriner's got us all killed," Preacher called to Smoke.

"Maybe not," Smoke said. "Since the baron missed, and they didn't start shooting back at us right away, maybe they'll be willing to listen to reason."

Keeping his hands lifted, Smoke got to his feet. The bluff was about thirty feet tall, so the Indians were well within hearing distance. Now that he had gotten a better look at the decorations on their buckskins and the way they wore their hair, Smoke was sure they were Pawnee. That was a good thing, since the Pawnee were slightly less warlike than the Cheyenne, at least these days.

"My name is Smoke Jensen," he called to them in their language, hoping there might be some among them who would recognize the name. He had fought Indians in the past but had never made war on them unjustly, and he had friends among many of the tribes. "I would talk with your chief so that I can apologize to him for the mistake made by my companion."

The warriors on the rim pointing their rifles at him didn't budge, except that two of them moved aside slightly to let another rider come forward. This man was older, Smoke saw, with a stern, weathered face.

"I know you, Smoke Jensen," he said in English.

"It is said you helped the Paiutes save their land from greedy white men not long ago."

"That's true," Smoke replied. "Near the settlement known as Helltown."

The spokesman for the warriors raised an arm and pointed at Matt and Preacher.

"The old man is the one known as Ghost Killer."

"I'd rather be called Preacher," the old mountain man responded, "but I'll answer to other names."

"And the young one is Matt Jensen," the Pawnee leader went on.

"That's right," Smoke said. "We're all friends to the Indians, as long as they're friends to us."

"Then who is the dog at your feet," the chief demanded angrily, "the one who tries to kill the Pawnee for no reason?"

The baron had caught his breath and gathered his wits enough to realized what had just been said about him. He started to get up, saying, "How dare that savage call me a dog! I'll teach him to respect—"

"You'll stay on the ground unless you want to get us all killed, blast it!" Smoke grated. He was ready to plant a booted foot in the middle of von Hoffman's back and shove him back down if he had to.

Growling something in German that was undoubtedly a curse, von Hoffman subsided. As he lay there, he snapped, "This is unforgivable!"

"No, it would be unforgivable for us to get ourselves killed for no good reason, so just keep your mouth shut," Smoke told him. He looked up at the Pawnee chief again and went on, "This man is a stranger to our land and knows little of our ways. When he saw the warriors of the Pawnee, he was afraid and acted without thinking. I ask you to forgive him."

For a long moment, the chief didn't say anything. Then, in a tone laced with dry humor, he responded, "If he was a better shot, you would all be dead now."

"Don't I know it," Smoke said with a smile.

"Stay there," the chief ordered. "I would speak with you."

Smoke nodded. He said quietly to von Hoffman, "All right, Baron, get up and go back to your horse. Leave your rifle. We'll get it later, if all goes well."

Von Hoffman climbed to his feet and tried to brush mud off his clothes.

"This is intolerable," he said. "I will not be treated like this, Jensen."

"I know you're a smart man, Baron. Keep your mouth shut and do what I tell you, and maybe we'll all come out of this alive."

Von Hoffman looked like he wanted to argue some more, but after a moment he turned and stalked toward Matt and Preacher without saying anything else. Smoke stayed where he was with several of the Indians watching him while the Pawnee chief and some of the other warriors rode to a spot where they could descend the ridge.

When they came up to him, the chief dismounted and regarded Smoke gravely.

"I am called Bone Striker," he said. "I lead this band of Pawnee."

Smoke had been thinking quickly while he was waiting for the Indians. It was unusual to see this large a group of warriors unless they were a hunting party or they had set out to make war. They weren't painted for battle, but that could be because they hadn't found their enemies yet.

"Something has happened, hasn't it, Bone Striker?" Smoke asked. "That's why you and your warriors are away from your village."

"We are hunting," the chief said. "Hunting men."

"Not us. We have done no harm to the Pawnee."

"Then why are you here?"

Smoke considered the question rapidly. It wouldn't do much good to lie to Bone Striker. The chief stood a good chance of finding out the truth anyway. The wagon train would be passing through his country.

"We are traveling to Wyoming with a group of settlers," Smoke explained. "Immigrants. They're camped south of here with their wagons."

"A wagon train?" Bone Striker's face remained expressionless, but Smoke saw a flicker of surprise in the chief's eyes. "Few white men travel in wagons anymore, since the iron horse goes so many places."

"I know," Smoke said with a nod, "but these are. And they've been pursued by enemies, which makes them nervous. That's why the baron took a shot at you."

"This baron is a foolish man."

"Sometimes," Smoke said under his breath. "Anyway, we mean you no harm, Bone Striker, and wish only to follow the trail northward."

Bone Striker nodded slowly.

"These enemies you speak of," he said, "is one of them a man as pale as the moon? The whitest white man anyone has ever seen?"

Smoke took a deep breath. That sounded like the description of Klaus Berger that the baron had given them.

"A man with pale skin and long pale hair and very dark eyes?" he asked.

Bone Striker nodded and said, "That is the man."

"You've seen him?"

"He and some other men came upon a small group of my people. They murdered the warriors, then dishonored the women and female children before killing them as well." Bone Striker's voice was as flat and hard as stone. "They thought they had murdered all the young men as well, but one of them lived long enough to tell us what had happened when we found them. Since then we have been looking for these men but have not found them."

"They were probably moving pretty fast," Smoke said. "I'm surprised they stopped long enough to harm your people. After everything that had happened, Berger probably wanted to keep his men from getting too impatient with him. He still needs them."

Bone Striker shook his head and said, "I do not understand."

"These are our enemies, too, Chief. They have

been pursuing us, but now they ride ahead of us because we defeated them. They probably intend to regroup and attack the wagon train again later."

"These are very bad men."

"I know," Smoke said. "The baron, the man who shot at you by mistake, is their biggest enemy." Smoke paused. "That means he and the Pawnee should be good friends."

Bone Striker thought about that for a few seconds and then nodded.

"This is true. I forgive the baron for his mistake." The chief's eyes narrowed. "But tell him not to shoot at the Pawnee again."

"Oh, I'll tell him, Bone Striker," Smoke promised. "You can count on that. Not only that, but I give you my word that if we find the pale man and his companions, we will avenge the deaths of your people."

"It is known throughout the land that Smoke Jensen is a man of his word." Bone Striker extended his hand. "We will be friends."

Smoke gripped the chief's hand.

"We will be friends," he agreed.

"Your wagons may pass unharmed through Pawnee land."

"Thank you."

"You and Matt Jensen and the old man called Preacher will come to our village," Bone Striker went on. "We will smoke and feast. Bring the one called the baron with you."

Smoke wasn't sure that was a good idea, but under the circumstances, he couldn't very well refuse.

"We'll be there," he promised.

Chapter Twenty-five

The baron was still upset when Smoke rejoined him, Matt, and Preacher, after the Pawnee had ridden off.

"I demand an apology, Jensen," he said with a scowl.

"Well, you're not going to get one," Smoke snapped. "I'll be damned if I'm going to apologize for saving your life."

"Maybe we're the ones you oughta be apologizin' to for that," Preacher muttered.

"Don't just make it worse," Smoke told him. He turned back to von Hoffman. "Listen, Baron, Bone Striker—that's the Pawnee chief—has invited the four of us to come to their village this evening. I told him we would."

"Ride into the camp of those savages so they can murder us?" Von Hoffman snorted in contempt and shook his head. "I think not."

"If they wanted us dead, we wouldn't still be

breathing," Matt pointed out. "They could have massacred us a dozen times over without any trouble."

"Anyway, most Injuns are hospitable sorts," Preacher added. "If you ride into their villages, they'll welcome you, feed you, make you feel at home. Of course, they might kill you when it comes time for you to leave, if they're of a mind to." He looked at Smoke. "I know, I still ain't helpin', am I?"

"Bone Striker considers us friends now, because we're enemies with Klaus Berger," Smoke said.

Von Hoffman looked surprised again.

"What does Berger have to do with this?" he asked.

"He and his men came across a small band of Pawnee and attacked them," Smoke explained. "They killed the men, raped and murdered the women, and even killed the children. One of the youngsters they left for dead lived awhile, though, and he was able to tell the warriors who found them what happened and describe Berger. So Bone Striker and his men are out hunting for him."

"Too bad they didn't find him," Matt said. "A war party that big would have wiped out Berger and his bunch."

"Yeah, but Berger probably had them moving pretty fast again once they finished with the Pawnee."

The baron said, "I fail to see what any of this has to do with me."

"There's an old saying about how the enemy of my enemy is my friend," Smoke said. "That's how

Bone Striker feels about you now, Baron, even though you shot at him. Which he's still not happy about, by the way, but he's willing to forgive and forget, especially since I told him that if we found Berger, we would avenge the deaths of his people."

"I have sufficient reasons of my own for wanting to see Klaus Berger dead, and they don't including placating some feathered savage."

Smoke suppressed a sigh of exasperation. Von Hoffman had his good qualities, but just when Smoke would start to think he wasn't a bad hombre, the baron would turn pompous and obnoxious again.

"Dead's dead, no matter what the reason. Let's just leave it at that. But we still need to go to Bone Striker's village and sit down to powwow with him. It's the smart thing to do."

Von Hoffman didn't look convinced, but he said, "How will we know how to find the camp?"

"He told me where it was," Smoke said. "It won't be hard to find. We'll dress out those antelope, take the meat back to the wagons, and let folks there know what's going on."

"What if Berger attacks while we're gone?" von Hoffman asked.

"That's not likely. After what happened with those Pawnee, probably the last thing Berger wants to do is double back. He'll keep going north so he and his bunch can put some distance between themselves and the Indians."

Von Hoffman thought about it for a moment and then shrugged.

"I suppose you're right." He looked down at his muddy clothes. "I must clean up. I wouldn't visit even savages looking like this."

The glare he directed toward Smoke made it clear that he blamed him for getting knocked down. It would have made more sense for the baron to blame his own stupidity and recklessness, Smoke mused, but clearly, that wasn't going to happen.

"Let's get busy," Smoke suggested. "We don't want any of that meat to spoil."

The wagons were in a circle, the teams were unhitched, and everyone had settled in at the camp by the time Smoke, Matt, Preacher, and von Hoffman returned. Even though the ground was muddy, there was enough dry brush around to fuel several fires, so some of the women got busy cooking the meat the four men had brought back with them.

Erica said, "When we heard shots, we knew you must have found some game."

"We found more than that," Matt said. "Or rather, they found us."

"They?"

"A Pawnee war party."

Erica's blue eyes widened in alarm.

"Wild Indians?" she said. "Like in the books Dieter reads?"

"Not exactly," Smoke said. Von Hoffman had disappeared into the wagon he shared with his cousin. "The baron took a shot at them, but he missed.

Lucky for us, the Pawnee were willing to listen to reason and accept our apology. It turns out they had a run-in with Klaus Berger, too, and were out searching for him."

Smoke didn't go into details about what Berger and his men had done. Erica didn't need to hear about all that.

"Is there no end to the evil this man Klaus can do?" she murmured.

"Not so far, it doesn't seem like," Matt said. "But there will be. Justice always catches up to buzzards like that sooner or later."

"I can only pray that you're right, Matt."

"In the meantime," Smoke went on, "the three of us and the baron are going to the Pawnee village for supper tonight. The chief invited us, and it didn't seem like a good idea to turn him down."

"Really?" Erica was surprised by that, too. "I cannot imagine Friedrich sitting down to eat with savages."

"To the Injuns, we're the savages," Preacher said. "I reckon most of 'em has got good reason to feel that way, too."

"You won't let anything happen to him, will you? He . . . he is all I have left in the world."

"He'll be fine," Smoke assured her, "as long as he doesn't do anything foolish."

From the look on Erica's face, she might be starting to think that was asking a lot of her cousin, Smoke thought.

Later that afternoon, the four men set out for the Pawnee village. Von Hoffman had cleaned up and put on fresh clothes. He was still dressed for riding, but he had added a cravat to his outfit.

He had also buckled on a revolver, Smoke noted. As long as he didn't plan on using it, that shouldn't matter. Smoke was going to keep a close eye on the baron the whole time they were in the Pawnee village, anyway.

After riding for several miles in a northwesterly direction, they came to a small creek. Bone Striker had told Smoke about the stream and instructed him to follow it to the west. They did so, and after a couple of miles they came to the village, which consisted of about fifty tepees scattered along both banks of the creek.

The village's dogs made quite a racket as the four white men approached, and the commotion drew the attention of the village's inhabitants. The warriors gathered to welcome the riders, with the women and children behind them watching in rapt attention.

Smoke glanced over at von Hoffman. The baron's face was set in taut, stern lines, but Smoke could tell the man was nervous. Von Hoffman had never seen this many Indians at one time before. Even though he never would have admitted it, his attitudes toward the frontier and its inhabitants had probably been shaped by the popular image fostered in those dime novels, just like Dieter's. Not to the same extent, since von Hoffman had visited America before, but some of the feelings were still there.

The baron wouldn't be able to see an Indian without worrying, at least a little, that his scalp was in danger.

But as long as he didn't do anything foolish, that didn't matter.

The four riders reined in and dismounted. Smoke clasped wrists with Bone Striker and said, "Thank you for inviting us to your village, Chief."

Bone Striker nodded gravely.

"Come to my lodge. We will eat and talk of our enemies."

For Smoke, Matt, and Preacher, it was nothing new to sit cross-legged in a tepee and eat stew from wooden bowls with their fingers, using pieces of frybread to mop up all the juices. Von Hoffman was visibly less comfortable with the procedure, but he didn't say anything and managed to nod with at least a semblance of enthusiasm when Bone Striker asked him if he liked the food.

After they had eaten, they smoked a pipe, passing it from hand to hand. Smoke quietly told the baron what to do, and von Hoffman followed his instructions. So far, so good, Smoke thought.

Bone Striker said, "Tell me of this pale man. Is he an evil spirit come to life in the form of a man?"

"That is a good description of him, Chief," von Hoffman agreed. "He works for political enemies of mine, and he will stop at nothing to carry out their schemes of vengeance."

Bone Striker frowned and shook his head.

"I do not understand this . . . political enemies. All I know about are enemies. What sort are these?"

A bark of laughter came from Preacher.

"Not understandin' politics is somethin' you got in common with most folks, Bone Striker," the old mountain man said. "I don't reckon anybody really understands the dadblasted stuff!"

Von Hoffman tried to explain anyway.

"It has to do with who has power in the government and who decides how to make the laws."

Bone Striker shook his head and said, "Only the Great Spirit makes laws."

"What about the government in Washington?" Matt asked.

"They say things, but what they say has little to do with us," Bone Striker answered serenely. "When it rains, the ground is wet. When the wind blows in the winter, it is cold. These are laws. What men say . . ." He made a dismissive gesture. "Only words easily blown away by the wind or washed away by the rain. They mean nothing."

The world might be a lot better off if Bone Striker was right, Smoke thought, but unfortunately, the words men said in Washington and in all the other world capitals did have an effect on people's lives. Someday, those words would mean that Bone Striker and his people could no longer live as they chose.

No one could. Smoke knew it was inevitable, the way things were going in this world.

He just hoped that day wouldn't come until long after he had gone on to his reward.

"The pale man's name is Klaus Berger," Smoke said, getting the conversation back on track. "He and his men have attacked the baron's wagon train three times and killed some of the baron's people."

Bone Striker looked at von Hoffman and said, "Baron is like chief."

"Yes, you could say that," von Hoffman replied with a nod. "In fact, I rather like the comparison."

"Every time Berger's men attacked us, we killed some of them, too," Smoke went on. "More of them than they killed of our people. They aren't strong enough anymore to keep on attacking us, so I think they've left this part of the country for now."

"But they will come back," Bone Striker said.

"Probably not here. Berger will have to hire more men. The closest place for him to do that is Cheyenne."

"We cannot pursue him that far," the chief said with a frown. "The deaths of our people will go unavenged."

"No, because sooner or later Berger will attack the baron's people again, and when he does, we'll deal with him, like I told you this afternoon," Smoke said. "When we kill him, it will be for all the people he has ever harmed."

"And I have your word on this?"

"You do."

Bone Striker looked at the others. Matt and Preacher nodded, and von Hoffman said, "I swear a solemn oath to you, Chief, that we will avenge your people as well as our own."

"This is not as good as killing him ourselves," Bone Striker said, "but as long as this man Berger dies, I will accept it. And in return I promise you and your wagons safe passage through the land of the Pawnee."

"We have struck a bargain," von Hoffman said.

"We smoke again, to seal it," Bone Striker decreed.

By the time the four white men were ready to leave and ride back to the wagon camp, von Hoffman had relaxed. Smoke was glad to see that. Whenever the baron took that stick out of his backside, he seemed to be a pretty decent hombre. Given his history, he might not ever fully adapt to the frontier, but at least there was some hope of that happening.

They said their good-byes and rode out of the Pawnee village. Night had fallen, but Smoke knew he would have no trouble following the stars back to the camp.

"That went well, did it not?" von Hoffman asked.

"It did," Smoke admitted. "You did good by promising to avenge Bone Striker's people."

Von Hoffman waved a hand.

"A promise to a savage means nothing," he said. "I want Berger dead for my own reasons."

That just showed how different he and the baron

were, and always would be, Smoke thought. He had given his word to Bone Striker, too, and he intended to keep it.

Because to Smoke Jensen, his word meant just about everything.

Chapter Twenty-six

A hard wind sprang up overnight, and that helped to dry out the ground. By morning, the wagons were able to move out with their wheels rolling much easier.

By the next day, the situation was even better, and the miles began to fall behind the wagon train. Day followed day, with Smoke, Matt, and Preacher alternating the scouting duties, one man riding far in front of the wagons while the other two flanked them.

The storm and the various troubles the immigrants had encountered had slowed down the wagon train to a certain extent, so by the time a week had passed since leaving the Sugarloaf, they had not yet reached their destination. Smoke estimated it would take them only a few more days, however.

"See those mountains in the distance?" he asked von Hoffman as they rode side by side and he pointed out the dim gray shapes on the northern horizon. "Those are the Medicine Bows. From what you told me, that's where your new ranch is located."

The baron nodded.

"I have a map the previous owner sent to me," he said. "The Rafter Nine is near a small settlement called Hawk Creek Station."

"I think I've heard of it, but I don't reckon I've ever been there," Smoke said. "I thought you told me there wasn't a town nearby, so you plan on starting one."

"This Hawk Creek Station does not amount to much, as you might say," the baron explained. "There is a trading post and tavern there, but that's all."

"Probably was a stop on the stage line at one time, and that's how the place got its name," Smoke mused.

"I want a *real* town," von Hoffman said firmly. "It will be called New Holtzberg, after the town where I was born."

"New Holtzberg, Wyoming." Smoke grinned. "Doesn't really have the same sort of ring as Laramie or Cheyenne, but I reckon you've got the right to call it whatever you want, if you're the one starting it up."

The wagon train had bypassed those two towns Smoke had mentioned. Supplies were starting to run a little low, but it would have been out of the way to visit either place, not to mention it would increase the chances of them running into Klaus Berger and more of the man's hired killers. Smoke still thought it would be smart to get to the Rafter 9 and dig in there while they waited for the next attack.

Dieter was strong enough now that he was able to sit up inside the wagon. Sometimes he even rode on the seat next to the driver for short periods of time while Erica was inside the vehicle.

He was upset that he had missed the chance to see the Pawnee village, telling Preacher one day, "That may be my only opportunity to become acquainted with some of the noble red men of the plains."

"I thought you was worried all the Injuns wanted to scalp you," the old mountain man said with a grin as he rode alongside the wagon.

"Well, it is true they are fearsome warriors, but they also possess a great deal of dignity and nobility."

"Some of 'em do," Preacher admitted, "but some of 'em are just low-down, good-for-nothin' skunks who are dumber'n dirt and nastier than snakes."

Dieter's eyes widened in surprise.

"I thought you were a friend to the Indians," he said, "and yet you talk of them this way?"

"Some of them, I said. Just like there are white men who are low-down, good-for-nothin' skunks who . . . well, you get the idea. I've knowed white men, red men, black men, brown men, and yellow men, and I've never run into a dang one of 'em you could say had to be a certain way just 'cause of what color he was. That's what some folks can't seem to understand. You can't say all white men are one way and all Injuns is another. That just ain't true. There's good and bad amongst all kinds."

"I suppose that's true," Dieter admitted. "And that may be the most I've ever heard you talk, Preacher."

The old-timer let out a snort.

"Just don't get me to speechifyin', that's all."

Things were still a little tense between Dieter and Matt, who hadn't been able to spend much time with Erica because she had been busy taking care of Dieter.

Smoke figured both young men were wasting their time worrying about Erica. Her cousin was never going to allow either of them to court her seriously, let alone marry her. And it was doubtful, in Smoke's opinion, that Erica would ever develop enough backbone to stand up to the baron.

From time to time the wagon train had passed an isolated farm or ranch, but southern Wyoming was desolate country and difficult to wrest a living from. Those were the only signs of human habitation.

But as they neared the foothills of the Medicine Bow mountains, eleven days after leaving the Sugarloaf, Matt came riding back in from his scouting position in front of the wagons and reported, "That trading post the baron talked about is only a couple of miles ahead of us."

"Did you ride in and talk to anybody?" Smoke asked.

"Nope," Matt replied. "When I saw the place I turned around to come back here and let the rest of you know. It's not abandoned, though, I can tell you that. I got close enough to see smoke coming from the chimney."

"Civilization," Erica said.

Matt grinned and said, "Calling it that might be a stretch. But it's as close as you'll find in these parts, I reckon."

"Matt and I will ride ahead and get the lay of the land," Smoke decided. "Preacher, you can bring the wagons in the rest of the way."

The old mountain man nodded his agreement.

"You're worried that fella Klaus might be layin' for us, ain't you?" he asked.

"It's a possibility," Smoke said grimly. "It won't hurt anything to take a quick look around first."

"Then I should come with you, too," von Hoffman declared.

Smoke shook his head, hoping this wasn't going to turn into an argument.

"I think it would be better for you to stay with the wagons, Baron," he said. "Now that we're this close, we don't want anything else happening."

Von Hoffman shrugged and nodded.

"As you wish, Herr Jensen."

He seemed to have gotten over his anger at the way Smoke had manhandled him during the first encounter with the Pawnee, but Smoke figured he was just bottling it up. He didn't really care one way or the other as long as von Hoffman didn't cause any trouble.

Matt pointed out the exact direction to Hawk Creek Station.

"Not that you could miss it," he added, "sticking up from the prairie the way it does. It's a two-story building, and looks to be the only building of any sort for miles around."

He and Smoke left the wagon train behind and rode toward the trading post. When the place came into view, Smoke saw that Matt was right: It was hard to miss the big, ugly building with the corral out back.

Half a dozen horses were tied to a couple of hitch racks in front of the trading post. A buggy was parked nearby.

"Place appears to be doing some business," Smoke commented.

"I'm not surprised," Matt said. "Where else around here are you going to get supplies or a drink?"

Smoke rasped his fingertips over the sandy stubble on his chin as he frowned in thought.

"What about women?"

"Wouldn't surprise me a bit," Matt said. "The proprietor's got to make some use of those upstairs rooms."

There were some single men among the immigrants, and they would probably welcome the chance to guzzle down some booze and take a soiled dove upstairs. In those respects, Germans were like every other nationality. After the long, dangerous journey they had made, Smoke didn't have any objection to the fellows cutting loose a little, but Baron von Hoffman might. If he tried to put the pleasures Hawk Creek Station had to offer off-limits, he might have a riot on his hands.

But there was no point in getting ahead of himself, Smoke thought. That was one reason he and Matt had ridden ahead of the wagon train like this, to find out exactly what sort of situation was waiting for the immigrants.

The trading post had a low porch with several chairs on it. Two of those chairs were occupied by men passing a jug back and forth. Smoke's eyes studied the men as he rode up, and he knew Matt was doing the same thing. Men such as them, men who all too often lived by their guns, couldn't ever afford to let down their guard.

The man on the left wore a buffalo coat despite the heat. Lank black hair hung from under his hat, which had a flat brim and a round crown. An equally dark mustache drooped over his wide mouth, the corners of which turned down in what appeared to be a perpetually sour expression.

The other man, in contrast, wore a broad grin on his freckled, sun-burned face. His hat was thumbed back on faded red hair. He gazed up at Smoke and Matt and nudged his companion in the side with a sharp elbow.

"Lookee here, Tyrone," he said. "We got strangers comin' into town."

"I see 'em," Tyrone grunted. "Don't give a damn."

"I think you better give a damn," the redhead said. "That there's Smoke Jensen. I don't know who the other one is, but if he's ridin' with Jensen, chances are he's pretty gun-handy, too."

Smoke didn't like the way this was shaping up. He hadn't liked it as soon as he laid eyes on the two men, because he recognized both of them, just as the redhead had recognized him. They all belonged to the same brotherhood.

The brotherhood of fast guns.

The man in the buffalo coat was Tyrone Wilkes. Some said he was from Canada. He had killed a dozen men in the Dakotas and Montana. Smoke hadn't heard anything about him drifting as far south and west as Wyoming, but here he was, big as life and twice as ugly.

The redhead was Conn Wheeler, from Texas originally, but he had made his reputation in the New Mexico range wars. And the reputation was that of a cold-blooded back-shooter who was fast enough to gun a man down from the front if he had to.

As far as Smoke knew, Wheeler and Wilkes had never ridden together before. He couldn't help but wonder what had brought the two gunmen together in an out-of-the-way place like Hawk Creek Station.

The answer probably wasn't anything good.

But Smoke didn't want trouble, so he just nodded and said, "Howdy, boys. This is Hawk Creek Station, isn't it?"

"It surely is," Wheeler replied, still grinning. His

next words echoed what Smoke had been thinking. "What brings you fellas here, Jensen?"

"Reckon that's our business."

Wilkes said, "Maybe he don't know who we are."

"Oh, I know who you are," Smoke said. "I recognized both of you."

"Then the only one who's got an advantage here is that fella beside you," Wheeler said.

"My name's Matt Jensen," Matt introduced himself. His flat, hard tone told Smoke that he knew what sort of hardcases these two men were. He was as ready for trouble as Smoke was.

"Matt Jensen," Wheeler repeated. "Matt Jensen his own self. I've heard of you, Matt. They say you're pert near as fast on the draw as ol' Smoke there. Is that true?"

"I don't bother worrying about such things," Matt said.

"Well, we do," Wheeler said as he sat up straighter. "It plumb annoys Tyrone and me when we hear folks talkin' about the Jensens and how fast they are. Yes, sir, them damn Jensens are just faster'n greased lightnin', everybody says. Makes me want to puke. You know why?"

Smoke was sick and tired of this. He had seen and heard it all before, too many times. He said in a harsh voice, "Because the two of you think you're faster than us, when all you really are is just road agent trash."

Wheeler and Wilkes both looked surprised, but

that didn't last long. Their shocked expressions were replaced a heartbeat later by furious glares. Wheeler came up out of his chair like a striking snake, and Wilkes was only a fraction of a second behind him, sweeping the buffalo coat aside so he could reach for the low-slung gun on his hip.

Chapter Twenty-seven

Both men cleared their holsters, but only because Smoke and Matt waited an instant before slapping leather.

Then guns appeared in their hands as if by magic, spouting flame and lead.

Smoke's Colt drove two slugs into Wilkes's chest, knocking him backwards. The buffalo coat flared out around him as he collapsed onto the chair where he had been sitting. Wilkes was a big man, and his weight made the chair legs snap and splinter. He crashed to the porch amidst the debris.

Matt's shots roared out only a shaved fraction of a second behind Smoke's. He fired twice, as well, and both bullets ripped through Conn Wheeler's body. One bullet perforated Wheeler's left lung while the other pulped his heart. Their impact made him spin halfway around. Even though he was dead, he stayed on his feet for a second or two before his muscles finally slackened enough to make him pitch forward on his face.

Smoke and Matt swung their guns toward the front door as it burst open. Heavy footsteps thudded on the porch planks as several men rushed out. They stopped abruptly when they saw that they were covered by the two grim-faced riders.

"What the hell!" one of the men exclaimed, followed by a volley of colorful obscenities. "You killed Conn and Tyrone!"

"They drew on us," Smoke said in a flinty voice.

One of the other men said, "These fellas must be pretty fast, Yancy, because Conn and Tyrone were slick on the draw!"

Yancy was the barrel-chested man who had spoken first. His jaw was like a belligerent wedge as he glared at Smoke and Matt and demanded, "Who are you?"

They didn't have to answer, because the third man, with the dark, narrow, haggard face of a consumptive, said, "The older one's Smoke Jensen. Somebody pointed him out to me down in Taos a couple of years ago. The man with him is his brother, Matt."

Yancy's glare didn't lessen any, but he moved his hand a little farther away from the butt of the gun on his hip, just so there wouldn't be any mistake.

"We got no quarrel with you, Jensen," he snapped. "Either of you."

"You don't want to settle the score for your friends?" Matt goaded.

Yancy snorted.

"I don't recollect sayin' that Wheeler and Wilkes were my friends. We rode together, that's all, and not for very long, neither."

Another man stepped out of the door of the trading post in time to hear this. He said coldly, "I thought you all rode for the brand, Yancy."

"We do, Mr. Kane," Yancy said, his face darkening and his jaw jutting out even more with anger. "But I ain't in the mood to get killed because a couple of hotheads decided to brace Smoke and Matt Jensen. In case you ain't noticed, they got the drop on us."

The man called Kane studied Smoke and Matt speculatively. He was below medium height but built like a tree stump, broad and hard to budge. The fabric of his brown tweed suit coat bulged with ridges of muscle along his shoulders and arms. His derby hat was pushed back to reveal a mostly bald head.

"My name is Jethro Kane," he said. "Those two men you just killed rode for my spread."

"They drew on us," Smoke said again. "A man does that, he's got to expect the other fella to fight back."

"I suppose so." Moving slowly, Kane reached up and withdrew a cigar from his vest pocket. He bit off the end, spat it out, and then clenched the cylinder of tobacco tightly between strong brown teeth, asking around it, "Did either of them even get a shot off?"

"No," Smoke said. "But they cleared leather."

Kane grunted, and it took Smoke a second to realize that the man had just laughed.

"Your name's Jensen?"

"That's right."

"Are you looking for work?"

Before Smoke could answer, Yancy said, "That's Smoke Jensen, Mr. Kane. He's not a hired gun. Fact is, I've heard that he's got a ranch of his own down in Colorado."

"Is that so?" Kane mused. "What brings you up here Wyoming way, Jensen?"

There was no point in concealing the truth. Folks around these parts would know about the immigrants soon enough, no matter what Smoke said here and now.

"We rode along with a wagon train that was bound in this direction," he told Kane. "Wanted to make sure it got where it was going safely."

Kane's somewhat bushy eyebrows lifted.

"A wagon train," he repeated. "Bound for here?"

"That's right."

"Why the hell are a bunch of immigrants coming here? This is ranching country. We don't need a bunch of damn sodbusters around here!"

"No offense," Smoke said, "but you don't strike me as a Western man."

"I'm from New York, originally," Kane snapped. "What's that got to do with anything? I'm a rancher now. The Boxed JK is my spread."

"The hombre leading the wagon train is going to be a rancher, too," Smoke explained. "He bought the Rafter Nine."

Kane stared at him for a second, then grunted again. Then he let out an actual laugh. The other men on the porch laughed, too. Of course, since they worked for Kane, they would be expected to, but it seemed to Smoke that they were genuinely amused.

"The Rafter Nine, eh?" Kane said. "Has this gent ever seen the place?"

"I don't think so," Smoke allowed.

"Then the damn fool bought a pig in a poke! The Rafter Nine failed years ago when a bad winter killed off the cattle its owner was running on it. He tried to build it back up, but bad luck did him in. The place is cursed."

"It's got a hoodoo on it," one of the other men said. "Bad water, not enough graze . . . A man who tries to make a go of it is bound to fail."

Smoke and Matt exchanged a quick glance. Smoke didn't know if these men were lying, but their words had the ring of truth. From the sound of it, Baron von Hoffman had been hoodwinked.

"I reckon we'll have to see the place for ourselves," Smoke said.

"Don't let me stop you," Kane said. "But I'd appreciate it if you'd put those guns away. You're starting to make me nervous. Nobody else is going to try to draw on you or bother you in any other way."

He looked hard at his men as he spoke that last sentence, as if to make sure they understood that was the way he wanted it.

Smoke and Matt pouched their irons. Matt said, "What about your spread, Kane? Is it as bad as you make the Rafter Nine out to be?"

"Of course not," Kane replied. "I have several good springs and plenty of grass. The Rafter Nine has waterholes that have dried up and taken the graze with them."

That sounded pretty bad. Smoke had seen things like that happen before. It sounded like a run of bad luck had ruined the previous owner of the Rafter 9, all right.

Whether Friedrich von Hoffman could turn that luck around was still open to question, but he would be facing an uphill climb, Smoke thought. And he'd have to worry about Klaus Berger and his enemies from the old country, too.

"Sorry about offering you a job a minute ago, Jensen," Kane went on. "I didn't know you were a cattleman, too. That was pretty nice of you, coming along with those pilgrims. Too bad it was a waste of everybody's time."

"We don't know that," Matt said.

"Oh, but we do," Kane said. His smug smile just added to Smoke's instinctive dislike of the man. "There's no chance in hell anybody's going to make a success of the Rafter Nine, especially not a bunch of wet-behind-the-ears pilgrims."

That was a pretty arrogant thing for an hombre from New York to be saying, Smoke thought, especially a man who had two of his riders lying dead practically at his feet.

Yancy spoke up again, saying, "Boss, you reckon we ought to get Wilkes and Wheeler out of here?"

"Put them over their saddles and take them back

to the ranch," Kane ordered curtly. "You can bury them there."

"Yes, sir," Yancy said. He motioned for his companions to give him a hand.

Kane jerked his head toward the door and said to Smoke and Matt, "Come inside and let me buy you boys a drink?"

"Thanks, but we need to get back to the wagon train," Smoke said.

"Yeah, somebody needs to break the news to those folks that they came all this way for nothing," Kane said. He nodded. "So long."

Smoke and Matt sat their saddles until Kane had gone to the buggy, climbed into it, and driven off to the north, using the whip on the two horses pulling the vehicle. Yancy and the two men with him followed on horseback, leading the two horses carrying the bodies of Tyrone Wilkes and Conn Wheeler.

"I don't like those fellas, especially that hombre Kane," Matt said quietly.

"Neither do I," Smoke agreed. He started to dismount. "Let's go inside."

"I thought we were heading back to the wagon train."

"Preacher can guide the wagons here. I want to talk to whoever these other horses belong to."

Smoke had already checked out the brands. One of the horses still tied at the hitch rack carried a Double Diamond brand. The other two had 7B4 burned into their hides.

"Seven before," Matt commented. "Before what, I wonder?"

"No telling," Smoke said.

They stepped up on the porch and went inside the trading post. The main room was shadowy and cavernous, with all sorts of goods hanging on the walls and packing shelves and counters. The saloon was off to the left, with a flimsy-looking wall between it and the rest of the building. A door was cut into that wall, and through the opening Smoke could see three men in range clothes leaning on a hardwood bar, nursing beers.

There was a counter in the back of the trading post, but nobody was behind it. In fact, that part of the building was empty. Smoke walked toward the saloon with Matt right behind him. Their boot heels rang loudly against the floorboards.

The cowboys at the bar had to hear Smoke and Matt approaching them, but they didn't turn around.

The three of them weren't packing iron, Smoke noted, although there were sheathed Winchesters on the saddles of the horses outside.

A balding man with a big gut and handlebar mustaches was behind the bar. He asked, "Something I can do for you fellas?"

"You're the owner?" Smoke asked.

"That's right. Clarence Fisher."

"My name's Smoke Jensen. This is my brother Matt. Pleased to meet you, Mr. Fisher."

The proprietor was about to respond when one of the cowboys said, "No need to get friendly with these fellas, Clarence. They're not gonna be alive long enough for it to matter."

"What makes you say that?" Matt asked sharply.

The man turned to give him and Smoke a bleak look.

"You don't think Jethro Kane's gonna let you live after you killed two of his pet gun-wolves, do you?"

Chapter Twenty-eight

Smoke and Matt looked at the young cowboy for a long moment, then Matt said, "Kane didn't seem too upset. In fact, he offered us jobs."

The puncher shook his head.

"That was just for show. He didn't want a gunfight where he might get in the way of a stray bullet. When there's killin' to be done, Kane's always a long way from it, even when it's on his orders."

"Especially when it's on his orders," another of the three cowboys said.

"And Wynn's right," the third man added. "Kane's got to have you killed now. He can't afford to have anybody stand up to him and get away with it. His own crew wouldn't like it, and it might give other folks around here too many ideas."

Smoke was starting to understand now. He said, "Kane's the big skookum he-wolf in these parts, is he?"

"You got that right," said the cowboy called Wynn.

"You boys don't need to be talking that way," Fisher said from behind the bar. "You're gonna give these strangers the wrong idea."

"You mean the idea that Kane's a land-hoggin' son of a bitch who means to own the whole Medicine Bow range and everything around it?" Wynn laughed. "Sounds to me like that's the right idea, Clarence. The exact right idea." He extended a hand to Smoke. "I'm Wynn Courtland. The Double Diamond is my spread . . . for now. It's a pleasure to meet you, Mr. Jensen. I've heard of you and your brother both."

Smoke shook with the man, and so did Matt. Wynn introduced his companions as Hank Jimson and Dusty Barnes.

"They ride for the 7B4," Wynn continued. "Hank's the foreman."

"Yeah, but when you consider the fact that Dusty and me are the only crew left, it ain't that big of a deal," Hank drawled. "In fact, I was thinking maybe we oughta start swappin' out, week to week."

Smoke felt a natural liking for these easygoing cowmen. He would have hired any of them in a second to ride for him on the Sugarloaf.

"Case Plowright owns the 7B4," Wynn said. "One of the finest old men you'll ever meet, Mr. Jensen. But he's bein' crowded out by Kane, just like I am. Just like all the other small spreads around here were. The Double Diamond and the 7B4 are about the only ones left." He smiled thinly. "And now the

Rafter Nine, I reckon, if this fella you brought up here really does take it over."

"We didn't bring him, we just came along with him," Smoke said. "And he's not going to turn around and go back where he came from. He can't. He doesn't have any choice but to settle here."

"Sunk everything he has into the spread, did he? Well, that's a shame, because Kane was right about one thing. The Rafter Nine is one sorry outfit and has been ever since he saw to it that the waterholes dried up."

Matt said sharply, "Kane did something to the waterholes?"

Looking more nervous by the second, Fisher said, "You shouldn't be spreading wild rumors, Wynn. It's not gonna do anybody any good—"

"Relax, Clarence," Wynn said. "I know you're gonna tell Kane everything we said here. It doesn't matter how much you suck up to him. He's already gunnin' for us. That's why he came in here today draggin' those hired killers with him. He thought he finally had his chance for them to prod us into a fight and be done with us."

"That's why you're not wearing handguns," Smoke guessed. "You knew you might run into Kane's men here."

All three of the cowboys nodded.

"He's had men keepin' an eye on us, just waitin' for the right time," Wynn explained. "But we needed some supplies, so we decided to all ride in together."

Matt said, "I'm surprised he hasn't just had you bushwhacked before now."

"It may come to that," Hank said with a wry grin. "Kane's got political ambitions, though. Figures he might be governor someday. So he wants things to look legal. That's why he won't let his men draw on a fella who's unarmed."

"But one of these days," Wynn said, "he's gonna get tired of waitin', and then we'll all catch a bullet in the back. Case'll be trapped in his house while it burns down around him. He's been in a wheelchair for the past ten years, since a mustang threw him and busted his back."

"What's this about the waterholes?" Smoke asked. He was intrigued by that, just like Matt was.

"Kane hired some smart scientific fella to figure out where the underground river that feeds the springs comes down out of the mountains. Don't ask me how he did it, but after he poked around the foothills for a while, he pointed to a spot and told Kane to dig there. It was on Kane's land, so nobody could stop him. He dug it up, set off some dynamite down there, and the Rafter Nine's waterholes all went dry, while Kane's springs are running better than ever."

Smoke nodded. He'd never had much book learning, but he had a wealth of practical experience. He knew that Kane had diverted the course of that underground stream to strengthen his springs and dry up everybody else's.

"Jack Newton at the Rafter Nine was the only fella

around here with a big enough spread to stand up to Kane," Wynn continued. "The rest of us are just little greasy-sack outfits. But with no water and his grass dyin' and his herd almost wiped out already, there was nothin' he could do. He pulled up stakes and left. I'm surprised he sold the place to somebody, knowing how bad off it is. Doesn't seem like something Jack would do."

"Maybe he died and his heirs did it," Matt suggested. "They could have wanted to get *something* out of the ranch, even if it meant taking advantage of somebody else."

"I reckon that could be," Wynn said with a nod. "Jack's wife always struck me as a hard-hearted sort, even if that ain't a gentlemanly thing to say."

Smoke turned as hoofbeats sounded outside.

"Must be Preacher and the baron," he said.

"Baron?" Wynn repeated in surprise.

"Baron Friedrich von Hoffman," Smoke explained. "He's a German aristocrat."

He left it at that, not explaining the troubles that had brought von Hoffman and his group here. That was the baron's business, and it was up to him to explain it to his new neighbors if he wanted to.

It would probably be a good idea to warn Wynn Courtland and the others about Klaus Berger, though. There was no telling what Berger might do, and the folks around here already had enough trouble with Jethro Kane and his hired guns, from the sound of what Smoke and Matt had been told.

"And that's the unlucky fella who bought the Rafter Nine?" Wynn asked.

"Yep," Smoke said. "And I reckon we'd better go tell him just what it is he's bought for himself."

The baron's eyes were wide with disbelief.

"This cannot be," he said. "It simply cannot."

"We'll have to see for ourselves," Smoke said, "but I believe what those fellas told us. They don't have any reason to lie about it."

"But I was assured that the Rafter Nine had the potential to be one of the finest ranches in Wyoming!"

"Maybe it would, if it had any water," Matt said. "But without any water on the range . . ."

Erica stood nearby, listening as the men talked beside the lead wagon that was now parked in front of the Hawk Creek Station trading post. She let out a little moan of despair.

"All for nothing," she said. "We came all this way, and there is nothing here for us. . . ."

"Stop that," her cousin snapped as he turned sharply toward her. "I don't believe this. Everything will be fine."

Not wanting to believe something didn't mean that it wasn't so, Smoke thought. He hadn't wanted to believe it when he first heard that his pa was dead, either, or his older brother Luke, or his first wife, Nicole, and their infant son, Arthur. Part of him had cried out in denial of those tragedies, but that hadn't changed the awful facts.

"We can head on out there and take a look," Smoke said. "Maybe things won't be as bad as they seem."

He wasn't trying to hold out any false hope to the immigrants, but he wasn't the sort of man to give up until he had seen the lay of the land with his own eyes. Even then, giving up didn't come natural to him. If somebody was willing to work hard enough, and fight hard enough if need be, almost anything was possible.

Wynn, Hank, and Dusty had followed Smoke and Matt out onto the porch of the trading post. Wynn said now, "We'd be glad to take you and your friends out to the Rafter Nine so you can take a look-see at the place, Mr. Jensen."

"We'd be obliged, Wynn. And call me Smoke."

He introduced the three men to the baron, who shook hands with them rather perfunctorily.

"Is there enough time left to get out to the ranch today?" Matt asked.

"Should be," Wynn replied, "if we go on pretty soon."

"There's nothing keeping us here," Smoke said. "You might want to pick up some supplies, Baron, but you can send somebody in to do that later."

Von Hoffman nodded, still looking a little stunned.

"Yes," he said. "We'll do that." He turned and called, "Everyone back on the wagons!"

Most of the immigrants hadn't heard the bad news yet, but Smoke could see their weariness anyway as they climbed back onto the wagon seats. They had come a long way, and some of them had to be wondering if their journey was ever going to be over.

It would be soon, Smoke thought, but probably not in the way they had hoped it would be.

There was no need for a scout now, since they had the three cowboys to guide the wagon train. Smoke, Matt, and Preacher rode with them in front of the column.

"So that fella's a real, honest-to-gosh European baron, eh?" Dusty Barnes asked.

"Yep," Smoke said.

"Can't you tell from the high an' mighty way he acts?" Preacher added.

"Well, he ain't much like the fellas around here, that's for sure," Dusty agreed.

Since von Hoffman was riding back alongside the lead wagon, Smoke thought this might be a good time to tell their three new friends about Klaus Berger.

"It's not my place to go into the whys and wherefores of it," he began, "but the baron's got some bad men gunning for him. Most of them are just hired pistoleros, but their leader is a man called Klaus Berger. He's not an albino, but next thing to it. Long, pale hair and really dark eyes. Any of you boys seen somebody like that in these parts lately?"

The three cowboys looked genuinely baffled. Wynn shook his head and said, "That don't sound like anybody I've ever seen, let alone lately."

"Klaus Berger," Hank repeated. "He sounds like a furriner, too."

"He's German, like the baron," Smoke explained. "But he speaks good English. I'm told that if you ever see or hear him, you'll never forget him."

"What do we do if we see him?" Wynn asked.

"Watch your back," Smoke advised. "And I'd take it as a personal favor if you'd let one of us know."

"We can do that," Dusty said. "So this is a really bad hombre, huh?"

"Really bad," Smoke agreed.

"And that's got something to do with why the baron can't go back home, I'll bet," Wynn said. "I don't go pokin' my nose in another fella's business, but it's good to know when there might be a lobo wolf roamin' around the vicinity."

"That's what I thought," Smoke said. "That's why I told you about Berger."

"We're obliged for that." They had reached the top of a low, rolling hill. Wynn reined in and pointed. "We've been on Rafter Nine range for a while now. There's the ranch headquarters."

Smoke brought his horse to a stop, too, as did the others. While they waited for the wagons to catch up, Smoke studied the layout in the little valley spread before them.

It wasn't too promising. There was a good-sized

ranch house built out of logs, but it showed signs of abandonment. Some of the windows were broken out, and the front door hung open and crooked on its hinges. That meant varmints had gotten inside and the place would probably need a lot of cleaning to make it livable again.

There were several outbuildings, including a barn and a bunkhouse, but they, too, were in disrepair. Some of the fence rails had fallen down around the big corral. The vanes of a windmill behind the house turned slowly in the breeze, but Smoke could hear them screeching even from up here on the hilltop. The apparatus was badly in need of oiling.

"Looks like it could be a nice place with some work," Matt commented.

Preacher said, "Yeah, but is it worth it to fix it up if there ain't no water on the spread?"

"Does that well work?" Smoke asked.

"The last I heard, before Jack Newton pulled out, it did," Wynn said. "But it just provides water for the ranch headquarters. There's not enough to irrigate the whole spread, if that's what you're thinkin', Smoke."

"It's not," Smoke said. "Just wanted to make sure these folks would have water if they decide to camp here for a while."

"Yeah, they'd be all right. But like Preacher says, what's the point?"

"That's not up to us to decide." Smoke turned his

horse and waved Baron von Hoffman forward. The baron trotted his mount up to join them.

His hard-planed face grew even more grim as he looked down at the desolate ranch headquarters.

"Is that . . . ?" he began.

"It is," Smoke said. No point in sugar-coating it. "That's your new home, Baron."

BOOK THREE

Chapter Twenty-nine

The inside of the house was as bad as Smoke feared it would be. Wolves and smaller critters had been in there, and the floor was covered with their droppings. Pieces of furniture that had been left behind by the Newton family had been shredded. Owls were nesting in the rafters. Erica was horrified as she looked around the place. Smoke imagined it was a far cry from the luxury she was accustomed to back in Germany.

"The servants will soon put things in order," von Hoffman said with a heartiness that sounded false to Smoke's ears. "We've been living in the wagons for weeks now. We can continue living in them for a while."

He had a point there, Smoke thought. At least the immigrants wouldn't be without shelter while they tried to get this place cleaned up.

Wynn, Hank, and Dusty had headed for their ranches, but not before explaining to Smoke, Matt, and Preacher how to find the half-dozen waterholes on the spread. Or where the waterholes had been, rather, since they had all dried up. Smoke figured they would take a look at the places tomorrow, since it was getting late in the afternoon now.

"Let's go see if that pump works," he said to Matt.

They walked behind the ranch house to the windmill. Matt said, "Looks like the baron got snookered, all right. Whatever he paid for this outfit, it was too much."

"Maybe not," Smoke said. "Structurally, the house looks sound enough, and so do the barn and the other outbuildings. They just need some repair work done on them, that's all, and there are several carpenters among the folks who came with him, the baron said."

"Oh, sure, they can do that," Matt agreed, "but what's the point if they can't raise any stock to make a living? And you can't raise stock without water and grass. You know that, Smoke."

"Yeah, I know." They had reached the pump. Smoke took hold of the handle and tried to work it. The mechanism was rusty and stubborn, but it was no match for the strength of Smoke Jensen. In a few minutes, he had the handle moving up and down relatively smoothly.

Matt put his ear close to the pipe attached to the pump and listened. After a moment, he smiled.

"I heard something gurgling," he said. "Keep pumping, Smoke."

After a moment, water began to trickle from the

pipe. It was slow and muddy at first, but as Smoke continued working the handle, the water flowed faster and began to clear. It wasn't long before he had a steady stream coming from the pipe to splash on the ground. Matt cupped his hand under the flow and brought it to his mouth to taste the water.

"It's good," he announced. "That's a break for the baron, anyway."

"I'll climb up there and oil that windmill tomorrow," Smoke said. "It'll work even better then."

They went back to the house to report that the well still worked and found that Erica had retreated to the wagon after looking around the house.

"She's very upset," von Hoffman said with a frown. "I tried to tell her that everything will be all right, but I don't think she believed me."

"I'll go talk to her," Matt said.

The baron's frown turned into a scowl. He still didn't like the idea of Matt paying too much attention to his cousin, Smoke knew. But as upset as she was now, he would probably be glad for anybody to comfort her and calm her down.

As Matt approached the wagon, he heard Erica sobbing inside the vehicle.

He heard something else that gave him pause: someone talking quietly in German.

Dieter.

Matt stopped before he got too close. A grimace tugged at the corners of his mouth. He had forgotten about Dieter. The young man had been inside the wagon, still recovering from his wounds, when Erica climbed in all upset about what they had found on the Rafter 9. That had given Dieter the perfect opportunity to step in and comfort her.

Not that Matt could blame him. Dieter had a good heart. He probably wasn't even thinking about anything other than trying to make Erica feel better. With a shake of his head, Matt started to turn away from the wagon.

That was when he saw a flash of something from the corner of his eye. He glanced in the direction of the more rugged hills to the north of the ranch headquarters and saw it again. The sun was reflecting off something up there, either glass or metal.

The glint was too far away for somebody to be aiming a rifle at him. That meant more than likely the reflection came from a telescope or a pair of field glasses.

Somebody could be watching the ranch. Spying to see when the baron and his followers arrived.

There had been only a tiny hitch in Matt's movements as he spotted the reflection, maybe not enough to be visible from that distance even with the amplification of a telescope or field glasses. He kept going, walking over to where Preacher stood talking to the blacksmith Rudolph Wolff and several other men.

The keen-eyed old mountain man noticed right away that something was bothering Matt.

"What's put a burr under your saddle?" Preacher asked.

Other than Dieter getting first crack at comforting Erica? Matt thought. But this new development allowed him to put that out of his mind.

"Looks like somebody's up in the hills spying on us," he said. "Don't look in that direction. Whoever it is, we don't want him to know that we've spotted him."

"You reckon it's Berger?"

"Could be. Or it could be one of those gunnies who works for Jethro Kane."

During the ride out to the ranch from Hawk Creek Station, Smoke and Matt had told Preacher about killing Tyrone Wilkes and Conn Wheeler, as well as explaining how the gunmen had worked for the local would-be range boss Jethro Kane. Preacher agreed that Kane's men were bound to come gunning for them sooner or later.

Nor would it help von Hoffman and the other immigrants for Smoke and Matt to leave the Rafter 9, because Kane would want to run off all of them in order to solidify his grip on the area. He just didn't have a personal grudge against them, the way he did against Smoke and Matt.

"Sounds like you and me ought to take a little ride," Preacher suggested. "We could start back toward the tradin' post, then loop around once we're out of sight and head up into them hills."

"So we can find out just who it is that's skulking

around." Matt nodded. "That's not a bad idea. We'd better tell Smoke what we're doing, though."

Smoke had come out of the ranch house with the baron. Matt and Preacher walked over to join them.

"Somebody with a spyglass up in the hills," Matt said, knowing that he didn't have to warn Smoke not to look up there. "Preacher and I figured we'd go find out who it is."

"It must be Klaus or one of his men," von Hoffman said.

Smoke shook his head.

"Not necessarily," he said. "It could be Kane's men."

"We thought of the same thing," Matt said with a nod. "Either way, it wouldn't hurt to know."

"You're right about that," Smoke agreed. "Just don't get yourself killed or caught." He paused before adding, "I've got a hunch that before this is over, we're going to need every gun we've got."

The sun was lowering toward the horizon as Matt and Preacher mounted up and headed over the hill to the south on the trail toward Hawk Creek Station. They had ridden about a mile when they swung back to the east.

There were enough ridges and gullies for them to avoid being skylighted as they circled toward the hills where Matt had spotted the sun reflecting off something. The possibility remained that what he had seen was totally innocuous and not connected to the baron and his party of immigrants . . . but Matt's instincts told him that wasn't the case, and Smoke and Preacher agreed with him.

Matt didn't know this area, but Preacher had been here before. He pointed to a broad stretch of flats and said, "A bunch of redskins chased me across there once, more'n forty years ago. They was mad as they could be at me."

"They probably had good reason to be," Matt said. "You must've gotten away from them, since you still have your hair."

"Yeah, that ugly ol' gray of mine I called Horse outrun 'em. He could get up and go when he wanted to."

"How many horses have you had over the years that you called Horse?"

Preacher frowned.

"I don't know, and what the hell does it matter, anyway? Horse is a perfectly good name for a horse!"

"And what did you call your dogs?"

"Called 'em Dog, as you durned sure know already. You gonna argue that Dog ain't a good name for a dog?"

"I'm not arguing about anything," Matt said. "Just saying that it's a mite unusual."

"A man ought to be consistent," Preacher declared.

"Well, you certainly are. According to Smoke, you haven't changed in the past twenty years except to get a little older and scragglier."

"Scragglier, is it?" Preacher combed his fingers through his tangled white beard. "I think I'm still a fine figure of a man—"

Matt reined in and held up a hand. They were riding along the base of a ridge. He pointed up with a thumb and whispered, "Somebody up there."

That was true. Hoofbeats sounded clearly in the late afternoon air as several men rode along the top of the ridge. Matt and Preacher crowded their horses closer against the steep slope and waited.

The riders were headed east. According to what Wynn Courtland and the other cowboys had told them, that was where Jethro Kane's Boxed JK spread was located.

"Reckon there ain't no doubt about it now," Preacher said as the hoofbeats faded. "They're headin' for Kane's place. Got to be his men."

"More than likely, but I'd rather get a look at them and be sure," Matt said. "Come on."

He turned his horse and started back the direction they had come. They followed the ridge until it petered out. Matt reined in and swung down from the saddle. Leaving his horse ground-hitched, he edged forward until he could see around a slab of rock that shouldered out from the place where the ridge started.

"Can you see 'em?" Preacher asked quietly.

"Yeah. Three riders about a hundred yards away, still heading east. I can't get a good look at them from here, though. Hell, one bunch of hired guns looks pretty much like another."

"But none of 'em got long white hair like Berger, do they?"

"No, that much I can tell," Matt said. "Berger's not with them. But they might be some gunnies he hired. Or they might be Kane's men. We're just going to have to follow them—"

He stopped as a bullet suddenly chipped rock from the big slab just above his head, followed instantly by the whipcrack of a shot.

Chapter Thirty

Matt crouched as he twisted in the direction the shot had come from. About a hundred yards away rose a small knob covered with scrub brush and aspen. Matt knew that was where the bushwhacker had to be hidden even before he spotted a puff of powder smoke and heard a second shot rip out.

"Son of a buck!" Preacher exclaimed. "I felt the heat o' that one!"

The old mountain man jerked his Winchester from the saddle boot and wheeled his horse toward the knob.

"I'll cover you, Matt!" he called as he started firing toward the hidden rifleman as fast as he could work the Winchester's lever.

Matt grabbed his horse's reins and leaped into the saddle. He and Preacher were out in the open here, with no cover nearby. Moving fast was their best chance of surviving this ambush.

"You go left, I'll go right!" he told Preacher as

both of them kicked their horses into swift gallops. They split up, angling away from each other as they rode toward the knob. That way the rifleman had to choose to target one or the other of them. He couldn't shoot at both of them.

Unless there was more than one bushwhacker up there, Matt reminded himself grimly.

But so far there was no sign of that. He had heard only one rifle, and now, as bullets kicked up dust around him, he looked over at Preacher and didn't see anything similar happening in the vicinity of the old mountain man. Matt supposed the bushwhacker figured he was the bigger threat.

The man might have made a mistake about that.

It took Matt less than a minute to reach a spot near the base of the knob where the hidden rifleman no longer had a good angle for a shot at him. He dropped from the saddle and left the reins hanging, knowing that the well-trained horse wouldn't stray very far. He pulled his own rifle from its sheath and started working his way through the brush.

That ambusher really should have made at least one of his shots count, Matt thought. Now the varmint was caught between him and Preacher, and that was a bad place to be.

Matt had a pretty good idea what had happened. The men who'd been watching the Rafter 9 had posted a man on the knob to make sure nobody was watching *them*. The bushwhacker probably had orders not to open fire unless someone was following the other men.

But that was exactly what had happened, and when it became obvious that Matt and Preacher were going to trail the spies, they had made themselves targets.

That theory worked whether the watchers were Berger's men or Kane's. Matt wished he could have gotten closer to them. He might have recognized someone from the encounter at Hawk Creek Station. As it was, the men would probably get away while he and Preacher were forced to deal with this bushwhacker.

He heard crackling and rustling in the brush somewhere above him. Someone was moving around, but he couldn't just open fire because it could be Preacher up there. Also, the sun was behind the mountains to the west now, and dusky shadows were starting to gather.

Suddenly, shots blasted out. Preacher yelled, "Comin' your way, Matt!"

Matt barely had time to swing his rifle up before a man crashed through the brush about twenty feet away from him and slightly up-slope. The man had a rifle, too, and he fired it as Matt dropped to one knee. The slug whipped over his head.

Matt wanted to place his shot carefully if he could. He brought the Winchester to his shoulder and squeezed the trigger as soon as the sights settled on his target.

The .44-40 round drilled through the meaty part of the man's right thigh. He let out a howl as that leg folded up underneath him.

The bushwhacker wound up on his belly, but he didn't drop his rifle or surrender. Instead, he thrust the weapon toward Matt and fired it one-handed. Matt rolled to the side as the bullet tore through the brush near his head.

Preacher appeared behind the man. The old mountain man leveled both his pistols and said, "Drop it, mister, or I'll take plumb pleasure in blowin' your dang fool head off."

Matt could tell that the bushwhacker thought about rolling over and trying to get off a shot at Preacher. He could see the desperate urge on the man's face.

But reason prevailed. The man placed the Winchester on the ground in front of him and lifted his hands well away from it.

"I can't stand up," he said in a voice wracked with pain. "My leg's shot out from under me."

"Reckon you must've done that, Matt," Preacher said as the younger man got to his feet. "You can get his gun."

Matt came forward and picked up the rifle. He tossed it out of reach, then did the same with the man's handgun, pulling it from the holster and tossing it after the Winchester.

Then he backed off and covered the man with his rifle.

"Damn it, ain't you gonna help me?" the bushwhacker burst out. "You shot me, and now I'm fixin' to bleed to death!"

Matt had already seen how slowly the bloodstain

on the man's trouser leg was spreading. He knew the man was in no danger of bleeding to death any time soon, or even at all, more than likely.

But the bushwhacker didn't have to know that, and the wound probably hurt like blazes.

Matt said, "Yeah, you look like you don't have much time left, mister. If you want to make your peace with the Good Lord, you'd better go ahead and do it."

"I might not die if you'd help me!" the man said. "Bind up this hole in my leg, for God's sake!"

"I don't know why I should," Matt said, "since you were doing your best to kill us."

"I didn't have any choice!" The man's voice was getting more strident and frantic. "Dick Yancy would've killed me if I hadn't done what he told me!"

"Yancy, eh? That means you ride for the Boxed JK."

"Yeah, yeah, so what? Damn it, mister, you and your friend killed two of our boys! Did you think Kane was gonna let you get away with that?"

"Would you be willing to testify to that in a court of law?" Matt asked.

Preacher's snort made it perfectly clear how he felt about that, but he added scathingly, "Court of law!"

The bushwhacker hesitated, obviously worried about what might happen to him if he testified against Kane and Yancy. But then Matt said, "Did you ever see so much blood, Preacher?"

"Not since the last time I was around for a hog-slaughterin'," the old-timer replied.

The bushwhacker said, "All right, all right, blast it! I'll say anything you want in court, Jensen. Just tie up this leg of mine before I . . . before I pass out. . . . Ohhh . . ."

As the man's head slumped to the ground, Matt leaned his rifle against a tree and strode forward.

"Keep him covered, Preacher," he said. "But if he tries anything, don't kill him. Just shoot him in the other leg. I don't care if he's ever able to walk again, do you?"

"Nary a bit," Preacher said.

Matt used his Bowie knife to cut away the leg of the man's jeans and expose the wound. The blood flowing from both bullet holes had slowed to a trickle. Matt sliced strips from the tail of the man's shirt and used them to bind up the wound, tying them tightly around the injured thigh.

"He's still pretty groggy. Let's get him on his feet."

Matt wasn't convinced that the bushwhacker was in as bad a shape as he was acting like, so he and Preacher were careful as they took hold of the man's arms and lifted him. The man didn't try any tricks, though.

"We'll have to find his horse," Matt said. "Set him on that stump, and then you can keep an eye on him."

"Don't take too long," Preacher warned. "My trigger fingers get mighty itchy whenever I'm around sneak-shootin' polecats like this."

It didn't take Matt long to find a saddled horse tied in some trees behind the knob. He led it back to where he'd left Preacher and the bushwhacker, and they lifted the man into the saddle with Matt doing most of the work.

"You'd better be able to stay on that horse," Matt warned him. "You fall off and you're liable to start those wounds bleeding again. I'm not sure we could save your life a second time."

He cocked his head so that the bushwhacker couldn't see him and closed one eye in an elaborate wink at Preacher.

"Don't worry," the man said. "I'm feelin' better now—"

His head exploded.

That was the way it seemed, anyway, as a high-powered bullet blew away part of his skull and sent blood, brain matter, and shards of bone spraying everywhere.

The distant boom of the shot sounded as the man's body toppled out of the saddle and fell to the ground. The spooked horse leaped away from the limp, gruesome figure, but the bushwhacker's right foot had caught in the stirrup. The horse dragged him through the trees and across the rough ground, slamming the body against tree trunks and making it flop and bounce grotesquely.

Matt and Preacher had gone diving for cover before the bushwhacker's body hit the ground, too. They could estimate the direction the shot came from, and they put some trees between themselves and the marksman. The slender-trunked aspens didn't provide much cover, but it was better than nothing.

"That was a Sharps like mine!" Preacher said as he knelt behind a tree. "Sounded like it was three, four hundred yards away, too. The varmint's got a good eye. That's some fine shootin' with the light fadin' like this."

"At least one of the men we saw earlier must have heard the shots and doubled back," Matt said. "But why shoot their own partner first?"

"To keep him from talkin'," Preacher said. "We know they got a spyglass of some sort. They must've looked through it, seen we had the hombre prisoner, and figured there was a chance he'd tell us who was behind it, just like he did. If they only got one shot, they wanted to make sure they got the fella who could testify against their boss."

Matt nodded and said, "That makes sense. They haven't fired again since we went to ground."

"No, they're probably headed back to Kane's ranch to tell him they got another score to settle with us. That makes three of 'em they'll hold against us, even though we didn't blow out this one's lights ourselves."

"Speaking of lights, in another ten minutes or so it'll be too dark to see us anymore, if they're even still out there. We can head back to the Rafter Nine headquarters then. At least we learned who was spying on us."

"And that fella we caught backed up what Wynn Courtland said about Kane wantin' us dead. Of course, we already had a pretty good feelin' about that bein' right."

A grim chuckle came from Matt.

"That's nothing unusual for us and Smoke, is it, Preacher? Somebody wanting us dead, I mean."

"Boy, varmints have been gunnin' for me a whole hell of a lot longer than you been alive," Preacher said with a grin of his own, "and I'm still here!"

Chapter Thirty-one

Smoke was about to put his saddle back on his horse and go looking for Matt and Preacher when they rode in, leading a horse with a dead man draped over its saddle.

Earlier, Smoke had heard some shots from the hills to the north, and he had almost gone after them then, stopping only when the shots died out quickly. If there was anybody he trusted completely to take care of themselves, it was Matt and Preacher. Whatever the problem was, Smoke was confident they had dealt with it.

Then, a while after that, he'd heard the faint, echoing boom of a heavy caliber rifle, probably a Sharps from the sound of it. But again, there was only one shot, so Smoke didn't know what to make of it.

Meanwhile, the business of setting up camp went on. Baron von Hoffman decided that it would be better to wait for morning to start trying to put things in order around the ranch, a decision that Smoke agreed with. Instead of arranging the wagons in a circle as they had been doing every night for weeks, this evening they were just parked here and there around the ranch buildings, and the oxen were led into the corral.

Fixing those fences was the only repair work that went on today. Smoke supervised that, and since there were plenty of willing workers among the immigrants, it didn't take long to make the corral sturdy enough to hold the massive, stoic creatures.

Other men gathered wood and built a large, roaring campfire. The circle of light reached out a long way from it once full dark had fallen, and that was why Smoke was able to see Matt and Preacher as they approached. Matt was leading the extra horse with its grisly burden.

Smoke had seen enough dead men that he didn't have to ask any questions about the blanket-wrapped figure draped over the saddle and lashed into place, other than who it was.

"One of Kane's men," Matt replied once he and Preacher had dismounted. He turned to the horse and started untying the rawhide strips that held the corpse. "He was bird-dogging those hombres who were spying on us. Best we can figure, they worked for Kane, too."

Von Hoffman had come up to listen, bringing several of his men with him. He motioned for them to unload the body. As they did so, the baron asked, "I take it you were forced to kill this man?"

Matt shook his head.

"No, we just wounded him and took him prisoner. His own compadres blew most of his head off with a long-distance shot from a Sharps."

Von Hoffman looked shocked. He asked, "Why in heaven's name would they do that?"

"To keep him from talking, would be my guess," Smoke said.

"That's right," Matt said. "We'd already gotten him to admit that he rode for the Boxed JK and that Kane wants our hides. He even said he'd testify to it in court. But then his pards double-crossed him."

Smoke ran a thumbnail along his jaw and frowned in thought.

"They'll go back to Kane's ranch and tell everybody that the two of you killed him," he said.

"Sure they will," Preacher agreed. "But they was already gunnin' for us, so it don't make much difference, does it?"

"Not much," Smoke admitted.

"I suppose we might as well see to it that this man is buried," von Hoffman said. "Although I doubt that he deserves such consideration." He turned his head to peer out at the darkness beyond the firelight. "It seems that we are surrounded by enemies. Klaus Berger is still out there somewhere, too."

Smoke didn't doubt that for a second.

He made sure the guards were just as diligent as ever, but nothing unusual happened that night . . . or for the next week after that. Smoke, Matt, and

Preacher all kept their eyes on the hills, but no one seemed to be spying on them. Matt and Preacher scouted on horseback in all four directions and found nothing suspicious.

Smoke stayed close to the Rafter 9 and used all the knowledge and expertise he had gained in building the Sugarloaf into a successful ranch to try to get the baron's people off to a good start. He showed them the repairs that needed to be made and explained how to go about them. He put men to work cutting down trees and building a smokehouse, something the ranch was in need of. He oiled the windmill, helped Rudolph Wolff put the blacksmith shop in order, even toted furniture and supplies into the ranch house once Erica and a number of the women had cleaned it from top to bottom.

Once she had gotten over her initial shock at the state of the ranch, Erica had stiffened her spine and gotten to work with surprising diligence and toughness. Smoke was impressed with her. It was like she had realized that she had no choice now but to grow up. She was no longer a pampered aristocrat and never would be again.

That was a good first step to becoming an actual frontier woman, Smoke thought.

Dieter continued to improve, and while he wasn't in good enough shape yet to handle any of the heavy work, he was willing to take on some of the smaller tasks and proved to be a good hand when it came to carpentry. There were plenty of minor repair jobs that needed to be done around the place.

And since that kept him around Erica a lot of the time, that was an added bonus for him. Smoke had a feeling that Matt had lost out on that short-lived competition for the girl's affections. Matt had never been one to take his romances all that seriously. Every time some gal started thinking about settling down with him, his fiddlefooted nature had him rattling his hocks for parts unknown pretty quickly.

Yes, the work was going well and there had been no trouble with either Klaus Berger or Jethro Kane, but a shadow still loomed over the Rafter 9.

No matter what the baron and his people did, the ranch would never be successful without more water.

So after a week had passed, Smoke, Matt, and von Hoffman headed into the hills to take a look at the waterholes, leaving Preacher in charge at the ranch headquarters.

"I greatly appreciate everything you have done for us, Herr Jensen," the baron said as they rode along. "But you have been away from your ranch for quite a while now. Won't your wife be starting to get concerned about you?"

Smoke smiled and asked, "Are you trying to run me off, Baron?"

"Not at all," von Hoffman answered without hesitation. "As I said, we are greatly in your debt, all three of you men. But you have your own lives, your own responsibilities."

"Smoke's got responsibilities," Matt said with a grin. "I've got a horse."

"Sally knows better than to expect me back at a

certain time," Smoke said. "She knows that things can come up that you don't expect. Like this ranch being in the shape that it's in. Now, mind you, if a couple of months go by without any sign of me, she might be liable to send Pearlie and Cal and some of the boys up here to look for me . . . but I don't think it'll come to that. When I do start home, I'll stop in Laramie and send a wire to Big Rock letting her know that I'm on my way."

"Very well," von Hoffman said. "I'll certainly take your help as long as you're willing to remain here."

Smoke had known all along that he and Matt and Preacher would probably stick around for a while, even if the ranch had been in fine running order. They couldn't ride away with the threat of Klaus Berger hanging over the heads of the immigrants.

Now, with the added menace of Jethro Kane thrown in, it was even more important that they not leave all those pilgrims to shift for themselves.

Smoke located the landmarks and followed the trails Wynn Courtland had told him about, and after an hour or so the three men came to the first waterhole. It was bone dry. The bottom of what had been a nice-sized pool had cracked in the sun.

Rocks surrounded the waterhole. Smoke and Matt dismounted and examined them, finding no sign of moisture. Smoke had brought along a shovel. He dug down into the hard ground for a ways, then handed the shovel to Matt, who deepened the hole even more.

"No mud," Matt said. "The spring that fed this hole has dried up good and proper."

"Is there any way to turn the water back in this direction?" von Hoffman asked.

"Maybe," Smoke said, "but we'd have to go onto Kane's range to do it. And if we go to blasting on the Boxed JK, he'd be within his legal rights to shoot us down on sight."

Smoke tipped his head back and looked higher in the mountains that ran in a rugged line from west to east, forming the northern boundary of the vast basin that housed the Rafter 9, the Boxed JK, and the few smaller ranches that were left.

That's where the answer lay, he told himself. Kane had diverted the underground river that fed the springs.

But that stream had another end somewhere else.

Smoke kept those thoughts to himself for now. He and Matt and von Hoffman checked the other waterholes and found that the situation was the same at all of them.

As they sat on their horses beside the last of the waterholes, the baron took his hat off and wearily scrubbed a hand over his face.

"We have water at the ranch from the well," he said. "What if we drilled more wells?"

"You might be able to do that," Smoke said, "and you could probably get enough water to support a small herd."

"Right now I have *no* herd," von Hoffman said

with a wry smile. "Perhaps starting small is what we should do."

"That's a decent plan," Smoke agreed. He had another idea in mind, but if it didn't work out, the baron would have something else to fall back on. It would be slow, building up the ranch that way, but it could be done.

Or at least, it could have been if the Rafter 9 hadn't had Jethro Kane squeezing in on it, trying to take over. Trouble was bound to come from that direction sooner or later.

For the time being, Smoke went on, "You can probably get somebody to come out from Laramie to drill a couple of wells for you. You might be able to buy some stock there, too. We'll figure on making a trip to town in a week or so. By then, all the repairs should be done."

That would give him some time to investigate his other idea, too, he told himself.

"Very well," von Hoffman said. "As always, I will rely on your guidance, Herr Jensen."

That was an awfully humble thing for the baron to say. Maybe the frontier was starting to knock some of the pompousness out of him.

Von Hoffman rode ahead as they started back toward the ranch headquarters. Smoke hung back a little, and as he expected, Matt joined him.

"I reckon you'll be going to Laramie with the baron to show him the ropes," the younger man said.

"That's right," Smoke said, "but before we do that, you and I are going to take another little trip, Matt."

Chapter Thirty-two

A few days after the wagon train had arrived at the ranch, the baron had sent one of the wagons back down to Hawk Creek Station with orders for the driver to load up on supplies in Clarence Fisher's trading post. Smoke had gone along to make sure the wagon got there and back safely and also to pick up a few things he needed.

The next morning after their survey of the dried-up waterholes, Smoke and Matt packed some supplies and saddled their horses. When von Hoffman saw them getting ready to ride, he said, "I thought you weren't leaving yet."

"We're not," Smoke said. "We're just taking a little trip up into the hills to check out an idea of mine. We may be gone for a few days, that's why we're taking along provisions."

"Is this something that might help us?" the baron asked.

"Maybe," Smoke said, "but I don't want to talk too

much about it just yet. It might not pan out, and I don't want to get everybody's hopes up for no good reason."

Von Hoffman nodded.

"I understand. And again I owe you a debt of gratitude."

"We haven't done anything yet," Matt pointed out.

"No, but you are trying to help. That is more than some people would do."

"Keep your guard up while we're gone," Smoke advised. "Listen to Preacher. That old man's mighty canny, and he's got the best instincts for trouble you'll ever find."

"Of course," von Hoffman said with a nod. "And it's possible we're still being watched, so the two of you should be careful as well. If spies see you ride out alone, they might try to come after you."

"They'll be sorry if they do," Matt declared.

He and Smoke rode out a few minutes later. They had already explained their plan to Preacher, so there was no need to tell the old mountain man that they were leaving. They were all practical men, not given to sentimental good-byes.

Smoke and Matt kept a close eye on the hills as they rode toward the more rugged terrain. They didn't see any signs of anyone watching them . . . but the spies could still be up there, being more careful now in their lurking.

In all the paperwork that had been sent to Baron von Hoffman when he concluded the deal to buy the Rafter 9 had been a map of the area showing the boundaries of the ranch. Smoke had spent quite a bit of time pouring over that map, studying all the details of the ranch and the surrounding area.

This was still open range country to a certain extent, although Washington was making efforts to get people to file legal claims on the land they were using. Jack Newton was one of the ranchers who had filed those claims, and the legal boundaries of the Rafter 9 stretched well up into the hills, even though they were too rugged and rocky to provide any good range.

They might provide something else, though, Smoke hoped.

As they rode, Matt said, "I reckon I've given up on Erica. Dieter's won her over."

"I was thinking the same thing the other day," Smoke said. "It's probably for the best. The two of them have a lot more in common."

"I'm not sure it matters. The baron's not gonna let Dieter marry her."

"She's a grown woman," Smoke pointed out. "That decision's up to her."

"You and I both know things don't always work out that way, Smoke."

"They do if the woman's strong-willed enough," Smoke said with a smile, thinking about Sally. Her parents back in New Hampshire had never been all that sure it was a good idea for her to marry him, but that hadn't made a lick of difference. Sally had been born with plenty of frontier spirit in her, although she'd had to go west to discover that. Once she had, there was no turning back for her. Smoke had a hunch Erica von Hoffman might be the same way.

"Well, I hope things turn out all right for them," Matt said. "I never figured on settling down just yet, anyway."

"I never thought you did," Smoke said.

By midday they had started to climb into the hills, which steadily grew more rugged and eventually turned into a range of small mountains. Smoke knew what he was looking for—the green of vegetation— but it took most of the afternoon to find it.

When they did, though, his spirits rose as he studied a line of trees and brush angling through the hills from northwest to southeast. He pointed it out to Matt, who said, "That looks promising, all right. But it'll depend on what we find there."

Smoke knew that, but the lay of the land was good. They climbed higher, aiming for the trees.

A short time later they came to the stream, which was bordered by brush and aspen as it zigzagged down a hillside. Smoke dismounted and knelt beside the creek. He stuck his hand in the water and felt how cold it was. Cupping his hand, he brought it to his mouth and tasted the water.

"Mighty good," he announced to Matt. "Let's see where it goes."

They turned their horses and followed the creek downstream, moving away from it some so they wouldn't have to fight their way through the brush. Late in the afternoon, they came to a spot where a hollow in the rocks had formed a pool. That appeared to be where the creek ended.

Smoke knew that wasn't the case. The flow of water into the pool had to be going somewhere, so that meant this was where the stream went underground. Assuming it continued in roughly the same direction, that would take its course across a corner of Jethro Kane's land before it entered the Rafter 9 to feed those springs that had formed waterholes.

And it was in that stretch of Boxed JK range that Kane had diverted the water.

Now, if Smoke's plan worked, they were going to give Kane a taste of his own medicine.

Matt studied the rocky walls of the pool and then stood up in the stirrups to gaze to the south.

"There's a little valley that runs right through the middle of the baron's range. If we can make a hole in that rock, the water ought to work its way down and eventually form a creek that runs across the Rafter Nine."

"That's the idea," Smoke said. "Maybe it'll start those springs flowing again, or maybe it won't, but at least the baron will have the creek. Put in a few wells here and there, and in time that'll be enough to water the range again. The Rafter Nine will be able to support some fine herds of cattle then."

Matt frowned slightly.

"It'll take a hell of a lot of hard work to chip out a new course in that rock using picks," he said.

Smoke smiled and said, "I know. That's why I brought dynamite."

Matt let out a little whistle.

"I didn't know you were carrying any of that hellish stuff. I would've ridden a little farther away from you if I had."

"It's safe enough as long as you know what you're doing. I've used it on the Sugarloaf. I didn't know if Fisher would have any at the trading post, but I asked him about it when I was there a few days ago. Turns out he keeps a small supply on hand for the prospectors who go up into the mountains looking for gold." Smoke patted his saddlebags. "I've got a few sticks of it wrapped up in here."

"Then what are we waiting for?" Matt asked with a grin. "Let's blow that rock wall to smithereens. We'll see how Kane likes it when all his water dries up."

Smoke shook his head.

"We'll wait until morning to set off the blast. I'd like to place the dynamite so we don't divert all the water, just part of it."

"You don't want to do to Kane what he did to that fella Newton?"

"I don't give a damn about Kane," Smoke said bluntly, "but his cows didn't do anything wrong, and they don't deserve to die of thirst."

"Well, you're right about that," Matt said with a shrug. "So we're going to make camp here for the night?"

"That's the plan," Smoke said as he swung down from the saddle.

He spent the rest of the afternoon closely studying the area around the pool, figuring out exactly where he wanted to place the dynamite. He would start out using just one or two sticks of the explosive, he decided, in the hope that would create a big enough gap to provide a sufficient flow of water without diverting the whole stream.

Matt gathered wood and built a small fire near the pool, then put a pot of coffee on to boil while he got out a frying pan and a side of bacon. The horses had plenty of water, and there was even some grass growing along the edges of the pool so they could graze. It was a pleasant spot, no doubt about that.

"I wouldn't mind spending some time up here," Matt said as he fried up a mess of bacon. "There's probably some pretty good hunting in these hills. Might be some fish higher up in that stream, too."

"Maybe we'll come back here sometime," Smoke said.

"When we don't have to worry as much about bushwhackers?" Matt asked with a smile.

"I didn't see anybody on our trail today. That doesn't mean they weren't back there, though."

"I know."

Matt set the bacon aside and started mixing up some dough for biscuits. Both he and Smoke were being careful not to look directly into the fire. That would ruin a man's night vision quicker than anything, and darkness had descended around the camp with the suddenness it always displayed in the high country.

"Have you figured out where you're going to put the dynamite?" Matt asked.

Smoke nodded and said, "I think so. I'll have to use a pick to chip out a place for it, but that's all. The dynamite ought to do the rest of the work."

"That's fine with me. I swung a pick enough when the two of us were mining down in Colorado, when I was just a kid."

Smoke remembered those days. Back then, the tragedy that had wiped out Matt's family wasn't that far in the past. He'd been Matt Cavanaugh then, but he had put that name aside and taken the name Jensen when he was old enough to set out on his own. That was his way of declaring that he and Smoke were brothers, and Smoke had always been touched by the gesture.

Earlier this evening, when he unsaddled the horses, Smoke had taken the saddlebag containing the sticks of dynamite and draped it over a rock that was well away from the campfire. The explosive managed the difficult trick of being unstable and hard to set off, at the same time. If you dropped a stick of dynamite and it landed hard enough on a rock, it might blow. On the other hand, you could burn it without it going off, at least sometimes. It was hellish stuff, as Matt had said, but Smoke was confident that it would accomplish their goals.

If they got the chance to use it, which was suddenly in doubt because as Matt reached for the frying pan to put the uncooked biscuits he had formed into it, a bullet whipped past his head and ricocheted off the cast-iron pan with a sinister whine like the keening of a lost soul.

Chapter Thirty-three

Smoke and Matt reacted instantly and instinctively, throwing themselves in opposite directions away from the campfire. More shots blasted out as they rolled across the ground, out of the circle of light cast by the flames.

By the time Smoke came to a stop, his gun was already in his hand without him even having to think about it. He lay on his belly and searched the darkness for muzzle flashes.

Whoever had ambushed them had already stopped firing, though. The echoes of the shots rolled away over the hills, but no more reports followed.

"Did they tag you, Smoke?" Matt called softly from the shadows on the other side of the fire.

"Nope. You?"

"I'm fine," Matt replied. "I'm not sure that frying pan will ever be the same, though. And since I dropped my biscuits, I reckon they're probably ruined."

Smoke grinned in the darkness. Leave it to Matt to make light of nearly being drilled by a bushwhacker, he thought.

"You see where the shot came from?"

"Not really. I think it came from over my shoulder somewhere."

Smoke's instincts agreed with Matt's. That would put the gunman somewhere above them in the hills.

Gunmen, rather, because the shooting started again, but this time at least two guns were cracking as slugs clawed through the shadows, searching for Smoke and Matt.

Smoke winced as he realized that some of the shots were coming pretty close to those saddlebags he had placed on the rock, away from the fire. He had half a dozen sticks of dynamite in there, and if a bullet struck them, it might set off all six sticks. That would produce an explosion big enough to blow the pool to Kingdom Come and take Smoke and Matt along with it.

"Matt, I'm going to draw them off," Smoke said. "When I do, you grab the saddlebags with that dynamite and toss them up in the rocks as far as you can."

"Isn't that liable to set it off?"

"I don't think so. I wrapped them up pretty good. But if they do blow, I'd rather they were farther away from us."

"You and me both," Matt said. "What happens after that?"

"We work our way up there and see if we can find the buzzards," Smoke said grimly.

"I like the sound of that. Good luck."

"You, too."

Smoke took a deep breath, gathered himself, and suddenly surged to his feet. He ran upstream, crashing through the brush and emptying his Colt in the direction the shots were coming from. He saw orange spurts of muzzle flame winking at him and sensed as much as heard bullets sizzling through the air around his head.

Behind him, Matt lunged through the firelight, grabbed the saddlebags from the rock, and whirled around with his arm extended. When he let go, the saddlebags whipped through the air above the pool, spinning around and around and vanishing into the darkness.

Matt threw himself back into the shadows. He heard the thud as the saddlebags landed high in the rocks that formed the southern wall of the pool, but that was it. No explosion. He lay there for a minute, catching his breath, and then crawled away, taking a different angle up the hillside than the one Smoke had taken.

Smoke lay behind a tree and thumbed fresh cartridges into his gun. When all six chambers were filled, he moved again, but this time he didn't fire and he used all the stealth at his command not to make noise as he ghosted through the brush.

Rifle shots continued to crack, but after a moment the guns fell silent as the would-be killers realized they didn't have any targets anymore. Firing now just gave away their own position.

That was the beginning of a deadly game played in the dark as Smoke and Matt searched for the men who wanted to kill them. Since their eyes weren't much good under these circumstances, they relied on their ears and even on their noses. It was Smoke's sense of smell that finally led him to his quarry. He homed in on the harsh scent of tobacco that told him one of the men he was after was fond of cheap, three-for-a-nickel cheroots.

On his belly, he moved closer until he heard an urgent whisper.

"Where do you reckon they went?"

"How the hell do I know?" a second man answered. "I can't see in the dark."

"Well, neither can I, so I say we get outta here while we still can!"

"You want to go back to Kane and Yancy and tell 'em we failed? Hell, Dick's liable to beat us within an inch of our lives if we do that!"

"Maybe so, but that's Smoke and Matt Jensen down there! Won't be even an inch of our lives left if those two get hold of us."

He was right about that, Smoke thought with a faint smile. Although there was a chance he and Matt might let them live, if the opportunity arose.

"I wish Hubbard hadn't spotted 'em ridin' up

here," the first man went on. "Then Dick wouldn't have sent us after 'em."

That confirmed that Kane's men were still spying on the Rafter 9. The news didn't surprise Smoke at all. Kane would want to keep an eye on how things were progressing on the ranch, and from the sound of it, his men had standing orders to kill Smoke and Matt if they got the chance.

By nature, Smoke didn't sit back and wait for things to happen. He was more likely to take the fight right to his enemies. It was about time to do that with Jethro Kane, he thought.

First, though, he and Matt had to get out of this trap and deal with the job that had brought them up here into the hills. As far as he could tell, there were only two bushwhackers. It would be easy enough to get behind them and get the drop on them.

He was doing that when a horse suddenly let out a sharp whinny somewhere nearby. Something had spooked the animal. There was a racket in the brush.

One of Kane's men cursed while the other exclaimed, "The horses are loose! Grab 'em!"

Smoke seized the opportunity to take advantage of the situation. He lunged to his feet and started toward the men. With the horses causing such a commotion, they wouldn't hear him coming.

A dark figure loomed up in front of him. Smoke brought his gun crashing down on the man's head. At the same moment, a rifle went off. Several shots blasted from a revolver. That had to be Matt trading shots with the second man, Smoke thought.

A stray bullet could be just as dangerous as one that was aimed. Smoke dropped to one knee to make himself a smaller target. He put out a hand and felt for the man he had clouted. His fingers touched cloth. He followed the man's arm up to his shoulder. The hombre was on the ground where he had collapsed, out cold.

A man groaned and wheezed in the darkness.

"Somebody . . . help me!" he gasped. "Please!"

That was the second man, not Matt, and it didn't sound like he was pretending to be wounded. But a trick was always possible, so Smoke didn't move, didn't make a sound. Neither did Matt.

"Walt! You gotta . . . do somethin' . . . I'm shot . . . in the gut."

Smoke waited. It was a little nerve-wracking, kneeling there in the darkness while a few yards away a man gasped and groaned away what was left of his life. When Smoke heard the breath rattle for the last time in the man's throat, he knew it was over. No cheap gunman was that good an actor.

"Matt?" Smoke called. "Are you hit?"

"No, I'm fine," Matt's voice came back. "What about the other one?"

"I've got him right—" Smoke began as he reached down with his free hand to touch the man he had knocked out.

But before he could do that, something smashed

into his stomach with stunning force. He realized in that instant of pain that the man had been shamming and had just kicked him in the belly. Agony filled Smoke, and he couldn't get his breath. The gunman rolled, hitting his legs and knocking them out from under him.

"Smoke!" Matt yelled. He had to know something was wrong, but he couldn't start shooting because he didn't know where Smoke was.

Smoke tried to force himself back up, but the desperate blow had been powerful enough to almost paralyze him. His muscles didn't want to work. He made a grab for the bushwhacker but missed as the man struggled to his feet and lunged away.

"Get . . . him!" Smoke managed to call to Matt as the gunman went crashing downhill through the brush.

Matt didn't know how bad Smoke was hurt, and he wanted to go to his adopted brother. But Smoke had said to go after the other bushwhacker, the one that was getting away, and Matt thought he knew why.

If the man made it back to the Boxed JK and told Kane that Smoke and Matt were up here poking around the creek that turned into the underground stream that fed the springs on Kane's ranch . . .

Well, if that happened, Kane might be smart enough to figure out what was going on, and then it wouldn't matter that they were on land legally claimed by the Rafter 9. Kane would know that his water supply was in danger, and he would come storming up here with his whole crew of gun-wolves and do anything to stop Smoke from changing the course of the stream. So the fleeing bushwhacker had to be stopped.

Colt in hand, praying that Smoke was all right, Matt bounded down the slope after the gunman. He could track the man by the racket he made. Matt triggered a couple of shots after him, but that just seemed to make the man go faster. Matt wasn't surprised he hadn't hit anything, firing blindly in the dark like that.

The campfire he'd built earlier was still burning down by the pool. Matt saw it ahead of him. He was moving so fast he almost lost his balance and wound up skidding and sliding down toward the water. As he caught himself, he spotted the fleeing man on the other side of the pool, clambering over the rocks.

Matt lifted his Colt and fired, but at that moment the gunman tripped over something and went sprawling. The fall saved his life as Matt's bullet whined over his head. He came back up in a hurry, and now he had a revolver in one hand and in the other clutched the thing he had tripped over.

The saddlebags full of dynamite.

Matt was in the edge of the firelight, so the bushwhacker could see him. The man snapped a couple of frantic shots at him, one of which came close enough that Matt heard the bullet rip through the air near his head.

But he couldn't return the fire, because he might

hit the dynamite. Smoke wanted to place the explosive carefully, not just set off a huge blast.

"Drop that, you fool!" Matt yelled. "It's dynamite!"

The gunman looked down in horror at the saddlebags, then opened his hand and let go of them. In that instant, Matt thought that maybe he had made a mistake. Just because getting thrown around earlier hadn't set off the dynamite, that didn't mean a jolt now wouldn't do the job.

But the saddlebags thumped harmlessly to the ground at the man's feet.

With his pistol leveled, Matt ordered, "Drop your gun, mister! It's all over!"

For a second, he thought the man was going to do what he was told. But then the man's face twisted with anger and hatred, and he yelled, "Go to hell!"

His gun came up, flame gouting from its muzzle.

Matt crouched and returned the fire. He saw his opponent stagger as one of his slugs drove into the man's chest. Smoke might have wanted to take one of them alive, but things hadn't worked out that way. The man's gun arm sagged as he pressed his other hand to his chest and blood flowed over his fingers, an even deeper crimson than usual in the firelight.

But the man hadn't dropped his gun, and Matt's eyes widened as time seemed to slow down while the barrel tracked closer and closer to the leather bag lying among the rocks. The man hunched over as a death spasm went through him. Even though Matt was too far away to really see it, in his mind's eye he saw the man's finger contracting on the trigger . . .

"Ohhhh, hellllll!" Matt yelled as he threw himself backwards and scrambled away from the pool as fast as he could.

Hell was right. Flame licked from the barrel of the gun, and an instant later an earth-shaking explosion seemed to engulf the entire hillside.

Chapter Thirty-four

Smoke had made it to his feet. He probed his midsection gingerly and decided that nothing was broken and no lasting damage had been done to his guts. The kick had been hard enough to paralyze him momentarily, and he would probably have a big bruise on his belly, but that was all.

As he started down the hill, he heard gunfire below, along with Matt's shout. Smoke broke into a staggering run, eager to reach his brother and help Matt corral the other bushwhacker.

He had taken only a few steps when the earth jumped under his feet and sent him tumbling down the slope as a roar like the mightiest clap of thunder in history filled the night.

There was only one explanation for that, Smoke thought as he rolled over several times and came to a stop with his arms over his head to protect it from what he knew was coming.

All six sticks of dynamite had gone off at the same

time, creating a huge explosion. That blast would have thrown a lot of rocks and debris high into the air.

And what went up . . .

Smoke lowered his head and tried to bury it even deeper under his arms as chunks of rock began to pelt down around him like big, hard drops of rain. Some of them struck his arms, back, and legs, and although they stung like blazes, none of them were big enough to do any real harm. The stone wall around the pool must have been completely pulverized by the explosion.

Smoke didn't know how that had happened and didn't care. All he was worried about at the moment was how close Matt had been to the blast.

The echoes rolled away over the hills and gradually began to fade. Debris stopped falling from the sky. Smoke fought his way to his feet and started down the hill again.

"Matt!" he called. "Matt, where are you?"

There was no answer. Smoke Jensen wasn't a man given to fear, but right then, he was afraid for Matt.

As he approached the pool, the stench from the explosion filled the air along with a cloud of smoke and dust that made Smoke cough. The campfire was gone, blown out and scattered by the blast.

He heard a groan somewhere nearby, and the sound made his heart leap.

"Matt!" he shouted, then realized that if Matt had been this close to the explosion, he probably couldn't hear anything. The roar would have deafened him, at least temporarily.

Smoke dug a match out of his pocket and snapped it into life with his thumbnail. By the flickering glare, he spotted a couple of booted feet sticking out from under some blown-down aspens. Hoping that was Matt, Smoke hurried to the trees, shook out the match, and began pulling the broken trunks aside.

It didn't take long to uncover the man buried beneath them. Smoke struck another match. Relief flooded through him as the light revealed Matt's face. He was scratched and bloody but didn't seem to be badly hurt. Smoke got an arm around his shoulders and lifted him.

Matt groaned again. His eyes fluttered open, and he said, "Wha . . . wha' happen . . . ?"

"All that dynamite went off," Smoke told him. "You were almost caught in the explosion. From the looks of it, you made it into these trees, and they broke the force of the blast enough to save your life, even though they sort of buried you when they got blown over."

Matt blinked groggily at him.

"Stop whisperin' . . . Smoke . . . You sound like . . . you're so far away. . . ."

Smoke realized that Matt hadn't understood much of his explanation. Just as he had thought, Matt was partially deaf from the blast. But the fact that Matt could hear anything boded well. His hearing would probably come back.

"It's all right," Smoke said, raising his voice. "You'll be fine."

"That other bushwhacker . . ."

"Did he get away?"

"He was . . . standin' on top of . . . that dynamite . . . when it . . . when it . . ."

Matt couldn't go on. He was still too stunned to form the words.

"That's all right," Smoke told him. Matt had said enough. If the second gunman had been right on top of the dynamite when it went off, he wouldn't be hightailing it back to the Boxed JK to tell Jethro Kane what they were doing.

In fact, there wouldn't be enough left of the unlucky varmint to bury, or probably even to pick up.

Dawn revealed what the explosion had done.

The pool was gone. The blast had sprayed it all over the hillside, vaporizing it.

But the creek still flowed, and with the rock wall that had formed the pool destroyed, there was nothing to stop the water from running on downhill. It was flowing steadily toward the headquarters of the Rafter 9.

"Well, that wasn't exactly what I intended," Smoke said to Matt as they stood beside the stream watching it run. "But since it was one of Kane's men who was responsible for it, I'm not going to lose any sleep over it, either."

Matt had recovered from almost being caught in

the explosion. He was battered and bruised, even more so than Smoke, but his iron constitution would allow him to bounce back in a hurry. He still had a little echo in his ears at times, but his hearing was mostly all right.

"That's going to make a good creek for the baron," he said. "He may have to have his men dig out a channel for it here and there, but I think there's a good chance he can bring it right through the middle of his range."

"It'll make a big difference, all right," Smoke agreed.

"But Kane's liable to declare all-out war once he realizes what's happened."

Smoke nodded grimly.

"I know that, too. But if there's got to be a showdown, it's better to have it sooner rather than later. If Friedrich's going to build this ranch into something and start himself a town, too, he doesn't need the shadow of a range war hanging over him."

"I guess we'd better let him know what's happened."

Their horses had been far enough away from the blast that they hadn't been injured, although the explosion had spooked them and made them run off. The animals were used to gunfire, so it took a lot to make them skittish. Six sticks of dynamite going off definitely qualified. Smoke had found them without much trouble, though, and brought them back to the former site of the pool where he and Matt had camped.

The two men mounted up now and started toward the Rafter 9 headquarters. They were leaving the other bushwhacker's body for the scavengers.

"Do you think that hombre meant to pull the trigger and set off the dynamite?" Smoke asked Matt as they rode.

"I don't know," Matt replied with a shake of his head. "He might have. Maybe he figured he could take me to hell with him. Or maybe he just jerked the trigger involuntarily as he was dying. I've seen that happen plenty of times."

So had Smoke. All it took was for nerves and muscles to contract as the death throes went through a man.

"I don't reckon we'll ever know for sure," Matt went on.

"No," Smoke agreed, "and it doesn't matter, either. Kane's lost two more men and a big part of his water supply. That's what's important."

They followed the new course that the creek was carving out for itself. From the amount of water that was flowing, Smoke figured the explosion must have closed off the underground route, possibly for good. All that water had to go somewhere, and geography dictated that it was going toward the Rafter 9 headquarters.

The new creek took some twists and turns along the way and formed some new pools here and there that would serve as waterholes for the stock that von Hoffman would run on his range. Smoke and Matt soon outdistanced the water, which would take time to work its way across the ranch. But it was coming, and it was going to make all the difference in the world, Smoke thought.

They came in sight of the ranch house and the outbuildings at mid-morning. Preacher rode out to meet them. Not surprisingly, the keen-eyed old mountain man had spotted the two riders approaching.

"What in tarnation happened up there last night?" Preacher demanded as he turned his horse and fell in alongside Smoke and Matt. "We heard what sounded like thunder, but there weren't a cloud in the sky! Matt, you look like somebody's been beatin' you with a stick."

"Something like that," Matt said. "Only it wasn't a stick, it was half a dozen aspen trees."

"What in blazes are you talkin' about?"

Smoke said, "That 'thunder' you heard was really half a dozen sticks of dynamite going off, Preacher."

"Jehosaphat! Did you set it off on purpose?"

"Well . . . not really. But it did the job we set out to do. Did it even better than I intended, in fact."

"You turned that crick in this direction?"

Smoke nodded.

"In a few days, the baron will have a nice little stream running right across his ranch. It ought to give him all the water he needs for his herds."

"That's mighty fine news," Preacher said. "And here he comes, so you can tell him all about it."

Von Hoffman was riding hurriedly toward them. Smoke lifted a hand in greeting and edged his horse ahead to meet the baron.

"That's not all of it," Matt said quietly to Preacher.

"Figured as much. What else happened up yonder in the hills?"

"Two of Kane's men tried to kill us again. They're both dead."

Preacher's snort made it clear he didn't regard that as a surprise.

"And the blast totally changed the course of the creek that fed that underground stream," Matt went on. "It's not running under the Boxed JK anymore."

"Which means that Kane's waterholes are liable to dry up," Preacher said.

"I think there's a good chance of it," Matt agreed.

"Which means he's liable to be mad enough to forget about doin' things legal-like and come after the baron and his folks with all guns blazin'."

"I wouldn't be a bit surprised," Matt said.

Chapter Thirty-five

Smoke figured Baron Friedrich von Hoffman wasn't the sort of hombre who let his mouth hang open in amazement . . . but the baron came close to that when Smoke told him what had happened in the hills.

"Let me make sure I understand," the baron said. "There will be water flowing across my land?"

"That's right," Smoke said. "You'll probably have to dig a few ditches here and there to direct it, but the general way it's flowing will bring it down here."

"And take water away from Herr Kane?"

"Yep."

Von Hoffman threw back his head and laughed.

"That's incredible!" he said. "How in the world did you accomplish such a thing?"

"Luck and half a dozen sticks of dynamite," Smoke said.

He explained what had happened up in the hills. While he was doing that, Erica, Dieter, and several more of the immigrants gathered around to listen. Some of them hurried off to tell their friends and families, and the word began to spread quickly around the ranch.

Dieter grinned, put his arm around Erica's shoulders, and said, "This is the best durned news we had in a coon's age, *ja?*"

Smoke returned the grin.

"I reckon so," he said.

Von Hoffman didn't look so happy about Dieter embracing his cousin, Smoke noticed, but the baron didn't say anything about that. The news was too good to ruin it with recriminations.

But von Hoffman was smart enough to know that this development had other implications. He grew solemn and said, "We should double our guard."

Smoke nodded and said, "That's a good idea. Kane might have been willing to wait you out before. His real grudge was against Matt, Preacher, and me. That's all changed now."

"I will issue orders for the men to be armed at all times."

That afternoon, Smoke and Matt took von Hoffman and some of the other men up into the hills to check on the progress of the water. The initial force from the pent-up pool being released was long gone, but the new creek still had a steady flow to it. The water followed the path of least resistance, as it was bound to do, so that meant it serpentined back and forth quite a bit, but its general direction of flow was still toward the ranch headquarters.

"Might have to build you a levee to keep the buildings from being flooded," Matt said with a smile. "I'll bet that wasn't something you were worried about a day or two ago."

"No," von Hoffman admitted. "I never dreamed I would see that day. I cannot express my gratitude toward the both of you."

"Save your thanks until things are settled with Kane," Smoke suggested. "Klaus Berger is still out there somewhere, too."

"I have not forgotten him," the baron said grimly. "And I assure you, Herr Jensen . . . he has not forgotten us."

Jethro Kane was at the big desk in his office when Dick Yancy appeared in the open doorway and said, "We got a problem, boss."

Kane glanced up from the ledger where he was entering figures and glared. He didn't like being disturbed while he was working, and he sure didn't like hearing the word "problem" from any of the men who rode for him.

"What is it?" he asked harshly.

"Walt and Lee followed those two Jensens up into the hills along the northern boundary of the Rafter Nine yesterday afternoon."

"I know that," Kane snapped. "Let me guess. They came back and said that the Jensens got away."

Yancy shook his head.

"They didn't come back at all, boss. We never saw

hide nor hair of 'em since they rode out. So I sent Jim Hubbard and a couple of other men up there to look for them."

Kane slapped the ledger closed, rested both meaty hands palms down on the desk, and pushed himself to his feet. Struggling to contain the angry impatience he felt, he barked, "Get on with it!"

"They found Lee. He was dead. Gutshot. Found both of their horses wanderin' around. But no sign of Walt."

Alarm shot through Kane.

"The Jensens may have taken him prisoner."

"Could be," Yancy agreed, "but that ain't the worst of it."

"Well, spit it out, for God's sake!"

"Something happened to that creek. Instead of going underground where it formed that pool, it's runnin' down across the Rafter Nine now. The pool's gone."

Thunderstruck, Kane sagged back into his chair. What Yancy had just told him was impossible. The Boxed JK depended on the springs fed by that underground stream. Without them, the waterholes would dry up, and without the waterholes . . .

Without the waterholes, he was ruined, Kane thought.

"How?" he managed to say. "How is that even possible?"

"Hubbard said it looked like they dynamited the place. Blew up the pool and set the water free to form an actual creek on the Rafter Nine."

"No." Kane shook his head. "No, it can't be."

"I'm about to ride up there and see for myself," Yancy said. "Want me to have the boys saddle a horse for you so you can come along with me?"

Kane stood up again. He was still stunned by the news, but anger was beginning to replace some of the shock.

"Damned right I do," he said. "I want to see this with my own eyes."

"It'll mean goin' onto that foreigner's range."

"I don't give a damn about that!" Kane bellowed. "Pick out a dozen men to ride with us! And tell them to be ready to fight!"

Jim Hubbard was one of the men who accompanied Kane and Yancy to the former location of the pool. He was the lean, dark-faced man with the occasional wracking cough of a consumptive. As he sat his saddle with the others, he pointed and said, "Right there is where the pool used to be, Mr. Kane. Reckon we should've put a guard on it to make sure nothing like this ever happened."

Kane stared in horror and dismay at the creek flowing merrily through the huge, gaping hole in the rocks. He had seen the results of a dynamite blast before, back in his mining days, and he knew that's what he was looking at now.

"It's a little late to be considering that now, don't you think, Hubbard?" he said.

"Sorry, boss," Hubbard muttered. "You're right.

But when the Rafter Nine was abandoned, there wasn't any need, and since those foreigners came in . . . Well, I guess nobody even thought about it."

Kane turned his head to glare at Yancy, Hubbard, and the other men. He wanted to roar curses at them, but he knew it wouldn't do any good. He knew, as well, that the blame here actually lay with him. He should have ordered them to post guards around the spot where the creek went underground.

But like he had told Hubbard, it was too late now.

"Can we dam it, change its course somehow?" he asked.

Yancy shook his head.

"It misses Boxed JK range by three or four hundred yards, boss. The whole thing is on Rafter Nine now. Unless you want to go all the way up to the headwaters and block it off there. But that's on government land, and it's against the law to go messin' with a water supply there."

Kane wanted to yank the derby off his head and slap Yancy across his big boulder of a jaw with it. Instead he said in a quiet but menacing voice, "Bushwhacking's against the law, too, but that hasn't stopped us in the past, has it?"

Yancy shrugged burly shoulders.

"If I have to, I'll bring that engineer back in, and we'll figure out a way to turn the water at its source," Kane went on. "But before I go to that much trouble, I want to find out just how stubborn that damned German is." He took a deep breath. "Make his life miserable, Dick. Make life a living hell for him and his people for a while, and then we'll see whether or not he'll sell out . . . at my price."

"And if he won't?" Yancy asked.

"This is a hard land," Kane said. "A violent land. And a man who just won't adapt to it . . . well, he won't survive."

The new creek missed the ranch headquarters, but not by much, maybe half a mile. A few days after the explosion, Smoke, Matt, and Preacher sat on their horses next to the stream and watched it flowing. Von Hoffman, Erica, and Dieter were with them. Erica and Dieter were practically inseparable these days.

"You're gonna have to give it a name," Preacher said. "You can't just keep on callin' it 'the creek.'"

"I have the perfect name for it," Erica said. "We will call it Jensen Creek."

The baron said, "I was thinking it should be something to honor our German heritage."

"But this stream would not exist if not for Smoke and Matt," Erica argued.

With a shrug, von Hoffman gave in.

"Jensen Creek it is," he declared. "But the town will still be called New Holtzberg."

"Of course," Erica said.

"Rider coming," Matt announced.

They turned their horses, and Smoke, Matt, and Preacher moved their mounts so that they were between the others and the man riding toward them.

Since it was just one horseman, Smoke didn't think the man represented much of a threat, and that was confirmed a minute later when the rider came close enough for Smoke to recognize him.

"That's Wynn Courtland," he said.

The young cowboy who owned the Double Diamond came up to them and reined in to stare at the creek.

"I don't believe it," he said. "I heard about this, but I swore I wouldn't believe it unless I saw it with my own eyes. How do you conjure up a creek out of thin air?"

"Easy as pie," Matt said. "All you have to do is come within a whisker of getting yourself blown to smithereens by a bunch of dynamite."

Wynn shook his head in amazement.

"Well, I'm glad to see it, however you managed it," he said. "Does Kane know about this?"

"He's bound to, by now," Smoke said.

"We ain't seen no signs of him or his gunnies, though," Preacher added.

"You will," Wynn predicted. "Kane's not gonna let this stand."

"We'll be ready for him if he makes trouble," von Hoffman declared. "Herr Kane may as well realize that we're here to stay."

"To do that, you'll need cows," Wynn pointed out. "There's an auction down in Laramie in a couple of days. That's another reason I rode over here, to let you know about that. You'll need to start putting together a herd before it gets any later in the year."

"An excellent idea," von Hoffman said. "Will you be attending this auction, Herr Courtland?"

"Me? No, I've got all the stock I can handle on my little spread."

"I'll go with you, Baron," Smoke said. "Matt and Preacher can stay here and keep an eye on things while we're gone."

"Dang it, I wouldn't have minded a trip to town," Matt complained.

"Next time," Smoke told him with a smile. "Kane's bound to try something soon, and like the baron says, we need to be ready when he does."

Chapter Thirty-six

Greta Schiller paced back and forth in the room she had managed to convince the baron to give her on the second floor of the ranch house. She wanted to stay close to him, and since she had no real skills or any place in the community of immigrants, she hoped to persuade him that they should marry. A baron needed a baroness, after all.

If it came to that. He was surrounded by enemies now, after all. That man Kane wanted him dead, Greta suspected. And Klaus Berger was still out there somewhere. At least she hoped he was. Berger would not want to disappoint their shared masters back in Germany. If he never showed up, that had to mean he had been wounded in one of the attacks on the wagon train and might even be dead now.

Greta had been close to von Hoffman often enough that she could have assassinated him several times already, if she had chosen to do so. But she would have to risk her own freedom, indeed, her very life, if she killed him, and she was only going to do that as a last resort. It was better that Klaus Berger or Jethro Kane or someone else killed the baron. That way Greta's hands would be clean, and the baron's enemies in Germany wouldn't care who killed him, only that he was dead.

When Greta came downstairs one evening, she found Erica sitting in the parlor with young Dieter Schumann. The simpering little fool was in love with the boy, Greta thought. Anyone could see that. Erica had enjoyed a mild flirtation with Matt Jensen, but in the end she had chosen the man who was more familiar to her, the man with whom she had more in common, which didn't surprise Greta. Erica had no adventurous streak. She wasn't willing to risk anything to gain a reward.

Erica and Dieter were sitting close together on a large, overstuffed divan. They moved apart as Greta entered the room. They probably wouldn't have been so intimate if Erica's cousin had been around.

"Where's Friedrich?" Greta asked.

"You didn't hear?" Erica asked, seeming genuinely puzzled.

"Hear what? I've been resting in my room."

Greta didn't bother trying to keep the irritation out of her voice. There was nothing to do in this godforsaken wilderness, so she wound up sleeping more than she ever had in her life.

"Friedrich has gone to Laramie with Smoke Jensen," Erica explained. "They're going to buy cattle for the ranch."

Greta's perfectly plucked eyebrows arched.

"Really?" she said. She was a little surprised and angered that he hadn't said good-bye to her before he left.

Erica nodded and went on, "That's right. They took several of the men with them to drive the cattle back here." She smiled. "Smoke says that he'll make cowboys out of them."

"I wanted to go along," Dieter put in, "but Smoke didn't think I had recovered quite enough from my injuries yet. I think I'll make a good cowpoke soon, though."

Smoke, Smoke, Smoke, Greta thought bitterly. Von Hoffman would be dead by now and the wagon train destroyed if not for that meddling American, Smoke Jensen, and his two friends or whatever they were to him. Berger would have wiped them all out, and she would have been free to return to a new life in Germany, a life of luxury and power. She had her sights set on the circle of men who wanted the baron dead, and she was sure it wouldn't take long for her to achieve her goal of becoming the mistress to one of them.

"How long will he be gone?"

"Several days," Erica said. "Friedrich wasn't sure, and neither was Smoke."

Greta nodded. Her hands were tied as long as the baron wasn't here. She might as well go back up to her room, she thought, and get some more rest whether she needed it or not. She turned toward the stairs, which were made out of logs split in half, then sanded and polished, but she hadn't yet started up them when a commotion of some sort erupted outside. Men shouted in the darkness. . . .

And then guns began to blaze.

Matt and Preacher had been staying in the bunkhouse with a number of the single men from the wagon train. Some of those men had gone with Smoke and the baron to Laramie, so there were empty bunks tonight. The men who remained were playing cards and talking in German, a lingo that the two Americans hadn't managed to pick up to any great extent, although Preacher claimed he was getting to where he could cuss pretty good in it. So they were sitting out on the steps instead, talking quietly while Preacher smoked a pipe.

"You know, it's a funny thing," the old mountain man said, "but I don't feel a whole lot older than I did when I first come out here."

"How's that possible?" Matt asked. "You're as old as the hills."

"And you ain't the least bit respectful of your elders, not to mention your betters," Preacher groused. "I got all the aches and pains you'd think I would, but I'm talkin' about inside. Inside I reckon I'm as young as I ever was. Hell, sometimes I think I'm gettin' younger! I can't stop thinkin' about goin' places I never been and seein' things I never seen before.."

"I didn't know there was any place you hadn't been."

"Bound to be some. And by Godfrey, I'm gonna find 'em all before I'm done."

Matt smiled and said, "You know what, Preacher? I believe you will. I sure do believe—"

He stopped short and lifted his head.

"You smell something?"

"If you're gonna gripe about this pipe tobacco o' mine—"

"No, that's not it," Matt said. "I've smelled this before, and not that awful long ago. That night on the prairie south of here. That's kerosene, Preacher!"

Both men came quickly to their feet. It wasn't unusual to smell kerosene around a ranch, of course. All the lamps and lanterns used it as fuel.

But to smell it this strongly meant that quite a bit was being splashed around, and that was never good. There wasn't much breeze tonight, but what there was came from the direction of the barn.

Matt and Preacher broke into a run toward the big building. As they came closer the reek of kerosene grew stronger, confirming Matt's hunch.

Somebody was up to no good.

They pounded around the corner of the barn and saw several shadowy figures.

"Hold it!" Matt yelled as his Colt came out of its holster.

A match flared to life. Matt didn't wait. He shot the man holding it.

The man flew backwards under the impact of

Matt's bullet. The match in his fingers went high in the air as he flung his arms up. Matt snapped a shot at the bit of flame as it arched above pools of kerosene spread over the ground at the back of the barn.

The match winked out as the slug from Matt's gun destroyed the burning head.

It was the sort of shot that legends were made of, but there was no time right now to even think about things like that. There were three more skulkers behind the barn, and all of them yanked their guns out and opened fire on Matt and Preacher. Preacher proved he could curse in German by bellowing guttural obscenities as he crouched and returned the fire.

Matt knew there was no time to waste. He and Preacher had to keep those three men so busy they wouldn't have time to strike any more matches. He couldn't count on making another miraculous shot to keep the barn from going up in flames.

The gun in his hand still roared and bucked as he dove forward. One of the would-be arsonists staggered and would have fallen if another man hadn't grabbed his arm to steady him.

"Let's get out of here!" the third man yelled.

The first man Matt had shot wasn't dead and didn't even appear to be mortally wounded. He lurched to his feet and joined his companions in fleeing. They sprayed enough lead around that Matt was forced to keep his head down and Preacher had to duck back around the corner of the barn.

Then they were gone, their footsteps pounding on the ground as they ran off into the shadows.

Matt scrambled up and would have gone after him, but Preacher holstered one of his guns and grabbed the younger man's arm.

"Hold on," the old-timer said. "Let 'em go. We stopped 'em from burnin' down the barn, and that's the main thing."

"That doesn't sound like you, Preacher," Matt said. "Usually you're breathing fire even more than Smoke and me."

"We got that kerosene to deal with," Preacher pointed out. "And listen."

Matt heard rapid hoofbeats dwindling into the darkness.

"They already made it back to their horses," Preacher went on. "It ain't likely we could'a caught 'em."

"No, I guess not," Matt admitted.

The shots had drawn most of the men from the bunkhouse. They came on the run, carrying rifles and pistols and shotguns.

"Hold your fire!" Matt called, not wanting any of the greenhorns to get trigger-happy. "It's me and Preacher. The varmints we were after have already gotten away."

Dieter had come from the ranch house to join the other men. He stepped out in front of them and asked, "What happened, Matt?"

"Some hombres tried to burn down the barn, but Preacher and I stopped them," Matt explained. He knew what a close call it had been. If the two of them had been inside the bunkhouse instead of sitting outside, he almost certainly would not have smelled the kerosene in time.

He went on, "Get some shovels. Once the kerosene has soaked into the ground, put more dirt on top of it. It won't be a danger to anybody that way."

Dieter took charge of that chore. While the men were tending to it, Preacher got a lantern from the barn and said, "We best take a look around, Matt. There were guards posted, and somethin' could've happened to them."

The same grim thought had already occurred to Matt. He and Preacher moved well away from the barn before he struck a match and lit the lantern. Then, with the lantern in one hand and his Colt in the other, he led the search for the guards.

A few minutes, he and Preacher found what Matt had hoped they wouldn't. One of the guards, a young man named Rolf Heisse, lay dead on the ground with a stab wound in his back. From the looks of it, somebody had buried a Bowie knife in his heart.

"Blast it," Matt said. "I was afraid they had killed at least one of the guards. They came through here to get to the barn."

"Yeah. Kane's men, you reckon?"

"I'd bet a hat on it."

"Could have been Berger's bunch," Preacher speculated.

"We can't rule it out," Matt agreed, "but this

doesn't seem like something Berger would do. Anyway, he hasn't made a move against the baron in several weeks."

"Nope, but that don't mean he's given up."

"True. This just seems more like something Kane would do. I expected him to try something before now, since Smoke and I dried up his water. Hell, I halfway expected him to gather up an army of gunmen and attack the ranch right out in the open."

"This might be the first move," Preacher said. "And if it is, you can bet that hat o' yours it won't be the last."

Chapter Thirty-seven

The German immigrants took to driving cattle sooner and better than Smoke thought they might. He had his hands full showing them what to do and making sure they did it correctly, but they were hard workers and managed to keep the cattle moving toward the Rafter 9. Even the baron pitched in and did his share, riding back and forth and eating dust like the rest of the men without complaining about it.

Von Hoffman had bought two hundred head of stock at the auction in Laramie. They weren't prime animals, but they weren't too bad. They ought to be good breeding stock, Smoke thought, and with time and hard work, they would form the core of a fine herd. As long as the weather cooperated with enough rain and no terribly harsh winters, in a few years the baron's ranch could be one of the best in this part of the country.

As they approached the ranch headquarters,

Smoke told von Hoffman, "We'll let them graze in those pastures on the other side of the new creek. There's enough grass there to support a small herd like this, and it ought to just get better now that there's water."

The baron nodded and said, "I agree." He lifted a hand to shade his eyes from the sun as he peered toward the ranch buildings in the distance. "I haven't seen anyone moving around. I thought perhaps someone might come to greet us—"

The whine of a bullet over his head made him stop short and instinctively duck lower in the saddle.

Smoke yanked his Winchester from its sheath and twisted around to search for the source of the shot. More guns went off, and the cattle began to run. Through the clouds of dust kicked up by their hooves, Smoke caught a glimpse of several riders with bandannas masking their faces galloping toward the herd, whooping and firing six-guns.

Smoke knew there was a fairly deep gully a couple of hundred yards off to their right. He figured the masked men had been hiding there, waiting for the herd to come along so they could stampede it and ambush the drovers.

Kicking his horse into a run, Smoke headed for the front of the herd. He was going to try to turn it and stop the stampede before it reached the ranch headquarters. Even two hundred head of stock could do a considerable amount of damage if they were running unchecked.

One of the masked men charged at him. Smoke

rammed his rifle back in the saddle boot and drew his Colt instead. As a bullet whipped past his ear, he fired and saw the masked man rock back in the saddle. The man was able to stay on his horse, but he was hunched over in pain as his mount flashed past Smoke's.

More hoofbeats pounding close by made Smoke glance to his right. He saw von Hoffman riding there, grim-faced as he tried to help Smoke turn the herd.

As the two of them reached the leaders, they crowded their horses against the bolting steers. A misstep now by either of the horses would be fatal. If Smoke or the baron fell, the hooves of the herd would pound and chop them into something that didn't even resemble a human being anymore.

The leaders veered away from the riders. Smoke and von Hoffman kept prodding them to turn even more. Suddenly, the herd was milling instead of running. They had succeeded in blunting the stampede.

But that still left the men who had caused it. As the cattle began slowing to a stop, Smoke and von Hoffman galloped around the herd. Through the dust, Smoke caught a glimpse of the masked men fleeing now that their efforts had failed. He charged after them with his gun roaring in his hand. Von Hoffman was right behind him.

The men they were pursuing turned in their saddles and flung shots at them. Smoke leaned forward over the neck of his straining horse to make himself a smaller target. He holstered his gun as he saw that one of the masked men had fallen behind the others. He urged his mount on to greater speed and closed in on the straggler.

The man twisted in the saddle and fired a couple of frantic shots at Smoke. The bullets missed, and then Smoke was in reach of the gunman. He kicked his feet free of the stirrups and launched himself out of the saddle in a diving tackle that drove the masked man off his horse. Both of them crashed hard to the ground, but Smoke managed to land on top so the impact wasn't quite so stunning.

The fall knocked the breath out of the masked man, but desperation made him fight even though he was gasping for air. He writhed in Smoke's grasp and drove an elbow against Smoke's chest. That gave him enough room to throw a punch that grazed Smoke's ear.

Smoke responded with a hard left that he hooked into the man's stomach. He followed that with a right to the jaw. That was enough to take all the fight out of the man. He sagged limply on the ground.

Von Hoffman had brought his horse to a stop. He lifted his rifle to his shoulder and fired several rounds after the fleeing gunmen as they disappeared over the top of a hill.

The baron lowered his Winchester and started to go after them, but Smoke called, "Wait a minute! If you go charging over that hill alone, they're liable to double back and ambush you. Let them go."

"Let them go?" von Hoffman repeated angrily. "They attacked me and my men!"

"I know that, but we've got this one." Smoke was on his feet now with his gun out again, covering the man he had battered into semi-consciousness. "Not only that, but we need to get back and see if any of your other men are hurt."

Von Hoffman caught his breath.

"You're right," he said as he turned his horse. "Can you handle this man?"

"Go ahead," Smoke told him. "I'll be along with the prisoner."

Von Hoffman galloped toward the still-milling herd. Smoke reached down with his free hand, grabbed the man's shirt collar, and hauled the groggy bushwhacker to his feet.

"Don't try anything else, mister," Smoke warned the prisoner. "I'll blow one of your knees apart if I have to. You won't ever walk right again, let alone ride a horse."

The man just glared at him. His bandanna mask had slipped down, revealing the dark, narrow face of one of the hired guns who had been with Kane that first day at Hawk Creek Station.

"Go to hell," the man spat.

"You'll be there before me," Smoke promised. "Get on your horse."

He kept the man covered while they mounted up and started back toward the herd. As they approached, Smoke's mouth tightened into a grim line when he saw a couple of huddled shapes lying motionless on the ground. Von Hoffman had dismounted and was standing near them.

The baron looked up at Smoke and said, "These men were shot!"

Smoke recognized them as two of the men he and the baron had taken along to drive the cattle back from Laramie.

"That makes it murder," Smoke said in a flat, hard voice as he pointed his gun at the man he had captured. "And this hombre's going to tell the law who was responsible for it."

"You can go to—" the man started to say.

"Shut up," Smoke said. "I'm in no mood to hear it, mister. Your testimony is going to put Jethro Kane behind bars, but all you have to be able to do is talk."

The prisoner seemed to understand the implication of Smoke's statement. He shut up.

Smoke glanced toward the ranch headquarters and saw a couple of men on horseback riding toward them. A moment later he recognized Matt and Preacher.

"It's sure good to see you, Smoke," Matt said as he and the old mountain man reined in. "When we heard the shooting we figured Kane's men might have jumped the herd."

"They did," Smoke said. "Where's everybody else? I didn't see anybody moving around the ranch."

"That's because everybody's lyin' low," Preacher

said. "Anybody who sticks his head out is liable to get it shot off."

"What in blazes are you talking about?"

"It's true, Smoke," Matt said. "We've been under siege for several days now. It started with Kane's men trying to burn down the barn. We managed to stop them from doing that, but ever since then they've been up in the hills taking potshots at us, keeping us pinned down in the main house and the bunkhouse. They've busted out all the windows and put bullet holes in most of the walls."

Anger boiled up inside Smoke.

"We'd better get these cattle across the creek and into that pasture while the varmints aren't shooting at us," he said. "Baron, you take the prisoner back to the house and make sure he's locked up tight. The smokehouse would be a good place to hold him. And you, mister, you better keep your head down. Kane's already had one man killed so he couldn't testify against him. He won't mind doing the same to you."

Calling orders to the drovers, Smoke got the cattle moving again. Matt and Preacher helped, and it didn't take long to push the small herd across the creek into the pasture.

"How many casualties so far?" Smoke asked while they were working.

"Three men killed, including a guard the night they tried to burn down the barn," Matt replied. "Five more wounded. All those pilgrims are mighty scared, Smoke, and I don't blame them. They've been under fire before, but they've never been through a siege like this."

"We're going to put a stop to it," Smoke declared.

"How do you figure on doin' that?" Preacher asked.

"The same way we always do," Smoke said. "Once it gets too dark for bushwhacking, the three of us are going to take a ride over to the Boxed JK and raise some hell of our own!"

Chapter Thirty-eight

No one shot at Smoke, Matt, and Preacher as they returned to the ranch house. Smoke thought that maybe starting the stampede had been the culmination of Kane's plan, and when that hadn't worked, the hired guns had pulled back to regroup and come up with some other scheme.

Smoke didn't intend to give them very long to think about it.

First, though, he wanted to check on the situation at the ranch. As Matt had said, three men had been killed and several wounded. Everyone else, men, women, and children alike, were crowded into the ranch house and the bunkhouse, both of which were sturdy enough to stop most of the bullets fired at them. Shutters had been closed over the broken windows that were equipped with them, and boards were nailed up over the windows that didn't have shutters. That was better than nothing.

Late that afternoon, there was a council of war in

the parlor of the main house. Smoke, Matt, and Preacher were there, along with von Hoffman, Dieter, Rudolph Wolff, and several of the other men.

"The three of us are going to hit Kane's ranch tonight," Smoke explained. "We probably can't do enough damage to stop him, but that should keep him distracted for a little while. That'll give you time to send a couple of men to Cheyenne, Baron."

"Why should I do that?" von Hoffman asked. "Don't we need every gun we have?"

"There's a U.S. Marshal in Cheyenne," Smoke said. "The law's on your side, especially now that you've got a prisoner who can testify as to what Kane's been doing in these parts."

Preacher let out a disgusted snort and said, "Never thought I'd hear you sayin' we got to depend on the law, Smoke. You must'a been around that dang Monte Carson too much. What we oughta do is go over there and clean out that mess o' hydrophobia skunks!"

"That's exactly what I'd do if we had Louis Longmont, Johnny North, Silver Jim, and some of those other old-timers with us, Preacher," Smoke said. "But Kane's got a small army of hired guns, and we've got . . ."

"Go ahead and say it," von Hoffman said as Smoke's voice trailed off. "You have a bunch of immigrants who don't know what they're doing."

"I don't mean any offense, Baron, and I'm not doubting the heart and spirit of you and your men. When it comes to defending the ranch, I'm sure you'll all fight like blazes. But you wouldn't be any match for Kane's men in a straight-up gunfight."

Von Hoffman sighed and nodded.

"What you say is true," he admitted.

"Yeah," Preacher grumbled, "I reckon it is. But I still don't like havin' to depend on the law."

"We'll work with what we've got," Matt said.

"And it might be over by the time those men get back from Cheyenne with the marshal and a posse of deputies," Smoke pointed out. "When we hit Kane, it's liable to be like poking a bear. He might just saddle up and come storming over here with every man he's got. In that case—"

"We will be ready for them," the baron said as he clenched one hand into a fist.

"That's just what I was thinking," Smoke said with a smile and a nod.

Jethro Kane seethed inside as he listened to his foreman explain what had happened. After a couple of minutes, Kane stopped Dick Yancy with a curt gesture and said, "So what you're telling me is that you failed again."

"We've kept those foreigners pinned down for days now, boss," Yancy protested. "Stampeding that herd when Jensen and the baron got back from Laramie was a good idea, but it just didn't pan out. Jensen's too damned fast, and I don't just mean on the draw. I've never seen anybody who can figure out how to meet every threat as quick as he does."

Kane sneered and said, "You can go work for him if you think that highly of him."

Yancy's face darkened with anger.

"That's not what I'm sayin', and you know it, Mr. Kane. Any time you want me to take the men and go over there to roust them all out and kill 'em, you just give me the word."

"I'm not sure we have enough men left to do that," Kane snapped.

"Then let me send word to Cheyenne," Yancy suggested. "I can have another ten or twelve men out here in a few days. Good men who know how to fight."

Kane pondered that idea. It was tempting, and those immigrants deserved to be wiped out. Stealing his water like that was the last straw. The level of his waterholes was already starting to drop. In another week or so, the situation would become desperate.

"Do it," he growled. "Send for more men. I'm tired of pussyfooting around with those European bastards."

"There's one more thing," Yancy said hesitantly.

"Spit it out," Kane told him.

"Jim Hubbard didn't make it back from the Rafter Nine."

"So?" Kane shrugged. "Jensen probably killed him."

Yancy shook his head.

"One of the boys says he thought he saw Jensen tackle him and knock him off his horse. Hubbard could be their prisoner. They might figure on using him as a hostage."

A short bark of laughter came from Kane.

"If they try to bargain for the life of one man, and a cheap gunman, at that, they're going to be disappointed. I don't give a damn what happens to Hubbard."

Yancy's eyes narrowed.

"I won't tell the boys you said that. They wouldn't care much for it. Hubbard's one of us. But I get your point. What I was worried about was if they tried to get him to talk to the law. We already got rid of one fella who wound up in that situation, and the men didn't like that very much, either."

"All right, I see your point," Kane said. "If they have him, we'll set him free when we wipe out that bunch. If he's already dead, then we don't have to worry about him, do we?"

"I reckon not." Yancy turned to leave the office. "I'll send a rider to Cheyenne right now."

"Do that," Kane said. "And don't waste any time about it."

He waited until Yancy was gone, then stood up and went over to a bar built into one corner of the room. He picked up a crystal decanter that was half-full of brandy and poured himself a glass of the smooth but fiery liquor. It warmed his throat going down and kindled a small blaze in his belly.

Kane didn't take much comfort from that. He couldn't forget how he had been well on his way to getting everything he wanted. His grip on this area was almost secure, with only a few holdouts like Wynn Courtland and old Case Plowright still holding on to their ranches. It was only a matter of time until he squeezed them out, as well.

All he needed to do was put some pressure on Clarence Fisher at the trading post, and Fisher would stop selling supplies to them. And with the contacts he had in Laramie and Cheyenne, it wouldn't be difficult to make sure that Courtland and Plowright no longer got top prices for their stock when they drove them to market.

Kane had started out as a young man getting what he wanted with his fists. When that didn't work, a sap or a knife or a gun did the trick. That ruthlessness had helped him rise in the gangs in New York, until the law had finally cracked down too hard and he had hopped on a freight out of town just in time to avoid being jailed.

Since then he had worked in the mines and driven freight wagons and anything else he had to do in order to survive out here on the frontier, and over time he had become a wealthy man. The Boxed JK was his bid for real wealth, real power. He was damned if he was going to let a couple of gunfighters, an old mountain man, and a foreigner take it away from him!

He wasn't sure how much time he spent brooding about that. All he knew was that at some point he had taken the brandy and the glass back to the desk with him, and he was slumped there nursing another drink when Dick Yancy knocked on the office door and said, "Boss?"

Kane sat up straight and scrubbed a hand over his face. He shoved the nearly empty decanter aside and growled, "What is it?"

"There's a fella here who wants to see you."

"Well, damn it, I don't want to see anybody! Send him away!"

"I really think you ought to talk to him," Yancy persisted. "He says he's got something to do with that baron hombre over on the Rafter Nine."

What the hell was this about, Kane wondered? Only one way to find out, so he shook off the stupor caused by the booze and said, "All right. I'll talk to him."

The door opened, and the man who stepped inside was like nobody Kane had ever encountered before, not even back in New York, which had had more than its share of bizarre characters. This man was tall and gaunt, with the palest skin and hair Kane had ever seen. That just made the deep-set eyes seem even darker, like chunks of black agate.

What it came down to, Kane realized, was that this man looked like he had just climbed out of a coffin . . . a few weeks after he'd been put into it and buried.

That thought shook Kane, and as he got to his feet, he looked past the visitor at Dick Yancy and saw that his foreman appeared to be shaken, too. It took a lot to get to a hard-bitten gunman and killer like Yancy.

"Mr. Kane?" the stranger said in a high-pitched, grating voice like the squeal of rusty hinges.

"That . . . that's right," Kane blustered, upset with himself for the way he had hesitated. "What can I do for you?"

"I think there is something I can do for you," the pale man said. "Or rather, we can help each other. My name is Klaus Berger, and there is a man we both want to see dead . . . Baron Friedrich von Hoffman."

Chapter Thirty-nine

"How many of 'em do you want me to kill?" Preacher asked as he, Smoke, and Matt rode through the night toward the Boxed JK.

Matt said, "You don't mean to sneak in there and start cutting throats like they were Blackfoot Indians, do you?"

"The Blackfeet and me never got along," Preacher said. "I ever tell you about how they was gonna burn me at the stake?"

"So you started preaching at them like that fella you saw in St. Louis and kept it up all night and all day until they decided you were crazy and turned you loose because they didn't want you siccing any evil spirits on them?" Matt laughed. "Yeah, I believe you've mentioned it a time or two."

"Well, that's what happened, dadblast it! And that's why I say me and the Blackfeet didn't get along. But I ain't sure they was much worse'n those hired guns Kane's got workin' for him. At least the

Injuns hated me 'cause they hated me, not 'cause they was paid to. And you didn't answer my question, Smoke."

"We've got to find the place first," Smoke said. "Then we'll decide how to— Wait a minute. You fellas hear what I do?"

"Sounds like horses," Matt said.

"A bunch of 'em," Preacher added. "And they're comin' this way."

That was the way it sounded to Smoke, too. He reined his horse to the side, and Matt and Preacher followed suit.

"There are some trees over there," Smoke said, pointing to a dark mass visible in the light from the stars and a quarter-moon. "Let's get out of sight."

They rode quickly into the shadows under the trees and dismounted. The sound of hoofbeats was louder now, loud enough to have masked the noises they'd made getting out of sight. As the three men stood there holding their reins, a large group of riders moved out from behind a ridge and came into sight.

"How many of 'em you reckon there are?" Preacher asked quietly.

"Fifty or sixty, I'd say," Matt replied. "And they're coming from the direction of the Boxed JK. Did you know Kane had that many men, Smoke?"

"I don't think he did," Smoke replied. "But if you put his crew together with the gunnies that Klaus

Berger's probably been rounding up over the past couple of weeks, it would add up to that many."

"Berger!" Preacher exclaimed, making the name sound like one of those German curses. "You reckon he's back?"

Smoke said, "I don't know for sure, but it makes sense. He probably found out that Kanc has a grudge against the baron and offered to throw in with him. Then they decided that the best thing to do would be to go ahead and attack the Rafter Nine and wipe out their enemies."

That was pure speculation, Smoke knew, but it made sense. And it made his own plans for tonight moot. With an armed force like that hurtling toward Baron von Hoffman and his people, a final showdown was inevitable.

The riders swept past the trees where Smoke, Matt, and Preacher were concealed. Before the men were out of sight, Matt said urgently, "We've got to do something, Smoke! The baron has guards posted, but they won't be expecting something like that."

Smoke nodded.

"That's why you've got to get around them and warn everybody at the Rafter Nine," he said. "Your horse is just as fast as mine or Preacher's, and you can organize a defense. There's no time to waste."

"What about the two of you?" Matt wanted to know.

"We're going to follow them, and when they

attack the ranch, we'll hit them where they least expect it . . . from behind."

"Damn right we will!" Preacher said. "We'll have those varmints in a trap, right where we want 'em!"

She had waited long enough, Greta Schiller had decided. Weeks now of this endless cat-and-mouse game, and Friedrich von Hoffman was still alive. In the aftermath of the stampede that had come tantalizingly close to wrecking the ranch that afternoon, everyone was still upset and distracted, but they were looking for threats from without.

They weren't worried about threats from within.

She adjusted the neckline of the dressing gown so that more of the creamy valley between her breasts was visible. In her other hand she gripped the neck of a bottle of wine. When Friedrich opened the door of his bedroom and saw her standing there, he wouldn't be able to resist her. Once they were alone . . .

Well, she would just have to wait and see about that. Should she wait until after they had enjoyed each other and then slip out the knife she had hidden in the pocket of the gown?

Or should she just go ahead and get it over with as soon as he closed the door behind them?

He wouldn't be expecting anything. It would be simple if she was waiting for him to turn around. One swift jab to the throat, a hard rip to the side . . .

Of course, some blood might get on her as it came fountaining out from his ruined neck, but she could wipe herself clean with the sheets from his bed and then slip back to her room to get dressed and wait for his body to be found.

Perhaps she ought to take the gown off first and toss it aside, she mused. That way it wouldn't get bloody, and the last thing he saw would be the compelling sight of her nude beauty. Surely that would be enough to transfix him long enough for her to put the knife in him.

He might even die with a smile on his face.

Yes, she thought as she raised her hand and poised it to knock on the door. That was how she would do it. Mere moments now, and it would all be over.

She froze as shots blasted outside the house, followed by a man shouting. Heavy footsteps sounded on the other side of the door. Before she could move, von Hoffman jerked it open.

"Greta!" he exclaimed. "What are you—"

The sight of her in the dressing gown, plus the bottle of wine in her hand, must have told him why she was here. Friedrich was thick and callous, but he wasn't stupid. A spark of interest flickered in his eyes, but only for a second.

"Sorry," he muttered as he pushed past her. "Something's wrong. I must go."

With that he rushed along the corridor to the stairs and clattered down them. She had missed her chance, she realized bitterly. Not that it had been much of one. Now she would have to wait until this latest commotion, whatever it was, was over.

But at least she had planted the seed in his mind. He would be more receptive next time.

And then he would die.

Matt asked everything he could of the rangy stallion he was riding. It wouldn't do any good if he ran the horse so hard that its heart burst. That would just leave him afoot before he got back to the Rafter 9. But he pushed the horse as hard as he dared as he swung wide around the group of gunmen heading for the ranch.

He was going to feel foolish if he charged in, scared everybody, and then the riders turned out not to be a combined force of hired killers working for Jethro Kane and Klaus Berger.

But the chances of that were so small that Matt wasn't going to worry about it. He couldn't afford to run that risk.

On and on he drove the stallion, hoping that the animal wouldn't step in a hole or trip over some other obstacle in the dark. That would be ruinous, too.

He was relying on his instincts and his natural sense of direction to guide him since he didn't know the baron's range all that well. Having to avoid the small army of gunmen meant that he couldn't just retrace the route he and Smoke and Preacher had taken. He had to strike out on his own and find a new trail that would take him where he needed to go.

From time to time he paused to let the horse blow. During those brief moments, he listened intently but didn't hear any hoofbeats. He took that to mean that he had gotten ahead of the enemy. That was what he was going to tell himself until he found out otherwise, anyway.

Finally, he spotted lights glowing up ahead in the darkness. Those would be coming from the ranch buildings, he knew. Even though some of the windows were shuttered and others were boarded up, lamplight could escape through the cracks around them. Matt homed in on those faint glows.

When he came in sight of the ranch headquarters at last, everything seemed to be quiet and peaceful. It wouldn't be that way for long, he thought as he slipped his Colt from its holster. He had beaten the gunmen here, but he didn't know how much time they had before the enemy arrived.

He pointed the revolver into the air and squeezed off three fast shots, the universal signal for trouble.

"Everybody up!" he bellowed as he rode into the ranch yard. "Baron! Dieter! Everybody! Trouble coming! Trouble!"

Where were the guards? Why had no one challenged him?

Was he too late already?

That wasn't possible, Matt thought wildly. If the

baron and his people had been wiped out, he would have heard the shooting. It would have sounded like a full-fledged war.

"Where is everybody? Baron!"

Someone flung open the front door of the ranch house. Matt swung his Colt in that direction but held off on the trigger as he recognized Dieter in the light that spilled through the door. The young man clutched a Winchester.

"Matt!" Dieter cried. "What's wrong?"

"A bunch of men are on their way here," Matt explained as he turned his horse in a circle in front of the porch. "Smoke thinks it's Kane's men, and maybe Klaus Berger's, too. Everybody needs to get ready to fight! Now!"

"Berger!" a new voice roared. Baron von Hoffman rushed out of the house to join them. "I knew that devil would return!"

More hoofbeats pounded. Matt swung around, thinking the attack was upon them, but he saw right away that there were only a few men riding in.

"Herr Baron! Herr Baron!" one of them called. "Someone rushed past us! We could not stop him—"

The guards, Matt realized. They weren't dead after all. He had just been moving so fast that he was past them before they figured out what was going on.

He swung down from the saddle and told von Hoffman, "Get all your men in defensive positions, Baron. Make sure they have plenty of ammunition. The women and children need to be in the house, lying low where they'll be safe. The house, the bunkhouse, and the barn are all sturdy. We can defend them. And the odds are pretty close to even."

"My men are not professional fighters," von Hoffman said worriedly.

"Maybe not, but this is their home now, and any man worth his salt will fight to protect his home!"

Dieter turned toward the door, saying, "I must speak to Erica—"

"Schumann!"

The baron's harsh voice stopped the young man. Matt figured Dieter just wanted to tell Erica that he loved her, in case he didn't make it through the fight. Even though they had been rivals for her affections for a short time, Matt felt a surge of anger that von Hoffman was going to stop Dieter from saying what he wanted to say, just because of some outdated ideas about nobility and commoners.

Maybe that was what von Hoffman had been about to do, but in the light that came from the house, something changed in his hawklike face. He drew in a deep breath and said, "Tell her to be careful, Dieter . . . and tell her that I love her, too."

Dieter swallowed hard and nodded.

"*Ja*, Herr Baron," he said. Then he ran into the house.

Von Hoffman turned to Matt.

"Now, Herr Jensen, let us prepare to meet the enemy."

The next few minutes were hectic ones. The commotion had drawn out most of the men, and Matt and von Hoffman placed them around the ranch in positions with good cover, so they could fight off the attackers. Matt rushed from place to place, checking on the defenses, and when he was satisfied that they were as ready as they were going to be with such short notice, he hurried to the house where von Hoffman stood on the porch. Dieter had returned and was waiting there, too.

"There are men at every window in the bunkhouse," Matt reported, "as well as inside the barn and in the hayloft. The men up there will have the high ground."

"As will the ones on the second floor of the house," von Hoffman agreed. "I took the liberty of placing a keg of blasting powder in that wagon there, as well."

He pointed to one of the immigrant wagons that was parked by itself in the middle of the open space between the ranch house and the bunkhouse and barn.

"What did you have in mind, Baron?" Matt asked.

"One more surprise waiting for them," von Hoffman said with a smile. "And when the wagon is burning, it will give us light to shoot by, will it not?"

"It sure will," Matt replied with a grin of his own.

He might have said more, but at that moment he heard what he'd been listening for. It was a faint rumble at first, like the sound of distant drums, but then it grew louder and all three men knew it was the hoofbeats of many horses.

"Get inside," he told von Hoffman and Dieter. "Everybody needs to hold their fire until that powder blows. I told the men in the bunkhouse and the barn not to shoot until the men in the house opened the ball, so pass that along to them, Baron."

"I must light the fuse," von Hoffman said, nodding toward the wagon.

"I'll do that," Matt said. "You and Dieter get in there and shut the door. We want those varmints to ride in thinking that we're not expecting them."

The baron looked like he wanted to argue, but then he nodded and said to Dieter, "Come." They hurried into the house and closed the door.

Matt trotted over to the wagon. He reached inside and found the keg of blasting powder the baron had placed just inside the tailgate. The fuse was cut short. It wouldn't burn more than ten or fifteen seconds, Matt estimated.

That was fine. He didn't want to give the attackers any more warning than necessary. He fished a lucifer from his pocket and stood waiting with it.

The thunder of hoofbeats was loud now. Riders swept down from the hill overlooking the ranch and charged toward the main house. If there was any doubt about their intentions, it vanished as they started shooting.

Matt snapped the lucifer to life and held the flame to the end of the fuse. It caught instantly and threw off sparks as it burned toward the keg. It moved even faster than he expected. Matt turned, charged toward the house as bullets whined over his head. . . .

For the second time in little more than a week, the world blew up behind him.

Chapter Forty

The force of the blast knocked Matt off his feet and sent him tumbling across the ground. He came to a stop against the porch, on his belly, and lifted his head to look across the ranch yard. Several horses and men were down, but the explosion would have done more damage to the attackers if it had come a couple of seconds later.

Too late to worry about that, Matt thought as he came up on one knee and drew his Colt, which had stayed in its holster despite his being tossed around by the powder keg's detonation. Riders crowded into the area in front of the house, shooting steadily at the house, the bunkhouse, and the barn. Return fire from those buildings ripped into them.

Flames shot up from the burning wagon, casting a flickering, hellish glare over the scene. That part of the plan had worked as von Hoffman intended, anyway. Aiming by that light, Matt drew a bead on one of the raiders and triggered a shot. The dull boom of his revolver sounded muffled and distant to him, telling him that the explosion had partially deafened him again. At this rate he would be lucky to have any hearing left, he thought.

Assuming he even lived through the next few minutes, he added grimly to himself as he watched the man he had just shot topple off his horse.

Twisting, Matt found another target and fired again, and again he was rewarded by the sight of a raider doubling over and then pitching from the saddle. Some of the raiders had noticed Matt, though, and bullets began to kick up dirt around him.

They would have closed in on him and shot him to pieces, he knew, but at that moment the front door slammed open and the baron and Dieter charged out onto the porch. The rifles in their hands spat fire and lead as Dieter called, "Come on, Matt, we'll cover you!"

Matt ducked under the porch railing and rolled across the planks. He came up on a knee again and added some shots from his Colt to the withering fire being poured out by von Hoffman and Dieter. A couple of horses went down directly in front of them, spilling their bullet-riddled riders.

The three men pulled back into the house then, still firing as they retreated. Matt pulled the door closed behind them.

"Thanks," he told the baron and Dieter. His voice sounded a little tinny to him, but his hearing was coming back.

Outside, the shooting died away.

"Are they leaving?" Dieter asked. "Did we win?"

"Not hardly," Matt said. "They're just catching their breath."

As if to prove his point, guns began to roar once more, and now the Colt thunder was louder than ever.

"Here they come again!" Matt called as he crouched at one of the windows, thumbing fresh rounds into his revolver.

Smoke and Preacher closed to within a quarter of a mile of the army of gunmen, then gradually got even closer as the riders neared the Rafter 9. The hired killers had their attention focused in front of them and weren't really paying much attention to what was behind them.

Not only that, but with so many men it was difficult to keep track of where everyone was. If anyone glanced back and saw them riding there, they would likely think the two of them were just lagging behind a little.

So when the horsemen topped the hill and started charging down toward the ranch headquarters, Smoke and Preacher were in perfect position. As guns began to go off, they urged their horses forward and drew even with the men in the rear ranks of the attackers.

Preacher drew both pistols, stuck them out to the sides, and started firing as he careened forward. He blew men out of their saddles without them ever knowing what had happened.

Smoke was more selective in his assault, twisting in the saddle to fire right and left. He wanted to find Kane and Berger, figuring that if he could cut off both heads of this monster, the rest of it might die.

The attackers had almost reached the ranch house before they realized that they had enemies among them, cutting them down. Smoke and Preacher had killed probably a dozen of the gunmen when an explosion rocked the night and sent fire shooting up into the darkness.

That was their cue to pull back. They had dealt out a lot of damage, but now they needed to join the Rafter 9's defenders.

"Come on, Preacher!" Smoke called as he wheeled his horse. The old mountain man followed him as Smoke galloped toward the barn. They leaned forward in their saddles as bullets whistled around their heads.

One of the barn doors swung open. Preacher rode through it, but Smoke reached up to grab the rope that dangled from a beam sticking out above the hayloft opening. The rope was attached to a block and tackle that was used to lift bales into the loft. Smoke scrambled up it hand over hand until he could grasp the beam and swing himself through the opening. Men were there to grab him and help him in.

They babbled at him in German. Smoke grinned at them and said, "I'm not sure what you're saying, fellas, but I reckon I agree. Grab your guns, because here come those varmints again!"

After a lull of a few seconds, the chaos of battle

rose to fill the night. Shots, curses, and screams blended to form an unholy melody. Clouds of dust and powder smoke rolled through the air and mingled into a sharp reek that stung the nose. The blown-up wagon continued to burn and cast its garish light over the ranch yard, although the flames were starting to die down a little now.

Just as Smoke expected, the baron's men fought valiantly in the defense of their new home. He wished he knew how Matt and Dieter and von Hoffman himself were doing, but that would have to wait. At least half the gunmen were down, and the others had to be thinking about bolting.

A bellowing voice urged them on, and Smoke followed the sound of it until he spotted Jethro Kane. The Easterner had lost his derby, and his bald dome glinted in the firelight. He was having trouble controlling his horse as it leaped around, maddened by the smoke and noise. The animal's spinning, jumping course carried it toward the barn.

Smoke holstered his gun and jumped up to grab the protruding beam again. He heard startled cries from the defenders in the hayloft as he swung himself out and let go.

His momentum carried him toward Kane. The man looked up and saw him coming at the last second. Kane's mouth dropped open in surprise, and then Smoke slammed into him and drove him out of the saddle.

Both men crashed to the ground. Smoke rolled away and came up on his feet. Kane was almost as fast to recover, though, and he charged forward like a maddened bull before Smoke could get himself set. Kane rammed into him and knocked him backwards against the barn wall.

The man might be from the East, but he was tough. Muscles bulged under his coat as he drove punch after punch into Smoke's body. Smoke's belly was still sore from getting kicked there several days earlier. He hunched forward a little to protect it and smashed a punch of his own into Kane's solar plexus. It was like hitting a rock wall.

Kane had come up against a man whose strength more than matched his own, though. Smoke hammered a right uppercut into Kane's jaw that rocked the man's head far back on his neck. That gave Smoke room to hook a left into Kane's face.

Whipping more punches into Kane's face and body, Smoke drove him back. Now that he wasn't pinned against the barn wall by Kane's weight, Smoke had room to really put some power behind his blows. In a matter of seconds, Kane's features were smeared with blood that had leaked from his flattened nose, and both eyes were swollen almost shut.

Kane kept on flailing punches of his own, but most of them missed. His strength was deserting him now. The blows that landed didn't have enough power behind them to hurt Smoke. Chopping punch after punch into Kane's ruined face, Smoke wondered why the man didn't just go down and stay down. Kane was just too damned stubborn for that, Smoke supposed.

Even the strongest man would eventually crumple before an onslaught like that, however. Kane slipped to one knee, then forced himself back up onto his feet only to have Smoke crash another hard right to the middle of his face. Flinging his arms out, Kane went over backwards. Dust puffed up around him as he crashed to the ground, out cold.

Smoke didn't have time to celebrate his triumph. A bullet ripped across his right side, plowing a bloody furrow in his flesh and spinning him halfway around with its impact. Fighting against the pain of the wound, Smoke saw one of the riders charging toward him. Long, pale hair flew out behind the man's head, and his agate eyes burned with hatred.

"We meet at last, Herr Jensen!" Klaus Berger cried as he drew a bead on Smoke and got ready to shoot him again.

The world had gone insane, Greta Schiller thought as she huddled at the top of the stairs and watched the men firing out the windows at the attackers. She had never been in the middle of a battle like this. She didn't know if she was going to survive.

And it was all Friedrich von Hoffman's fault, she told herself. If he had not been such a fool, he could be back in Germany, living the life of a pampered aristocrat, and she would be his wife by now, plotting how to best get rid of him and take over his estate.

Instead they were in this godforsaken wilderness with crazy men yelling and shooting everywhere.

But if she lived, von Hoffman still had to die, she thought. Her masters back in Germany would reward her for his death. And there was a way. . . .

She had fetched the little pistol from her trunk. If she could lure him upstairs, she could shoot him, and no one would ever know that he hadn't been killed by a bullet fired by one of the raiders. For a second, she curled her fingers around the butt of the gun in the pocket of her dressing gown and gathered her courage. The weapon was small. She would have to be close to him in order to shoot him and be sure that he died.

She hurried down the stairs and went to his side.

"Friedrich!" she cried as she grabbed his shoulder. "Friedrich, there's a man upstairs! I think he's one of them!"

Von Hoffman jerked around. His face was grimy from powder smoke.

"Where?" he demanded. "Show me!"

That was exactly what she wanted, Greta thought exultantly. Grasping his arm, she tugged him toward the stairs.

"I'm so afraid," she babbled. "Friedrich, you have to stop him. He was going toward Erica's room."

Fear for his cousin's life would make the fool even less suspicious, Greta knew. As they reached the landing, von Hoffman jerked away from her and bounded ahead.

Greta pulled the pistol from her pocket and ran after him. Before she could stop him, he reached the door of Erica's room and pounded on it with his free hand, shouting, "Erica! Erica, are you all right?"

Greta jammed the pistol against his back and pulled the trigger.

Von Hoffman cried out in pain and arched his back. Greta fired again and sent another bullet ripping into his body. He dropped his rifle and sagged against the wall, slapping his hands against it as he tried to hold himself up. He twisted his head around to stare at her in disbelief.

"You made too many enemies, Friedrich," she told him.

"You . . . you work for . . . them!" he gasped out.

"Of course," she said. She lifted the pistol to shoot him in the head and finish him off.

Before she could do that, he swung an arm and smashed the back of his hand across her face. The blow sent her staggering backwards.

At the same time, Erica opened the door and screamed as she saw her cousin's bloody form swaying there. The last of von Hoffman's strength finally deserted him, and he crumpled to the floor.

Greta caught her balance and lifted the pistol again. Now she would finish wiping the slate clean by killing Erica, and no one would ever know the part she had played in their deaths except the men back in Germany who would be in her debt.

Erica dived to the floor as Greta fired. Greta watched in amazement as Erica scooped up the rifle her cousin had dropped. She tried to lower the pistol and fire again, but she was too late. Flame lanced from the Winchester's muzzle.

The .44-40 slug punched into Greta's soft belly and blew her spine out her back.

She collapsed, filled with the most incredible pain she had ever experienced in her life. The world spun crazily around her as the pistol slipped from her fingers. She was barely aware of Erica standing up and stalking along the corridor toward her.

"You killed him!" Erica cried as tears coursed down her face. "You killed him, you bitch!"

"And you've killed . . . me. . . ." Greta whispered.

Those were her last words as Erica worked the rifle's lever and began to fire again and again. The roar of the shots washed Greta Schiller away like a black river.

Matt heard the shots upstairs and could tell there was something different about them. Defenders were manning some of the windows up there to fire down at the raiders, but these shots sounded closer somehow.

That could only mean there was trouble up there.

"Dieter!" Matt called to the young man who crouched at one of the other windows. "Where's the baron?"

Dieter looked around the room, his eyes widening. "I don't know!"

Neither of them had seen von Hoffman leave the room, but the baron must have gone upstairs,

Matt thought. He surged to his feet and said, "Come on!"

They ran to the stairs and started up, and as they did, more shots blasted. As they reached the landing and peered down the hall, both men were shocked to see Erica standing over what had been a woman. She had a Winchester in her hands, pointing down at the gruesome remains.

"Erica!" Dieter cried.

She looked up at them, her face wet with tears.

"She . . . she killed Friedrich! Frau Schiller killed Friedrich . . . and tried to kill me!"

Matt didn't know what was going on here, but he saw the sprawled shape on the floor of the hallway beyond Erica. He rushed past her and dropped to a knee beside the bloody form of the baron.

Von Hoffman was still alive, but he was shot to pieces, Matt saw. He probably didn't have long. Matt lifted the baron's head.

"Erica . . ." von Hoffman said weakly. "Erica . . ."

"Dieter!" Matt called to the young man who had put his arms around Erica to comfort her. "Bring her over here! Her cousin's still alive!"

"Erica, come!" Dieter said as he urged her along the corridor. "The baron still lives."

Erica knelt beside von Hoffman and hugged him, heedless of the blood she was getting all over her.

"Friedrich!" she cried. "Friedrich, you must not die!"

"It is . . . too late," he managed to say. "I am sorry . . . sorry for the harsh things I did . . . sorry for the way I treated you. . . ."

"All you ever did was love me and try to protect me," she told him through her sobs.

"Dieter . . ."

The young man was kneeling, too. He leaned forward and said, "Yes, Your Excellency?"

A faint smile tugged at von Hoffman's mouth.

"I would rather now . . . that you called me friend," he whispered. "And you must promise me . . . you will take care of . . . of Erica. . . ."

"Forever, Your Excellency," Dieter choked out.

Von Hoffman lifted a shaking hand. Dieter grasped it. Erica had hold of his other hand.

Matt saw the life go out of the baron's eyes.

He left the two of them there to mourn the loss. Von Hoffman might be dead, but the gunfire continued outside.

The defenders of the Rafter 9 still had a war to win.

Smoke's Colt was still in its holster, but the bullet wound in his side had deadened that arm and shoulder for the moment. He willed the muscles to work, to draw the gun and blow a hole in the fish-belly hide of Klaus Berger, but his right arm refused to budge.

The left one worked just fine, though, as he whipped his Bowie knife from its sheath and threw it underhanded at Berger.

The blade buried itself in Berger's body and caused his second shot to go wild. He didn't get a chance for a third one because Preacher burst out of the barn just then with both guns blazing. The old mountain man's shots slammed into Berger's body, rocking him back and forth in the saddle. Berger dropped his gun and grabbed frantically for the saddlehorn instead, managing to stay mounted as his horse plunged around in panic.

Berger grabbed the handle of Smoke's knife, ripped the blade from his body, and flung it at Smoke. The knife fell short, landing at Smoke's feet. Berger couldn't control the horse. It bolted, carrying its bullet-riddled rider out of the ranch yard and into the darkness.

Preacher ran up to Smoke, who had his right arm clamped tight against his body now, and said, "Are you all right, son?"

"I will be," Smoke said. "This is just a scratch. We'd better find Matt."

"Shouldn't be hard to do," Preacher said. "Looks like the fracas is about over."

There were only scattered shots now as the defenders finished off the last of the raiders. A few of the hired gunmen had thrown down their weapons and surrendered already, and the other survivors were quick to do so.

As Smoke and Preacher hurried toward the ranch house, Matt came out onto the porch and called their names. He leaped down and came to meet them.

"Smoke, how bad are you hit?"

"Not bad," Smoke assured him. "I'll be all right. How about you?"

"Not a scratch. Preacher?"

"You know I'm too old and ornery to die," Preacher replied. "Them dang bullets just go around me."

"Smoke," Matt said, and something in the younger man's voice told Smoke there was bad news. "The baron wasn't so lucky. He's gone."

"Blast it!" Smoke said. "One of those hired guns got him?"

"Well . . . not the way you think. That redheaded woman, Greta Schiller, killed him."

"What!"

"Best I can figure it out," Matt said, "she was working for the baron's enemies, too, just like Berger, only she was spying on him and waiting for a good chance to assassinate him."

"Were you able to grab her?"

"No, but she didn't get away. Erica killed her."

The news that von Hoffman was dead had shaken Smoke, but at least the baron's cousin had been able to avenge his murder. There was something fitting about that.

"Where's Kane?" Matt went on.

Smoke pointed with his good arm.

"Over yonder. He's out cold."

Matt went over to Kane to check on him and came back shaking his head.

"He's dead, Smoke. Looks like he must have choked on his own blood when he couldn't get any air through that nose of his after you smashed it."

Smoke shook his head. He wouldn't lose any sleep over Kane's death, but he honestly hadn't meant to kill the man. He would have left it up to the law to hang him.

But maybe Preacher was right. Maybe he was getting too soft in his old age.

On the other hand, he thought, looking around at the carnage that surrounded the three of them, maybe not.

Epilogue

The small cemetery on the Rafter 9 grew considerably more crowded the next day as a dozen of the ranch's defenders were laid to rest, including Baron Friedrich von Hoffman.

After the funerals, Smoke, the wound in his side bandaged up now, sat down with Erica to have a talk with her.

"I reckon this is your ranch now," he told her. "You don't have to make any decisions yet, but eventually you'll have to figure out what you want to do with it."

"I know what to do with it," she replied without hesitation. "I will make it the very best ranch in this part of the country, just as Friedrich intended. And New Holtzberg will be a fine settlement, as well." She gave an emphatic nod, despite her pale, tear-streaked face. "Dieter has promised to help me, and I know the others will, too."

Smoke smiled and patted her hand.

"You know, I think you'll be just fine," he told her. "All of you."

A worried frown creased her forehead.

"But what about Friedrich's enemies, back in the old country? I am his heir. They may come after me, now that he is gone."

"I don't think so," Smoke said. "I hate to say it, but they got what they wanted."

Erica's mouth tightened into a grim line, and her features hardened.

"Someday they will pay for what they have done," she vowed.

"The settling up comes to everybody sooner or later," Smoke said, "for the good and the bad alike. Best we can hope for is that the good we've done outweighs the rest of it."

"In your case, Herr Jensen," Erica said, smiling now, "I think there is no question about that."

Smoke waited a few days to let the wound in his side heal a little more before he saddled his horse and got ready to ride for home. Preacher was going to join him.

"I think I'll stick around here for a while, just to make sure Erica and Dieter get the ranch off on the right foot," Matt said as he stood on the porch. Smoke and Preacher had led their saddled horses up to the house to say their good-byes.

Erica hugged both of them, and Dieter shook their hands.

"Don't worry about us, Smoke," Dieter said. "We will be fine."

Smoke grinned and said, "With a true Western hombre like you around, Dieter, I'm sure of it. I'd like to stay, but I've got a ranch of my own to run, you know."

"Maybe the Sugarloaf and the Rafter Nine can do some business sometime, *ja*? I mean, you reckon?"

"I reckon we just might," Smoke told him.

As they rode away, headed south toward Colorado, Preacher said, "It's a damn shame the baron didn't make it. I never did like him very much, mind you. He still had too many o' them high-falutin' European ideas. But I got a hunch he would've come around in time."

"I think so, too," Smoke agreed. "He had a dream for this land where he brought his people, and at least that dream is still alive. I don't think Erica and Dieter will let it die."

"I don't reckon they will, either . . . but they ought to have a little easier time of it with both Kane and Berger dead."

Smoke rubbed his jaw and frowned in thought.

"You know, we never did find Berger's body," he said quietly.

"Oh, hell, the wolves got it! You know that. I shot him full o' holes, and you stuck a Bowie in him. You don't reckon anybody could live through that, do you?"

"I wouldn't think so," Smoke admitted. "But I'd

feel a mite better about it if I knew he was in the ground where he belongs."

Preacher snorted and said, "You need to stop worryin' about things that ain't gonna happen. You got a pretty wife waitin' for you at home, remember, and by now I'll bet she's missin' you somethin' powerful!"

"You know, I believe you're right," Smoke said with a grin. "Let's go home."

The porter took the man's bag and helped him up the stairs into the private railroad car in the depot at Cheyenne. It was a warm night, but the fella was all wrapped up in an overcoat anyway, and he moved gingerly, like he was sick or hurt. And when he spoke, his voice rasped like a rusty gate.

"Thank you," the passenger said. He pressed a coin into the porter's hand, and the porter couldn't help but notice how thin and pale the man's fingers were.

"You're mighty welcome, sir. You headed east on business?"

"No. I travel . . . for my health."

Well, that was no surprise, the porter thought. The poor varmint looked and sounded like he had one foot in the grave already.

"But when I come west again . . . it will be for pleasure," the passenger went on. "To look up an old friend . . . a man named . . . Jensen."

That name was familiar to the porter for some reason, but he couldn't place it just then. He didn't worry about it, just tipped his cap to the passenger instead, and said, "You enjoy your trip now, sir."

He left the car and started back across the platform toward the station. Behind him, with a hiss of steam and a clanking of its drivers, the train pulled out, heading into the night.

The porter paused, looked over his shoulder at it, and shook his head. His shoulders moved as a shudder went through him. The night seemed a mite colder all of a sudden.

He didn't think about it for long. He had work to do. With another little shake of his head, he went back into the station.